THE OLD GIRLS' CHATEAU ESCAPE

KATE GALLEY

B
Boldwood

First published in Great Britain in 2025 by Boldwood Books Ltd.

Copyright © Kate Galley, 2025

Cover Design by Lizzie Gardiner

Cover Images: Shutterstock and Adobe Stock

The moral right of Kate Galley to be identified as the author of this work has been asserted in accordance with the Copyright, Designs and Patents Act 1988.

All rights reserved. No part of this book may be reproduced in any form or by any electronic or mechanical means, including information storage and retrieval systems, without written permission from the author, except for the use of brief quotations in a book review. This book is a work of fiction and, except in the case of historical fact, any resemblance to actual persons, living or dead, is purely coincidental.

Every effort has been made to obtain the necessary permissions with reference to copyright material, both illustrative and quoted. We apologise for any omissions in this respect and will be pleased to make the appropriate acknowledgements in any future edition.

A CIP catalogue record for this book is available from the British Library.

Paperback ISBN 978-1-83533-872-8

Large Print ISBN 978-1-83533-873-5

Hardback ISBN 978-1-83533-871-1

Ebook ISBN 978-1-83533-875-9

Kindle ISBN 978-1-83533-876-6

Audio CD ISBN 978-1-83533-886-5

MP3 CD ISBN 978-1-83533-867-4

Digital audio download ISBN 978-1-83533-870-4

This book is printed on certified sustainable paper. Boldwood Books is dedicated to putting sustainability at the heart of our business. For more information please visit https://www.boldwoodbooks.com/about-us/sustainability/

Boldwood Books Ltd, 23 Bowerdean Street, London, SW6 3TN

www.boldwoodbooks.com

For Rex <3

COMPANION WANTED FOR ELDERLY COUPLE – SOUTH OF FRANCE

Temporary position
Live-in
BOX: 843982

Job Specifications:

Live-in companion urgently needed for an elderly couple. You will have adjacent accommodation in the grounds of a hotel in Aix-en-Provence.

It will be necessary for you to stay while the couple's daughter is out of the country. Knowledge of dementia isn't essential, but will be useful. Light domestic chores and personal care as required. You will be asked to escort the couple on outings to the surrounding area to help them adjust to their new arrangement.

English-speaking applicants only, but if you have a little French it could be useful.

This is an open-ended position as reflected in the salary.

Salary £1500 per week.

Please apply with CV.

PROLOGUE

Dorothy let her eyes scan the wanted advertisement for a second time before she clicked her mouse to exit the page. She sat back in her late husband's chair, her fingers resting on his walnut desk as she looked out of the window down the stretch of garden to the boathouse.

So, it was official, Meredith and Gerald really did need a companion. Dorothy's friend Barbara had been right when she'd spoken to her on the phone; it wasn't just gossip. The ad didn't mention the book, though. Barbara had heard that Meredith was writing her memoir and she had suggested it was going to be a tell-all affair. Dorothy shuddered at the thought.

They had made a pact not to ever talk about what they had done in the summer of 1970, but perhaps Meredith had changed her mind. Dorothy hadn't seen her for years. How could she know what she might or might not write about now?

Of course, Gina must go; she was perfect for the position. As soon as the thought entered Dorothy's head, she felt a pang of guilt. Gina Knight – the woman Dorothy had dismissed as a mousy nobody when she'd first seen her, had since become one of her greatest friends and was now occupying the boathouse at the end of Dorothy's garden. If she could get Gina to accept the role and fly to the south of France, she would be in the perfect place to report back to Dorothy on the contents of this memoir.

Was it too much to ask of her new friend? She pushed her chair back and reached for her walking stick, which she'd left propped against the filing cabinet. Dorothy was eighty-nine and only operated at one speed now, and she used it to get her out of Philip's office and down the garden to the boathouse. This might very well be asking too much of her new friend, but there was a lot at stake and she was going to ask, regardless.

1

GINA

'First time in Marseille?'

The man seated next to me had been tapping away on his laptop for the majority of the flight from Heathrow, but now, with me craning across him to look out of the window to the city stretching out below, he closed the lid, momentarily catching the cuff of my blouse in its grip. I gently pulled it free.

It had been raining when we'd left London. Rivulets of water streamed across the glass as we'd taxied down the runway, but here, in the south of France, the sunlight glinted off the wing of the aeroplane and the sea sparkled enticingly below.

'First time in the air?'

The man tried again and I realised I hadn't answered. I was transfixed by the view getting closer as we came in to land. I wasn't expecting it to be so mountainous, the landscape pinched into folds like pleated fabric. We were over houses now with white-painted walls, red roofs and azure-blue pools in their gardens. It was the furthest I'd been from home in years.

'First time to Marseille,' I said, 'but not the first time in the air.'

The last time I was on an aeroplane had been when my

husband Douglas and I flew to Scotland for a few days. It was just after he'd retired, when I still had hope that we would have a future together, but that seemed like a joke now. Douglas was living happily in a flat many miles from me with *Little Miss Maidenhead* and I was living in a boathouse in Hampton at the end of an elderly friend's garden. It really was quite amazing how, at the age of seventy-one, my life had changed immeasurably.

'Is Marseille home?' I asked him, making an assumption based on his lovely French accent. The deep tone of his voice made the words sound quite sexy. Good God! What a thought. He was at least ten years younger than me and besides, Douglas may have moved on but we were technically still married. I shuffled back in my seat a little to give the poor man some space.

'It is. I've been visiting my daughter and grandson in London and now I'm home. Do you need recommendations for places to visit in the city?'

'That's kind, but I'm actually moving on to Aix-en-Provence.'

'Ah, the home of Paul Cézanne. You're an artist also?'

'No,' I said, amused, but my mind did conjure up an image of the portraits I used to paint, now stored along with my mother's old car and a lot of other distant memories in my rented garage in Oxfordshire. 'I'm here for a job, so I doubt I'll have much chance to be a tourist. I'm a companion,' I added as he took a closer look at my face. 'I'm here to look after an elderly couple.'

It appeared as if he was going to say something else and then seemed to change his mind.

Yes, I didn't expect to be rejoining the workforce at my age, either.

The wheels of the aeroplane touched down on the runway and I let go of the tense feeling I'd been holding on to during the two-hour flight. Of course I knew, statistically, you were safer in the air than you were on the road, but loading myself into a metal tube and hurtling through the sky without any control was not a naturally comfortable place for me.

'*Welcome to Marseille Provence Airport.*'

The voice of a member of the cabin crew interrupted us and everyone began to gather their possessions, turn on their phones and stretch in their seats. The man offered me a smile and a *bonne chance* as we left the plane and he disappeared into the bowels of the airport.

Once I'd navigated my way to the baggage reclaim and wheeled my suitcase through passport control, I was out into the arrivals hall and looking for signs pointing me in the direction of the railway station or, actually, *la gare*. I had my phone open on a Google translate app and was trying not to feel completely out of my depth.

I passed a line of taxi drivers holding up placards and as my eyes travelled the group I saw my own name scrawled on a piece of paper.

GINA KNIGHT

My heart relaxed a little when I realised someone had been sent to collect me and I let out my held breath. I wasn't at all sure what to expect as I'd had little to no information and everything had been arranged at considerable speed, through third parties. I hadn't even had a chance to talk to either of the elderly couple that I was here to look after, nor even their daughter, who usually took up their care. I looked up to the face of the person holding my name and found an attractive man, I guessed in his late thirties or early forties – he certainly looked to be a similar age to my son, Chris. His dark hair had fine flecks of grey and it was on the longer side, flopping into his eyes. He had a pair of sunglasses tucked into the opening of his white linen shirt. His sleeves were folded over and I noticed a tattoo on his forearm. It looked like an old-fashioned compass, the sort you might see illustrated on a fantasy book cover. When he pushed his hair back with his hand, our eyes met and he offered me a tentative smile.

'Gina Knight?' he asked, stepping forward.

'*Oui*,' I answered, immediately feeling foolish. 'Yes, that's me.'

I thrust out my hand and he took it and shook it, his smile broadening.

'Lucien DuBois,' he said. 'You had a good flight?'

'It was quick, uneventful and we stayed in the air for all the time we needed to,' I said and he laughed.

'*Formidable*.' He reached for my suitcase. 'I'll take you to the car.'

'I was expecting to get a train, but thank you.'

'I was at home in Marseille anyway. Things to sort out. And now on my way back to the hotel, so *pas de problème*.'

I followed Lucien and my wheelie case outside into the busy and sunny afternoon and I breathed in the unmistakable warmth of a Mediterranean climate. The sky was a blue so intense it didn't seem real after the grey mass of the London sky I'd left behind at Heathrow. The sun was dazzling and I could feel the immediate prickle of heat on my face. Despite the sheer fabric of my blouse, I knew it wouldn't be long before there would be a trickle of perspiration running down my skin.

Lucien was charging ahead in some desperate hurry to get back to his car and I wondered if the parking charges were as steep in France as they were in UK airports. He glanced back over his shoulder as he crossed the road and began following a line of cars parked opposite the airport building.

'*D'accord*, okay?' he asked me and I stuck up a feeble thumb in response before I could embarrass myself with another *oui*.

His car was a neat and tidy blue Citroën, and he bundled my

large case into the back and opened the passenger door for me. I had overpacked, I knew, but this job was open-ended and I had no idea how long I would be needed. I slid onto the hot seat and was immensely glad that he got the engine going and the air con on before he swung out of the car park at some speed. He drove like he walked – rapidly!

The radio was blasting out some music I didn't recognise followed by some animated and busy French chat. Lucien seemed to realise suddenly how loud it was and reached forward to turn it off.

'So, you work at the château?' I asked him and was mortified to hear my voice was doing that silly half-accent thing. I remember Douglas doing this whenever he had to talk to anyone who wasn't a native English speaker. Instead of attempting the other person's language he would adopt a strange accent of his own while still only speaking English, or worse, start shouting. 'I'm sorry,' I said quickly. 'I don't speak much French.'

'No problem,' he said. 'I have worked for the Guérin family for three years. Rose and Hugo are good employers. Hugo is my uncle, my mother's brother, although he is actually only thirteen years older than me. My mother had me when she was very young.'

'Oh, okay, and Rose is Meredith and Gerald Harper's daughter isn't she?'

It was Meredith and Gerald I was here for. Gerald had dementia and Meredith, after a recent fall, had broken her arm. They were to be my second companion job. My first had been Dorothy Reed, an eighty-nine-year-old woman who, it turned out, had an ulterior motive for employing me for the week-long wedding party of her grandson. I thought I'd be helping her get dressed and making sure she'd cleaned her teeth, but she'd had me on an altogether different mission. We'd become good friends, though, and it was her boathouse I was now resident of while I waited for the sale of my own house to go through.

'Yes, she is their daughter,' Lucien said. 'And it is bad timing, because now she and Hugo are in New Zealand. But, of course, that is why you are here – to look after her parents. Their son is in a bad way after his accident and it is right they are with him as he leaves the hospital, but things are a bit *écrasant* – overwhelming – here at the hotel. We have a lot to do without them. I am the temporary manager until Hugo comes back.'

I noticed it was twice he'd used the word hotel rather than château. Dorothy had told me it was a château. I was preparing myself for disappointment.

But, Lucien looked pleased with himself for a moment, proud of his position despite how busy he clearly was. My heart sank for a moment. I didn't want to be arriving into chaos. I wasn't really sure I even wanted to be *here*, but Dorothy had arranged it. I had been bulldozed, again. She could be a very persuasive woman when she put her mind to it.

We left the airport heading north and were soon on an uninspiring stretch of dual carriageway. I looked out of the side window back towards Marseille and the sea, and felt a bit disheartened that we weren't going into the city. Lucien must have sensed my thoughts.

'You should go on a trip when you have time. I could show you around, if you like.'

I imagined what a tour of the city with Lucien would be like and saw myself racing to keep up with him. He'd probably be an enthusiastic tour guide and I'd be left out of breath and sweaty in his wake. Not so much the beautiful heroine with a carefully tied silk headscarf, but more the huffing and puffing older woman with clicking knee joints. I didn't want to offend him, though, and it seemed as if he'd probably be too busy with work anyway.

'That would be very kind,' I said, simply.

'We have the oldest city in France,' he said, proudly. 'We are old, but we are also new here; we are glamorous and gritty. We are not only French, but Moroccan, Italian, Spanish and Armenian, Algerian. We are known for a good bouillabaisse, but really we do the best pizza, of anywhere. But, you know, check out the North African food – is *délicieux*.'

He suggested a trip to *Vieux Port* – the old port – to eat seafood and take a boat trip. He told me that the view from the *Basilique Notre Dame de la Garde* was *magnifique*. When he asked me what I used to do in my younger working days, I told him of my time as an art historian, a museum curator, although that had been a very long time ago, another life ago. He then began an excited spiel about the oldest part of Marseille, the *Panier Quarter*, and its colourful street art, funky sculptures and open-air art gallery.

'You can go for the art; I go for the food,' he said. 'And you know, we have Brutalist structures too; you know, concrete?'

'I know,' I said, smiling. 'Le Corbusier pioneered it.'

'*Exactement*! You know the *Cité Radieuse*?'

'I've seen pictures.'

'You must go see it in the flesh. In the concrete.' He laughed then and swerved violently to overtake a lorry.

'I really don't expect I shall have a lot of time to be honest.'

Clinging onto the side of my seat, a thought of not making it to the hotel alive crossed my mind. But Lucien was passionate about his city and extremely likeable, if a little hyperactive. I felt I had an immediate friend if I should need one.

We were driving up into the mountains now and the rocky terrain had gone from a rich terracotta colour to a chalky white. The vegetation was like a thick gorse and the trees were mostly pine.

'But of course we are going to Aix-en-Provence, the home of

Cézanne and name place of our hotel. People come from all over to see his studio and to see where he painted, walk in his footsteps. You will be among friends.'

My research about the area had been limited by the fact I'd had so little time to prepare. I'd mostly been looking up how to care for someone with dementia. But, of course I knew Paul Cézanne and his work. His paintings of *Mont Sainte-Victoire*, in particular seen from *Bellevue*, in its panoramic and delicate beauty, came straight to my mind, although my favourite by far was the brooding and intense *L'Estaque, Melting Snow*. To know I was heading into these locations and into the home of Cézanne himself gave me a frisson of excitement.

I began to see signs for Aix, but Lucien told me we were going straight to the hotel and he took the road that skirted south of the city itself. Before long we were onto small woodland lanes that could easily be mistaken for some of the roads around my house in Oxfordshire. The way the trees created a tunnel was very familiar. Then after a short time we were at the entrance to the hotel itself. There was a long driveway made to look even longer by the line of cypress trees that flanked it, and then we came to the main building. Dorothy had been quite right; it was a château that was for sure.

My eyes travelled up from the fountain in the middle of the driveway to the large doors of the main entrance, flanked by two large olive trees standing sentinel. The building was made of cream-and-ochre-coloured stone with warm-grey-painted shutters on all of the many windows. The roof was steeply pitched with ornate gables at either end and four turrets dominated each corner of the building. I gave up counting the finials after eight. It was truly a château you'd want to escape to.

The borders to one side of the building were filled with flowering shrubs and woody herbs. There was a large square of lawn with tables and chairs set underneath a sprawling tree, which cast a dark shadow of its silhouette.

There, in the shade, a lone woman sat with a coffee and her newspaper, looking a little like a model with her props for a château photo shoot. It was all very perfect and because of that perfection I suddenly felt a bit disconcerted and ever so slightly intimidated.

'*Hôtel and Spa du Cézanne,*' Lucien said, rather grandly as he swung the car past the main building and into a small car park on the side, spraying gravel towards some hedging as he skidded to a halt.

'What can you tell me about the Harpers before I meet them?' I asked him as he switched off the engine.

'Well, Gerald is very quiet and I don't see him much. And Meredith, I don't think she likes it here – she is homesick, my aunt told me. Perhaps you can get her out of her shell. She is...' He paused for a moment while he tried to find the word. 'Well, it's best if I leave you to meet her,' he said and then offered me an apologetic smile as if Meredith's temperament were his own fault. But, a homesick old woman I could easily empathise with.

'And the hotel? It looks big and expensive.'

'It is both of those things,' he said with a smile of pride. 'The building was abandoned and neglected when Hugo and Rose took a chance and bought it. Now, we are fifty *chambre* in the main *hôtel* and eight villas in the grounds, but most of those are still to be *rénové* – fixed up. Meredith and Gerald live in one of the good ones. It's very nice. Follow me and I will get the key to your room.'

Lucien pulled my case from the back seat and I followed him inside. The entrance was charming and light with huge doors leading out behind the reception area to an inner courtyard with a glimpse of sculpted gardens beyond. A staircase swept up to the right of us, but I could also see a lift had been discreetly installed in the far corner. Everything, from the seating to the artwork on the walls to the curtains and the furniture, was luxurious. Rich tones of blues and golds and greens were followed through all the soft furnishings and carpets and someone had taken great pains to put together the most beautiful floral display on a large mahogany table in the middle of the space. I could never afford to stay in a place like this and yet, here I was. I felt exactly as I had when I'd arrived at Walstone Hall – the country estate in Norfolk where I first met Dorothy back in August – overwhelmed. I hadn't been there as a guest, either. I was staff and I had to be mindful of that.

And then I remembered what Dorothy had asked me to do while I was here. She'd sent me on a mission that was far more than should be asked of any companion. Dorothy had learned that her former friend, Meredith, was writing her memoir. A mutual friend of the two women had told her. It had sent Dorothy into a spin.

'What I need you to do,' she had said at the time, 'is to see what Meredith is writing. We were involved in something, many years ago, and if she is now going to uncover that long-held secret, I need advanced warning. I'd be surprised if she would, but you never know with us oldies when we get to the winter of our lives. Some of us feel the need to offload. It would be uncomfortable for more than just me if this comes out now. I would need to take action.'

'Dorothy, let me be clear,' I had said. 'I'll be there as a companion and perhaps a carer for Meredith and Gerald while their daughter and son-in-law are away. I won't be poking around in their business.'

'But you do poking around so well,' she had reminded me with a smile, which didn't quite meet her eyes. I realised that this really was bothering her.

'Why don't you just ask her not to write whatever it is?' I had said.

'Ah, well, that is because we haven't spoken in years,' she'd said. 'We had a falling-out.'

Now, here I was in the château and on the brink of meeting the couple themselves. I had a huge lump in my stomach that had nothing to do with the croissant I had stuffed into my mouth at the airport. I suddenly had a horrible feeling I would be seeing it again.

2

GINA

I hung back, holding on to the handle of my case for a little support while I collected my thoughts. I needed to pull myself together and concentrate on the fact that I was here to look after a nice old couple. Whatever Dorothy had planned in her mind didn't have to interfere with my simple job as companion.

A gentle chatter filled the space from the guests who were coming and going and also those who were waiting. A couple relaxed on one of the sofas, leafing through the magazines that littered the coffee table; a woman with a dog was standing by the door organising her rucksack and reminding me that I'd read about all the walking trails in the area; a family were holding a map, deciding on their route; and staff busied about, back and forth, clearly rushing, but with smiles arranged carefully on their faces. As they passed Lucien, I noticed they would acknowledge him with a nod or a smile and one man patted his shoulder. He was liked – that was clear – and I wasn't surprised.

Lucien chatted to a woman behind the main reception desk; in fact, I'd say he was flirting, the way he leaned into her as she passed him what looked like my room key. She was wearing a blue skirt and a green silk blouse with a lovely gold brooch pinned to one side. Her hair was so blonde it was almost white and fell down her back like a waterfall. She was very beautiful and I wasn't at all surprised that handsome Lucien was taken with her. He walked back towards me with an envelope containing the key to my room. I was keen to dump my case and freshen up before meeting Gerald and Meredith.

'She is very attractive,' I said, nodding in the woman's direction and his smile lit up his entire face.

'Béatrice,' he said. 'I don't mind telling you, I'm half in love with her.'

His cheeks went a delicate shade of salmon then and I couldn't help but smile.

'She's your girlfriend?' I asked him.

'*Non*! We are too old for those terms. Béatrice is thirty-six and I'm nearly forty and anyway, she is with Cristòu. He is the head chef here.'

'You have a rival?' I said and he laughed.

'I have no chance with her, not any more. He is famous for his food. I would expect a Michelin star soon.'

As he said this his face fell and all the warmth disappeared.

'A good thing for the hotel, though,' I said.

'*Oui*, I agree, but he is an *imbécile*. She should have better.'

He took my suitcase and offered me his other arm, then guided me out of reception, across the courtyard and towards the garden.

We navigated our way past a swimming pool surrounded by sun loungers, several of which were in use. It was one of those infinity pools that appeared to drop away into the landscape beyond. The gardens below were perfectly planted with a mix of yellow and white flowering shrubs and then cypress trees stood tall to bring order to the space. It was as if they had been stuck into the ground like spears.

Lucien led me away from the pool and on towards a wooded area and I glanced back at the turrets of the château with a small pang of disappointment. It would have been wonderful to stay in one of its rooms.

'Am I staying in the shed?' I asked him with a chuckle.

'Rose thought it would be better if you had one of the villas, so you could be closer to Meredith and Gerald. And actually the hotel is almost full. We have a festival next week and Rose and Hugo offered a discount to encourage people to come. And it worked – we haven't seen so many guests. She also asked me to apologise, because the villa isn't finished. You will have more space, but it is, how can I say it... basic.'

'I don't mind at all,' I said. 'I'm very happy with something simple.'

'Hmmm,' was his response. 'Only two of the villas are finished so far. Meredith and Gerald have one and an English guest is staying in the other. It is all part of a bigger project to expand. It is why the accident of their son and the arrival of Rose's parents is such bad timing.'

'Meredith and Gerald haven't been here long then?'

'*Non*, only three weeks. It is still very new to them.'

There was a shingle path that weaved its way through the trees and as we got further away from the main hotel it was clear where the improvements had ceased. It became overgrown quite quickly and the beautifully stocked borders of the formal gardens were not mirrored here. Everything needed a good going over and for the first time in a while I wanted to pull on my gardening gloves and get stuck in. Perhaps I would, given the opportunity.

It was the garden I missed the most about losing my house. I'd spent years out there making it perfect, testing which plants worked and which didn't, finding the sunniest spots for my blooms and the shadiest for my ferns. It would soon belong to someone else and I kept resisting the urge to tell the agent we'd only sell to a keen gardener. What did it honestly matter? I'd never see it again anyway.

My heart tugged for my old life for a moment and then I thought about the lovely boathouse at Dorothy's and Dorothy herself who had become such a close confidante. Then I allowed a small thought of Erik, her neighbour, with his piercing blue eyes, strong tanned arms and his hands that were usually holding a paperback book. He'd invited us to an impromptu book club on his narrowboat, a couple of weeks back, to talk about the thriller he'd lent us. We'd opened some wine, sat back, laughed for a good hour and then relaxed in his gentle company.

A villa stood to our left with a small patio behind a low, clipped hedge. It was covered in wooden boards with freshly painted cream-coloured window frames. The blinds were pulled down on all of the windows. Its neighbouring villa looked exactly the same, although the hedge needed cutting. Then we walked a little further and there were a couple more. This time, though, the boards were missing and the paint on the rendering was flaking around damp patches. Instead of a neat hedge there was a forest of weeds and a broken chair. I smiled at Lucien to let him know that I wasn't worried at all. I was sure the inside could only be better than the outside. Lucien walked forward then and opened the door so that I could see I was entirely wrong.

It was certainly a work in progress; that was for sure. We were straight into a living area that had an old lumpy-looking sofa, an armchair and a coffee table. There was also a kitchenette in one corner. At the moment there was a worktop with a small sink and some cupboards – one of which looked dangerously close to falling off the wall – and a single induction ring on a plug-in unit that had perhaps been an afterthought, but there was a small fridge and a kettle. Thank goodness for the kettle. There were a couple of doors leading from the space, which I assumed would be a bedroom and bathroom, but I was keen to explore those alone.

'This is perfect for me,' I said. 'But I'm sure you have better things to do than show me around. Please point me in the direction of Meredith and Gerald and then I can get on with why I'm here.'

'*D'accord*, and you're all right with this?' Lucien said, waving his hand around in the air and almost knocking the paper lampshade from its fitting.

'Of course.'

'I forgot to ask if you'd had lunch.' He glanced at his watch, seemingly surprised at the time. 'The kitchen stopped serving food at two, but I could find something for you, if you'd like?'

'Honestly I'm fine,' I said, thinking about that croissant still lodged in my stomach.

'And the other thing is that Rose has arranged an online meeting with you later so she can talk to you. I will bring you a laptop.'

'Oh, okay,' I said, surprised. But, really it did make sense to talk to her. She could let me know what to expect from her parents.

'You'll find the Harpers in the first villa we walked past.'

The neat one with all the blinds closed. I didn't like to think why, on such a beautiful day, the occupants wished to sit inside. But, then Gerald wasn't well and perhaps they preferred peace and quiet. At that moment there was an almighty crash from the villa behind the one we were in and Lucien winced.

'*Rénovations*,' he said with a shrug.

'The guests don't mind the noise?' I asked him.

'There is only the Harpers and the Englishwoman on a research trip in the villas. She accepted the reduced price too and seems happy enough. We are away from the hotel here. The other guests won't hear much.'

I will, I thought, at the sound of a low rumble and another crash. I took a breath, thanked Lucien for his time and then closed the door behind him as he left.

* * *

Villa number one was oddly quiet. The building team on the renovation job had downed tools for an afternoon break – a French siesta I supposed – and we were too far from the main hotel to hear anything from the guests there. I did wonder if I could make out a splash from the pool, but maybe that was wishful thinking, because the afternoon was becoming blistering. It was early October, but still rather too hot for me here on the south coast of France. A freak heatwave or climate change, it was hard to tell, but I would strongly guess at the latter.

I walked up to the front door and hesitated as something caught the corner of my eye. A ball of fur was curled up under a shrub by the edge of the villa. A black and white cat, by the looks of it. I stepped across the strip of grass and crouched down to pet it, and it unfurled with my touch. I'd lost my dog the previous year and had often thought of finding another pet to love, but with Douglas leaving me and my life at a time of change, it really wouldn't be fair.

'You're lovely,' I told it as it rolled onto its back and stretched.

Just then, the blind on the window above my head snapped up and a face appeared behind the glass. A woman with a pinched nose and narrow eyes stared at me and I scrambled ungainly to my feet.

'Hello,' I said brightly, lifting my hand to wave. 'I'm Gina, Gina Knight.'

I wasn't sure if she could hear me from behind the glass, but her mouth stretched into a thin, tight line before she leaned forward and opened the window.

'Come to the door,' she said, brusquely. 'And don't bring that bloody cat with you.'

I paused for a moment while she slammed the window shut and lowered the blind. It took me a second longer to reassess my assumptions, because I thought I might have just met Meredith Harper and she wasn't the kindly old woman of my imaginings.

3

LUCIEN

Lucien felt terrible about leaving Gina in the villa in its unfinished state. He made a mental note to go back and replace that broken chair for her, at least. The trouble was they'd been given next to no time to get the villa in a reasonable condition and on top of everything else that needed his attention, well, it was all starting to look like too much.

He had a couple with a leaking shower; a guest who couldn't handle the full sun on their balcony and wanted to swap with someone on the other side of the hotel; Helena, a member of kitchen staff, who was on the brink of leaving because she couldn't bear Cristòu's outbursts; and a man with a spider that needed removal from his bathroom. The spider was next on his list. The spider was *pain grillé*. The spider was toast.

Lucien unfolded the sleeves of his shirt and buttoned up his cuffs when he caught his reflection in the mirrored lift. He used to love his tattoo; it meant a lot to him. It had been a while since he'd had it done, but he still remembered the sharp scratching of the needle on his skin, then pulling back the plastic wrap to show his friends and girlfriend at the time. A compass to symbolise all the directions his life could go in. He'd been young, good-looking and his future was full of endless possibilities. Then his father had died and his mother, Solène, had become... well, difficult.

Just over ten years had passed now and occasionally those points on the compass taunted him. He'd spent most of that time looking after his mother. What had he achieved for himself? Nothing.

He loved the artistry of the tattoo still, but less so its original meaning. Either way, he tried to keep it covered for work. He wanted so much to be taken seriously. His uncle Hugo had left him in charge and he fully intended to keep everything ticking along smoothly.

The trouble was they were hosting the food and art festival in only a week and had so much to do. Lucien had mad dreams that Hugo would come back early and leave Rose in charge of Oliver's recovery, but he knew this wouldn't be the case. Hugo adored his boy, and even though he was now a man, there was no way he wouldn't be by his side as he navigated this new path. Lucien loved Oliver too, he'd been like an older brother to him rather than a cousin and he couldn't bear the thought of him having to deal with this new life he had; a life that might see him on wheels rather than on his legs. But, he was strong and young and one thing that Lucien knew about Oliver was that he would never give up on anything. Oliver should be the one with the compass tattooed on his arm.

Lucien exited the lift on the second floor and checked his WhatsApp for Béatrice's message. *Monsieur Moreau, chambre numéro dix,* Béatrice had typed. *Grosse araignée poilue* – Big hairy spider!

Monsieur Moreau was standing outside on the landing, looking distressed with a bath towel around his middle and his hair dripping onto his chest. He didn't seem to have a waist and with the sun he had clearly caught, he reminded Lucien of a slightly undercooked sausage. His door was propped open with a chair and he glanced up when Lucien arrived beside him.

'I keep hoping it will just walk out by itself,' he said in French.

'Don't worry, I will deal with it,' Lucien said, his chest puffed up a little.

'It's in the bathroom, but I don't want you to kill it, just catch it and let it go.'

'I like spiders and I'm not afraid,' Lucien said and walked confidently into the room and over to the *en-suite*. The door was open and he glanced inside. The bath mat was wet and pushed half up the side of the bath, no doubt in the man's rush to make his escape. Lucien wished Béatrice was here to witness his heroic actions, but he would just have to enjoy telling the story later.

Stepping into the middle of room, he was beginning to think the spider had indeed left of its own accord when a flash of black caught the corner of his eye. It was huge and running down the shower curtain towards Lucien's feet. Despite himself he let out a high gasp and went to take a step back, but slipped on the edge of the wet bath mat and as he reached out to steady himself he brought the shower curtain down off its pole with one yank.

'All okay in there?' Monsieur Moreau called from the landing.

Lucien scrabbled around on the tangle of curtain, mat and wet floor until he was back up on his feet.

'All is well. I nearly have him.'

When Lucien pulled up the curtain, though, he did indeed have the spider, but it was a wet, dead pancake of a spider. He rehung the curtain, folded the mat over the edge of the bath and flushed the spider's corpse down the toilet. Then, cupping his hands together, he rejoined his guest on the landing.

'I'll take him outside. You are safe to go back in.'

'*Merci, monsieur,* I am most grateful to you.'

Lucien kept his hands cupped until he was back inside the lift and then wiped them on his trousers when the door had closed. He definitely wouldn't be telling this story to Béatrice.

He was about to step out of the lift into reception when his phone started buzzing in his pocket. He had set it to silent once the calls had started to arrive, but he couldn't quite bring himself to stop the vibration as well. He certainly couldn't turn his phone off as Hugo liked to check in from time to time. He demanded updates to make sure that everything was running smoothly. It wasn't Hugo's name on the screen, though. Lucien ran a hand through his hair and wiped a bead of sweat from his upper lip. Then he pocketed his phone with it still buzzing like an irritating wasp.

'Lucien!'

Béatrice called to him as he stepped out of the lift. Her eyes were wide, indicating that she had a bit of a problem. Lucien couldn't help but feel that all of her problems could be solved by ditching Cristòu.

There were a couple standing in front of her wearing expressions that told of trouble. Lucien recognised them as the American people that arrived a few days ago. Mr and Mrs Roberts were in their fifties, courteous, well dressed and equally well spoken. It was also the second time they had stayed at *Hôtel and Spa du Cézanne.* They were from Washington they had told him when he had checked them in this time and had apparently enjoyed themselves so much last time that when they had received the email about the art and food festival they decided to *'hop over the pond'.*

'*Nous avons un petit problème,*' Béatrice hissed at him, despite Hugo and Rose asking them all to speak in English.

It didn't bother Lucien. His English was good and he'd lived in London for five years when he'd finished *université*. It made sense to him for a hotel that looked after guests from all over the world to try and simplify communications. Most of the staff had good English, certainly a lot better than the French that most of the guests attempted, but some resented not being able to speak in their own language. He understood, but he was someone who followed the rules. His thoughts went briefly to the phone call he'd just ignored. Mostly he followed the rules.

'Mr and Mrs Roberts. How may we assist you?' Lucien asked as the couple turned to him.

'Ah, Lucien isn't it? Please call me Bradley. We have a situation, but I certainly don't want to bother any other guests, so could we take this somewhere private?'

Lucien thought about Hugo's office that was currently a bit of a mess. He just hadn't had the time to sort it, but there was nowhere else that offered as much privacy.

'Please, follow me,' he said, sweeping them out of reception and away from the raised eyebrows of Béatrice. She liked to make fun of him, but Hugo had left him in charge and he would have to sort out whatever situation Mr and Mrs Roberts found themselves in. He couldn't see how they could have a problem with their room, because they had one of the best suites and Béatrice was in charge of the cleaning staff. She was usually on top of everything, but if something wasn't quite up to scratch he could offer complimentary spa treatments and a basket of fruit, perhaps a bottle of something from Hugo's cellar.

That would have to be a last resort, though, and would certainly be done with a lot of thought. When he'd first started working at the hotel he'd taken the wrong bottle of wine when he had a shift in the restaurant and instead of a reasonably priced Châteauneuf-du-Pape, he'd actually handed over an eye-wateringly expensive bottle of Château La Violette – Pomerol. He'd tried to make a joke about it with Hugo, about having wine in his cellar that was out of the region and what did he expect, but it had fallen flat. Lucien guessed, correctly, that when a man was down by about three hundred euros, it wasn't the time for jokes.

He opened the door to the office ready with an apology on his lips, but was surprised to see all the papers that had earlier been strewn across the desk were now tidied away. Béatrice – it had to be her and just that thought gave him the tiniest glimmer of hope.

'Please take a seat,' he told the couple, but only Mrs Roberts sat down.

'I'm afraid to say,' Mr Roberts began, holding on to the back of the chair rather than sitting in it, 'we have had a theft from our room. My wife, Laura, has a valuable gold necklace that is now missing. No obvious break-in has occurred that we can see and our balcony door was shut and locked. I'm afraid to say that I think it was perhaps the cleaning staff.'

'I'm very sorry to hear that!' Lucien said, surprised. It was honestly the last thing he'd expected the American to say. He couldn't remember there ever being a theft at the hotel. Of course, it would have to be on his watch. 'If I may speak for the cleaning team, I would have to vouch for them not to have taken your necklace, Mrs Roberts. They are very trustworthy. Do you mind if I suggest it may have fallen on the floor, or it has been caught in your clothes? We have a small lost property and I will certainly check in there. In fact I will do that now.'

'We have looked and looked and it's not in our room. I'm not a man to cause a fuss, but would appreciate it if you would talk to your cleaning staff and see if they can shed any light on the matter.'

'But, of course. I will see if there has been some kind of accidental slip-up. I do have every confidence in them, though,' Lucien said.

'It is a favourite,' Laura Roberts said, quietly, 'but I don't want anyone to lose their job. It's probably me; I've probably mislaid it.'

Laura's husband put a gentle hand on her shoulder and she lifted her own to cover it.

'Honey, you know you haven't mislaid it, but I love you for suggesting it.'

'Just give me a moment and I will check the lost property.'

He left them in the office and scuttled back round to reception.

'What's going on?' Béatrice asked him.

'They've lost a gold necklace and I'm going to check lost property before I call the police.'

'The police! Lucien, we have the festival in a week. You want the police here?'

'*Non,* of course not, but I have to be seen to be doing something. We've never had a theft. They have probably just lost it.'

Lucien moved past her to the room behind the desk and unlocked the door to the lost property cupboard. In it were a few coats and clothes, washed, ironed and probably never to be reunited with their owners. Their policy was to do their utmost to find who these items belonged to, but things weren't always left in the rooms the guests had recently vacated. There was the spa where stray items were abandoned. Coats were left on the backs of chairs and hooks in reception. They had power leads and phone chargers left plugged into various ports in the hotel common areas, not to mention the number of books, hair clips and shoes. Béatrice would email guests if things of value were unaccounted for; she had an eye for the good stuff. Lucien called it her Magpie Radar.

He took a smaller key and opened a safe that was tucked in the back of the cupboard, behind the coats. There was never much in here, because most guests returned for jewellery or passports et cetera and all there was currently was an old cameo brooch Béatrice had still to find the owner of and a sliver chain with a pink, butterfly charm hanging from the end. He scooped it up, knowing it wasn't what Mrs Roberts had lost, but thought he'd show the couple he had at least looked.

Mr Roberts actually laughed when Lucien held it up to him.

'I don't think you understand,' he said. 'My wife's necklace is an eighteen-carat-gold snake chain with a substantial locket on it. The locket is studded with twenty-five brilliant-cut diamonds.'

Lucien gulped, audibly, and shoved the pink butterfly into his pocket.

'What I will do, is have my colleague talk to the staff to double-check it hasn't found its way into some sheets or towels and then our laundry. And if that isn't successful, I will phone the police. How does that sound?'

It sounded pretty lame to his own ears, but he was pleased to see Mr Roberts taking it in.

'I'll give you until tomorrow lunchtime and if it hasn't been accounted for, I will be expecting you to call the police.'

Mr and Mrs Roberts refused the offer of coffee or tea and there was a firm shake from both of their heads at the suggestion of a glass of pastis. Then they left with Mr Roberts pulling his wife out of the office by her hand.

4

GINA

Inside, Meredith and Gerald's villa was as gloomy as I expected with the blinds pulled down and only minimal lighting. It was carefully decorated, though, certainly compared to the one I was staying in. A quick glance around and I could see that all of the soft furnishings were in neutral tones. The carpets, furniture, blinds and wallpaper were all varying shades of fawn, pale coffee and beige. In contrast to that was the artwork. The whole place was adorned with colourful glass and ceramic sculptures: on shelves, on the floor and even secured into stands in the corners of the room. On the walls, the pictures were modern, angular and mostly of architecture. I remembered then that Dorothy had told me Gerald was a retired architect. It was clear that Meredith and her old friend Dorothy shared a love of the glass that Dorothy used to work with. Perhaps Meredith and Gerald were also collectors, just as Dorothy's husband had been.

There was a stack of novels on the coffee table, a couple of empty mugs and a notebook with scrawled handwriting across the page. Also, a laptop with an open document on the screen.

The cursor was blinking at the end of four words: What is the point?! Meredith stepped forward and quickly shut the lid.

There was no sign of Gerald.

Meredith didn't offer me a seat, her hand or a cup of tea, but instead she walked over to the sofa and sat down while cradling her plastered arm.

She was a tiny bird of a woman who was dressed impeccably in smart grey trousers and a neat cream blouse with a frilled collar, which on closer inspection looked as if she was wearing it inside out. Her hair sat on her head like a perfectly coiffured helmet of gold and grey. She was perched on the edge of the seat with her knees pressed neatly together. She didn't smile.

'I'm Gina Knight,' I said, overly friendly in the hope she might warm up a bit. 'And I'm here in any capacity that you might need me.'

I was about to say I was a friend of Dorothy's and then remembered Dorothy's plan. I wasn't to mention her at all. 'Can I ask how your grandson is? I think he's coming out of hospital?' I continued when she didn't answer.

Surely I could win her round with talk of grandchildren. My own two granddaughters were a delight. Megan and Louise, or Meg and Lou to everyone now, were eight and eleven years of age respectively. Meg was a sunny child with a love of games, crafts and books. She collected flowers and pressed them before fixing them onto handmade bookmarks and birthday cards. I've had many a pretty gift from her. Lou was perhaps a little more demanding than her younger sister. But, she was funny, smart, ambitious and had big plans for her life, combining travel with earning an awful lot of money. Meg just wanted to have lots of pets and live by the sea.

Meredith's beady, bird eyes were fixed on me as she slowly opened her mouth to speak.

'Oliver was discharged from intensive care yesterday and my daughter and her husband are with him now as he begins his rehabilitation. Would you like to take a seat and we can discuss what I'd like you to do for me.'

I walked over to the armchair across from her and lowered myself into it, remembering that I hadn't taken my shoes off, but didn't want to draw attention to that fact now.

'As you can see, I've broken my arm, which does render me a little useless. I'll be looking to you for assistance with... well, the thing is, Gerald has dementia and...'

She broke off for a moment and her face lost a lot of its severity.

'I imagine it's very difficult,' I said gently and she nodded.

'He's lost the ability to do a lot of things now. He struggles with getting dressed by himself; he doesn't seem to understand where to put his arms if you hand him a shirt. He can still communicate for now, but is often silent. He hasn't anything familiar around him because we've had to move here and now, honestly, I think that was a mistake. Quite frankly, Gerald is the love of my life and I'm losing him.'

Her voice broke on those last words and I got up from my chair. I would have offered comfort to a friend, but I didn't know this woman and was pretty sure she wouldn't have wanted me to hug her or hold her hand.

'Shall I make us a cup of tea,' I offered instead and she gave me a small nod.

'The kitchen is through there,' she said, turning around and pointing to the door behind her. I scurried away to be useful while Meredith collected herself.

Their villa was a lot bigger than the one I was staying in and had a fully equipped kitchen with granite worktops. I couldn't tell in this light what colour the kitchen was, because the window was covered the same as in the rest of the villa. The place felt oppressive and I pulled the blind up an inch so I could see what I was doing without having to turn on the light. As soon as the afternoon sun filled the room, the worktops sparkled in silver and copper flashes and the cupboard doors revealed themselves to be a warm, elephant grey. I imagined the riot of colour that would be unleashed if the blinds were to be opened in the living room. How that glass would sing.

I filled the kettle and switched it on to boil, then set about looking through the cupboards for everything I needed. Each door had a large sticker with a list of what was inside. There was red tape across some of the plug sockets and instructions listed on a whiteboard pinned to the wall. All signs to help Gerald to navigate this new world he found himself in. And I imagined it wasn't just this French villa that was new to him, but what was going on in his head too.

I walked back through to Meredith who had returned to her perched position on the edge of the sofa, knees together and lips pinched. I put the cup of tea and a bowl of sugar I'd found on a shelf in the kitchen down on the table in front of her and collected the empty cups, which I left by the sink before returning to the living room with my own cup of tea.

'What can I do for *you*, Meredith? I'd really like to help in any way I can while I'm here.'

She sighed and looked me up and down. I tried not to be offended when she then sighed again as if I wasn't quite up to scratch. I silently cursed Dorothy for arranging this. I could think of several places I'd rather be right now.

'You're a little older than I thought you'd be,' she said and then had the good grace to look a bit embarrassed.

'I'm seventy-one,' I told her. I might as well be frank about it. 'Is that going to be a problem?'

'To be honest, I don't really need much help. My daughter thinks I do, which is why she organised this, but I'm more than capable, I believe.'

I wanted to say that's great, I'll book the next flight home, but I didn't. This was exactly how Dorothy had been when I first met her. I could tell, at the time, she was a bit resentful of the suggestion she might need assistance. She had said she didn't need any help and then proceeded to ask me if I would help her. Perhaps Meredith needed to settle into the idea.

This woman wasn't happy. Whether that was because of her husband's dementia, her move to France, her daughter's absence or me, it was hard to say. I assumed it was all of those things and wondered if I could really make a difference. Glancing again at the inside seam and the label of her blouse on show I felt a wave of compassion for that tiny display of fragility. I decided to take it slowly and get to know her.

'There is one thing,' she said, seeming to be weighing me up again as her eyes wandered from my face to my shoes and back up. 'I'm writing my memoir at the moment and I shall need you to type up my words. I can't be doing it one-handed – it will take too long and I have a deadline.'

'Won't your publisher be lenient?' I'd learned from Dorothy that Meredith used to write romance novels. 'If you talk to them, they might—'

'It's a personal deadline,' Meredith interrupted. 'I began to make notes before I broke my arm, but I still hold most of it in my head so I shall have to dictate now that my writing hand is useless. Can you type?'

I imagined if Dorothy was here, she'd be actively encouraging this. *Go on, Gina, get into her notes and report back.*

'I can type a little. I won't be terribly fast, to be honest.'

'Well, you'll be a lot better and quicker than me at the moment using one finger on my left hand; that's for sure.'

The door behind Meredith suddenly opened and a man appeared, looking confused and crumpled. He was wearing bright green corduroy trousers and a pale-lemon-coloured shirt. He had the look of an older Michael Portillo about him.

'I can't find my binoculars,' he said, in a voice that suggested he'd just woken up.

'Oh, my love,' Meredith said, getting to her feet using her good arm for support on the edge of the sofa and a bit of a rocking momentum. 'I will help you find them.'

Her face was flooded with love and warmth and she suddenly looked quite beautiful. I could imagine this couple in their younger years, turning heads as they went along. She reached his side, took his arm and guided him back into the bedroom.

'Let's get you sorted,' she said to him in a gentle voice.

I noticed a photograph of the two of them in a silver frame, sitting on top of a long wooden sideboard. It looked professional, like the sort you'd have taken at a gala event or maybe at the beginning of a cruise. Meredith was beautiful in a black and silver gown, her hair a mane of rich chestnut. Gerald was in black tie sporting a moustache he didn't have now, and somehow he seemed a little vulnerable without that facial hair.

'Can I help at all?' I asked.

'No,' she said, sharply. 'I can look after my husband, thank you.' She turned away from me for a moment and then seemed to remember her manners. 'You can come here in the mornings at eight-thirty for a bit and give me a hand getting us going. Then we can do our own thing, but I'd like you to return here for one-thirty each afternoon. We can work on the book while Gerald rests.'

She didn't ask if that was okay with me. There was no: *How does that sound, Gina?* Or: *Will that work for you?* I couldn't quite decide if she was just naturally rude or if I was actually in awe of her self-assurance. And then I thought that both of those things could be true, and reminded myself I was here to do a job.

'Okay,' I said in response. 'It was nice to meet you, Gerald,' I added, although I hadn't actually met him at all.

5

GINA

I wandered back towards my villa, then had a change of heart and decided to have a stroll through the gardens. The black and white cat had disappeared. Sensible chap.

Cutting back past the villa next to the Harpers' I noticed a woman sitting on the little terrace. I assumed she was the English guest that Lucien talked about. She looked to be in her sixties with curly chestnut hair. I noticed the odd white hair sticking up across her parting as if she'd just finished painting the ceiling, or maybe her roots needed touching up. She wore a pretty pale-blue summer dress that pooled on the ground where she sat in the chair. I was about to walk straight past as she was tucked away behind her unclipped hedge with her head down, seemingly engrossed in her mobile phone and not looking for company. But then, with only three villas occupied it was hardly neighbourly.

'Hello,' I offered.

She lifted her hand to shield the sun from her eyes and smiled tentatively at me.

'Hi,' she said, turning her phone face down on the coffee table in front of her. 'Have you just arrived?'

'Yes,' I said, taking a step toward her. 'Flew in a couple of hours ago. I'm staying there.'

I pointed to my villa and she followed my finger with her eyes before wrinkling her nose.

'What did you do to deserve that?'

She laughed and I joined her, glad to have the tension of being with Meredith lifted.

'I'm Gina.'

'Adele,' she said.

'I'm here to look after the couple in villa number one and to be honest mine isn't that bad. It's clean, at least,' I said.

'You're here for that elderly couple?' she asked, surprised, and it seemed for a moment that she also looked a bit eager, sitting forward in her chair. I couldn't imagine why Meredith and Gerald would be of that much interest to anybody, though.

'Yes, their daughter usually looks after them, but she's had to fly off on a family emergency, so I'm stepping in.'

'Oh, I see, like a carer then? I haven't actually seen them; they don't come out of that place at all. It can't be healthy never going out, but then I suppose it is a little warm and if you're not used to the climate...'

She trailed off and I was going to ask her how she knew they were an elderly couple if she'd never seen them, but I assumed Lucien or another member of staff must have told her who the neighbours were.

'Are they nice people? To work for, I mean.'

'Meredith is finding the move here from London difficult, I believe, and her husband, Gerald, has dementia, I've barely met him. And you're holidaying alone?' I asked her, to change the subject. I really had no business talking about the Harpers.

'I'm a photographer,' she said, simply.

'Weddings?'

'People and places.'

'For books and magazines?' I asked her as she didn't seem to be that forthcoming.

'Well, I've decided to write a travel vlog and I thought that the Marseille area and in particular here, in Aix, would be a good place to start. I'm going out to take photos tomorrow.'

It was really strange, because as she said this her voice sounded quite wooden as if she'd practised the words – like a spiel she'd got fed up repeating.

'I should have offered you a drink, sorry,' she said, leaning forward to pick up her glass from the table. The sunlight caught her hair and the chestnut curls shone. I was reminded momentarily of my old friend Carmen. She had the most wonderful head of curls, although hers were red, quite fiery red. I hadn't seen her since she moved back to Spain many years ago. The occasional Christmas card now was the only reminder we were ever friends in the first place. She wouldn't know I no longer lived in Thame. I'd have to send an early Christmas card with a change of address. I wonder what she'd think of my new situation. She had never been Douglas's number-one fan, so she'd probably be delighted. For a brief moment I entertained the idea of going to visit her; after all, I could do whatever I liked now and I'd made it to the south of France easily enough. It wasn't much more of a stretch to get to Malaga.

A wave of sadness suddenly took me when I thought of all the years I'd let slip through my fingers, but then I shook it off as Adele was saying something.

'So, would you like a drink?'

'Oh, that's kind, but I was going to have a walk through the gardens and then I really do have things I need to do.'

'With Gerald,' she said and it wasn't really a question.

'More Meredith, to be honest. She's broken her arm and she

wants me to write her memoir for her. Not sure how good my typing is, though. When I say write her memoir, I obviously mean type it. She'll have all the words for her own life story,' I said with a smile.

Adele just stared at me.

'She's writing her memoir?'

'Yes, she used to be a romantic novelist, apparently, but now she's writing her own story.'

'How lovely,' Adele said and she had that look again, eager. Perhaps it was just the interest from one new writer to an established one.

'If you need any help with the typing, then let me know. I'm pretty good.'

'I'm sure you have better things to do, but thank you,' I said getting to my feet.

Adele got up too and stepped forward with an extended hand.

'It was lovely to meet you,' she said, seemingly a lot more engaged than she had been at the start of our conversation.

I left her standing on her patio, fiddling with the gold chain that hung around her neck and disappeared down into the body of her dress. For a moment I wondered what was hanging on the other end. As I briefly glanced back I thought that she looked uncomfortable. She didn't seem like a relaxed holidaymaker; she looked like a woman who was waiting to meet someone and was rather apprehensive about it.

* * *

It was really too hot for me to walk in the gardens and I turned back for my villa after only traversing one flower bed and one line of cypress trees. The swimming pool was crowded with bodies keeping cool, but there were also some die-hard sunbathers stretched out on loungers, books and magazines in hand. Someone was sketching the view and I followed their eye to see what looked like *Mont Sainte-Victoire* in the distance. Of course, this was the home of Paul Cézanne after all. Lucien had told me that guests flocked to see his studio and walk in his footsteps, witness the views he would have seen and what he'd gone on to depict in his paintings. I would have to make sure I made time to go into Aix; after all, Meredith had given me most of the mornings to myself. This really didn't seem like that much of a job at all.

I opened my suitcase and began to fill the tiny wardrobe in the bedroom. The linen was fresh and the room was beautifully clean, but it still had a sad appearance and would greatly benefit from the *rénovations*.

A couple of hours later Lucien arrived with a basket of tea, coffee and sugar, and little packets of biscuits.

'This should have been here when you arrived,' he said. 'There's some milk in the fridge.'

He also had the promised laptop and set it up on the small table behind the sofa.

'Do you know how to use a computer?' he asked me with a worried expression and, I noted, a look that suggested he'd be surprised if I knew what a computer actually was.

'Of course,' I said, with a pointed look.

Douglas bought a laptop a couple of years back, but he never really used it. Out of the two of us, surprisingly to me, I was the more tech-savvy. He didn't take it with him when he left and I used to bring it up to bed with me in the evenings to watch movies or catch-up TV, rather than sit in our living room alone. I do the same now in Dorothy's boathouse because there isn't a television set in there.

'Rose has set the call to go through at seven *ce soir*. It will be six tomorrow morning for them.'

'Fine with me. It will be good to talk to her.'

'And, of course, you must eat all your meals as a guest in the restaurant, on the house. I forgot to say. The staff know to expect you and all the timings we serve food are in there,' he said, pointing to a booklet on the table that I had failed to notice before.

I was glad to hear I'd been made welcome for a meal and that would be perfect tonight as I had no alternative, but I'd much rather provide for myself here than sit in the restaurant alone night after night with guests enjoying themselves around me. Here I could read, relax and be alone without an audience to see I *was* actually alone.

Lucien's phone began vibrating then. I could hear it buzzing in his pocket and he pulled it out, glanced at the screen and with a frown he hissed the word *merde*.

'Problems?' I asked him, but he quickly shook his head before backing towards the door.

'All is *très bien*,' he said with a look that suggested quite the opposite.

'Hopefully Rose and Hugo's son will make a speedy recovery and they'll be back home soon. It must be tricky having to take over while they're away.'

'Do you know, Gina, if it was only the hotel it would actually be okay,' he said, cryptically before taking a card from his shirt pocket and dropping it onto the table. 'If you need anything then please call me.'

I picked up the card after he'd left and turned it over in my hand.

Lucien DuBois
Directeur de l'hôtel

The card felt and smelled fresh out of the printer and I wondered, with a smile, if Lucien had them printed as the Guérins were leaving for the airport. He was proud of his city and proud of his aunt and uncle's hotel it seemed. He reminded me a little of my son Chris – enthusiastic, caring and principled. He was one of the good guys too.

I glanced at my watch and realised I should get myself ready. It was already six o'clock and I wanted to freshen up and be prepared to talk to Rose. The afternoon had slipped away. I felt really that I ought to get back to Meredith. She hadn't specifically said she didn't want to see me again today, although it had been heavily implied by her dismissive back to me as I left, but surely she would need some personal care. This job couldn't all be about typing her memoir. The woman had a broken arm after all. The thought didn't fill me with cheer, but maybe I could just tap on her door, clarify what was expected. I should really have done that earlier.

I took a breath and then found a glass in one of the cupboards, one that wasn't falling off the wall. As I filled it with some water from the tap there was a rumbling sound and then a crash. At a time I'd expect them to be finishing, it seemed the *rénovations* were back up and running.

6

LUCIEN

'You seem to keep missing my calls and you're never at *la tua casa* when I pop round.'

Isabel's voice was low and a little husky. It could have been seductive apart from the fact that Lucien had an image of her smoking a cigarette like a Bond villain. Her fingers lifting it to her red-painted lips, a trail of smoke curling up into the air. Smoking caused damage, though, and there wasn't anything sexy about desiccated vocal cords. He took a moment to adjust to the change in language from French to Italian.

'I'm so sorry, I have been busy with a family situation.'

He answered her, slowly and carefully in simple Italian. The last thing he wanted was miscommunication. It was also news to him that she knew where he lived. He gulped and it was so audible they must both have heard it.

'Another family situation? Signor DuBois, how many do you have?'

More than I can handle, he thought with a grimace, as he readjusted the phone to his other ear so he could try to pull the large bunch of keys from his pocket, and he laughed darkly.

'*Sotto controllo*,' he said as lightly as he could, but he'd never felt less in control in his whole life. 'I'm still waiting to hear how much is actually owed and I want some proof of that too,' he said in a moment of bravado.

He then imagined climbing out of his car one night, being wrestled to the ground and having both of his kneecaps blown off. And, perhaps he was watching too many action movies.

'We will let you know, don't you worry.'

Lucien almost didn't want to know how much money his mother owed these people. It wouldn't be a small amount, it never was, but this was the first time *he* had been contacted. It meant that she wasn't prepared or able to pay it herself.

'I have to go now, but I will be in touch as soon as I can,' he said then, as if he was talking to an old friend.

'Don't leave me wanting, Lucien. This needs resolving and, you know, it's becoming increasingly clear that Solène cannot resolve it herself,' she said, pointedly and then with a brief *ciao*, she was gone.

The keys were wedged – his pockets were too small – and as he yanked them sharply upwards in frustration he tore the corner of the fabric.

'*Merde!*'

He tucked the loose flap of materiel into the pocket it had been torn from and began to work his way through the keys to find the one for the door to the wine cellar. It would be easier to wear this bunch clipped to his belt, but he already felt like the janitor; he really didn't need to look like one too.

The cellar was cool and ever so slightly damp. There was a sweet smell from the residue left after the wine-tasting sessions that Hugo was fond of. Red sticky rings where bottles had been left and not cleaned. Lucien took a moment to collect himself.

At first he had just thought someone was watching him. It had begun a couple of weeks back and he was able to laugh it off as him having watched too many Netflix dramas. But, then there had been silent phone calls from an unknown number and a message saying that *they were waiting and their patience was running low*. Now, of course Isabel had been in touch and there was nothing mysterious about it. Somehow, though, that was easier than the sinister silence that had come before. It was less intimidating when someone came out and told you exactly what it was they wanted. Money was owed and it wasn't going away. He'd have to talk to his mother tonight. He'd been too quiet about it for too long. They would have to come up with a plan together, no matter how vulnerable she seemed. His love for her had clouded his judgement. It was Solène's fault they were in this mess, after all.

The wall of wines in front of him took his attention then and he began to make a list of what he thought suitable. There was a party of local business owners who were getting together to finalise plans for the food and art festival. Hugo wanted to show off the renovations on the hotel and secure its place as one of the best, if not *the* best hotel in the area and so had offered his grounds for the event. Now, of course, he wouldn't be here. He had hinted a couple of times that he might be able to pop back for it, but Lucien thought it was all bluster. He was pretty sure that once Hugo saw how much his son needed him he wouldn't be popping anywhere, least of all embarking on a twelve-thousand-mile journey.

His eyes roamed the wall of bottles in front of him and he used the app on his phone as a guide. Hugo had suggested he download it after the last costly wine debacle. He said it was trustworthy. Of course, what Hugo needed to do was to hire a sommelier, but there were a lot of things that Hugo needed to do. Cristòu could do it, but he would pick and choose when it suited him. It was like a game and sometimes he would rather lose his shit when Lucien got it wrong than bother to put down his knife and go and choose the wine himself, complaining that he really didn't have the time. Well, neither did Lucien.

He picked up the odd bottle and made a note. He stacked those he thought would work well together in front of one of the many shelves. These weren't the best of Hugo's collection. Walking towards the darker, dustier corner, his eyes travelled the *supérieur* bottles. This lot in front of him was worth a small fortune and he quickly tucked that thought away. Far away.

* * *

Lucien made his way to the hotel kitchen where *dîner* preparations were underway. It was a noisy atmosphere and what seemed like organised chaos.

Cristòu, the head chef, was ordering everyone about as usual and round after round of *oui, Chef* punctuated the clatter of pans and the chopping of vegetables, the hissing and whirring of machines and the deep tones of Cristòu's instructions. Lucien stood and watched him for a moment. He was a large man with a perfectly bald head and a neatly clipped goatee. He wasn't fat, he was solid and muscular. Everything about him was powerful: the way he wielded a knife, the tone of his voice as he commanded his staff and his very presence in the room. Lucien couldn't help but always be surprised, though, when he saw him stooped over a dish with a tiny pair of tweezers, placing micro herbs onto perfectly grilled fish or edible flowers around beautifully presented desserts. Lucien was amazed by him, but he also despised him.

Hugo had a way to deal with Cristòu that Lucien did not. But Hugo had also left Lucien in charge and it was his job to make sure the hotel was running smoothly. He knew that Cristòu had everything under control and really he could leave him to it, but there was this little part of him that liked to wield his senior position, however temporary it was. And besides, he also didn't mind the opportunity for an argument with the head chef. He felt it energised him.

He put the bottles he'd collected from the cellar on the stainless steel counter: one red, one white and one rosé. He didn't want to overcomplicate things.

Cristòu turned and narrowed his eyes at someone in his kitchen who wasn't working directly on the dinner service and then narrowed them further because it was Lucien.

'*La Sobilane* for your *poulet* and *Montpeyroux* for your *bœuf*. And, of course Whispering Angel for the rosé. That goes without saying.'

Lucien squared up and leaned against the counter, trying to make himself bigger while he waited for Cristòu to have an opinion. Cristòu put down his knife and took a bottle opener from a drawer, then pulled the cork from the *Montpeyroux* and poured a lot of it into a glass before tipping it all down his throat.

'*Idéal*,' he said simply and turned back to what he was doing.

The kitchen had momentarily gone quiet, everyone seeming to be holding their collective breath, but now the noise started up again and it was back to business. Lucien walked away on slightly shaky legs. He'd been prepared for a fight, but had been denied. He wasn't sure how he felt about that.

7

GINA

I made a cup of coffee in preparation for the conversation with Rose, then sat down at the table and opened the laptop, arranging my expression into one that would best resemble a confident and competent companion, although the reality was that I still wasn't exactly sure what I would be doing for Meredith.

'Gina, hello.'

The screen came to life when the call connected and a younger version of Meredith appeared in front of me. She had the same tiny features as her mother, but she looked brighter, sunnier, more likely to welcome a conversation and that was mostly because she was smiling, not something I'd seen her mother do, yet.

'Hi, Rose, it's lovely to meet you.'

'Have you settled in okay? I'm sorry the place isn't finished, or, let's be honest, even started. We bought extra land, behind the château which already had several neglected holiday lets on it, but we haven't had time to do them all up yet.'

'It's no problem at all, I promise. I'm very happy to have my own space. Please, tell me how your son is.'

Rose took a deep breath and rubbed at her temples with her fingers. I didn't know this woman, but she looked exhausted. I couldn't imagine how I would feel if it was one of my children on the other side of the world, injured.

'He's strong,' she started. 'I'm honestly blown away by how resolved he is to get better. I know it's only early days, but with this attitude it makes me hopeful. Did my mother tell you what happened?'

'No, but Lucien gave me a little information.'

I hoped I wasn't getting him into trouble. I didn't want her to think we'd been gossiping about her family. Although, Lucien was her family, really.

'Dear Lucien, such a lovely guy.'

'I get that impression too.'

'Oliver had a motorbike accident and has hurt his back. He had an infection that stopped them from operating for a week, but now they have done what they can and we wait and see.'

She looked over her shoulder, and then leaned closer to the screen and lowered her voice.

'We don't talk about him not walking. He doesn't talk about that either. It's all about getting him well enough to come home and that's what we are here for, to get him better. It's going in the right direction and as soon as he's recovered properly from the operation and we can get him on a plane, he can rehabilitate at home.'

She leaned back and picked up her mug at the same time as I did, which made us both laugh.

'So, I assume you've met Mum.'

'Yes, this afternoon. She seems very…'

'Depressed,' Rose cut in. 'She's not happy and I'm sorry that you've been thrown in at the deep end. It's all such bad timing. They had only just moved in with us when Oliver had his accident, and to be honest, that was after extensive persuasion. Mum needed me, but so did my son. We did have someone who stepped in to help with them as we left, but they let us down after only a week and that's why we were lucky to find you. It's ironic after all the time I spent getting her to see that being close to me and Hugo was the best way and as soon as they make that monumental move, we're suddenly on the other side of the world. I was hoping to have time to settle Mum and Dad in with us and take them out into the city, acclimatise them to being in France. It's not healthy hanging around the hotel all the time. Especially for Dad. I think he needs stimulation and Mum is keeping him prisoner in the villa. Well, not prisoner maybe, but you know what I mean.'

I nodded. I did know exactly what she meant.

'I'm sure she will love the area, given time. Mum has always been outgoing and adventurous. I'd love for her to capture some of that again.'

It was hard to imagine Meredith as adventurous, but I knew from experience that judging someone on how they appeared now with what you think they may have achieved in their life was ignorant.

'I completely understand, Rose, and I want to assure you that I will do everything I can to help her to settle until you return.'

'That does give me comfort. I've heard only good things about you from Barbara. She said you were a calm and trustworthy person, which is good enough for me.'

'Barbara? Is she Dorothy's friend?'

I said this without thinking. I wasn't to mention Dorothy, but honestly did it really matter?

'I don't know Dorothy,' Rose said, 'but your reference came to us through Barbara. You were highly recommended. We were rushing, perhaps I didn't ask enough questions.'

She looked worried for a moment and I gathered my thoughts.

'Barbara must be associated with the family from my previous companion job. No matter,' I said, quickly. 'Calm and trustworthy, that's me. Can I ask what you would like me to do for Meredith? What do you feel she really needs? Because she gave me the impression that she can cope perfectly well herself. Gerald too – what can I do for him?'

Rose seemed to be mollified. Perhaps she was too tired to care, or maybe she simply liked the look of me. How much of a problem could I possibly be? I felt that the answer to that hinged on whether I was going to do as Dorothy said and report on the memoir. But, perhaps Rose already knew about whatever it was Dorothy and Meredith did in their past.

'Mum thinks she's capable, but I don't think she is, not now she's broken her arm. If you can, get her to let you help her a little in the villa. I usually help her to bathe and dress Dad, but she might prefer to muddle through with that until I get back. Really, though, if you can get her and Dad out, that would be amazing. Just to know you're there with her is a big help and if you need anything at all Lucien will be there for you. He can easily contact me, but I can give you my number for anything urgent.'

She reeled off a number I could contact her on and I scribbled it down on the edge of the hotel booklet.

'I know it isn't ideal, this being an open-ended position, but we just can't be certain how long it will take to get him ready for the journey.'

'I completely understand,' I said, but truthfully I was hoping for some clarification. Would it be days, weeks or, I gulped at the thought, months?

'Do you have any responsibilities at home that you'd need to get back for?' she asked me.

'No,' I said truthfully and the reality of that brought me up short for a moment. I had nothing I had to return for. I could quite literally stay here for months and I wouldn't be missed. Well, Dorothy would miss me a little, my granddaughters might ask when Granny was coming home, but the world would still turn; everyone would carry on with their lives.

'The doctors suggested a couple of weeks was likely, but I will keep you updated on what's happening.'

'Thank you and I'll do my very best to get them out and about. Oh, where do they take their meals? I can cook for them if they'd like – they have that lovely kitchen.'

'That's very kind, Gina, but I doubt Mum would like that. She's actually a very good cook herself, but is struggling at the moment with her arm. She doesn't like to eat in the restaurant, even though I've tried to persuade her. The kitchen make up meals and send them over to the villa, so you don't have to worry about that.'

'Okay, and what about her book? She needs help typing, doesn't she.'

'Oh, she's not writing at the moment. I'm pleased she's decided to take a break. She's published twenty-five books over the last thirty-nine years, she deserves a little time off. The last thing she needs to be worrying about at the minute is a book deadline.'

The word memoir got caught in my throat and instead I chose to ask about her career.

'Oh, so she didn't write as a young woman, then?'

'She was forty-four when her first book was published. *The Whispering Tide*, a story of a woman living by the sea and waiting for her lover to return. Spoiler: he drowned. Quite bleak really. Her books picked up a bit after that. She worked with ceramics years before that, shared a studio with a group of artists. I get the impression they were quite the set back in the day.'

So that was why Meredith had all the pottery and glass art in her villa and also explained her connection with Dorothy. When I first met Dorothy she told me about her own glass work. She has pieces displayed in her home and garden in Hampton. They were one of the first things I noticed when I had arrived for my interview back in the summer.

On reflection, it would have been much easier if I had let Dorothy tell me about her and Meredith and what happened in their past, what it was I was looking for in her memoir, or just simply so I wouldn't feel so wrong-footed now, but then I had said not to, that I wouldn't be digging, that I wasn't intending to get involved in someone else's business, their drama.

Dorothy must have known I'd be interested, though.

'What sort of ceramics did Meredith produce?'

'You wouldn't think it to look at her now, but she made very quirky pieces. Odd statues and heavily painted large bowls. She was quite bohemian in her approach. She has a few of her own in the villa and some she's collected of other artists over the years too.'

'I saw those, I didn't know they were her own work. Why did she stop?'

'I don't really know, to be honest. Dad said there was some upset with a fellow artist, but he didn't elaborate and Mum never really said anything, just sold her equipment, stopped paying the rent on her studio and that was that. It was around the time she had me, so probably a simple case of too busy being a mum.'

I thought about that time in my own life, when I had children and wasn't working outside of the home. Douglas had told me, recently, that I'd been lucky to able to stay at home, while he went to work to provide for us. I used to think that too, but lately I had begun to feel very differently about that time. If my head had been in a better state after the tragic death of my mother, I'm sure I would have liked to have gone back to my job at Ham House in Richmond. I accused Douglas of using me, taking advantage of me while I wasn't in a good place, turning me into a housewife and mother, but was that really fair? Didn't I actively choose those things myself? The truth was, I just didn't know. I really couldn't remember.

* * *

The restaurant was alive with clatter and chatter and I waited just inside the doorway to be seated. It was impressive how Rose and Hugo had managed to retain the old charm of the château while bringing some modern touches too. Looking up I could see the ceiling appeared to have its original intricately carved plasterwork, but the light fittings that hung from various points were explosions of glass with metal worked entwined.

I was surprised when Lucien arrived to show me to a table.

'Goodness, is there any role in this hotel you don't fill?' I said with a gentle laugh.

'*Non*, well, I'm not allowed to cook, which is to everyone's advantage.'

He showed me to a table for two and the empty seat opposite mine glared at me.

'Will you be okay dining alone?' he asked me and I nodded and showed him the book I had in my handbag. It was another crime thriller Erik had lent me and I had a sudden yearning for a lazy afternoon on the river with him and Dorothy, easy chat, a pot of coffee and one of her home-made lemon drizzle cakes. I took the seat and he handed me the menu.

'This is all on Hugo and Rose,' he reminded me when he saw my eyes bulge at the prices. 'And you know, it won't be that quiet in here tonight. We have a group of local people getting ready for the festival.'

'What's the festival to celebrate?'

'It's uncle Hugo's idea for getting his hotel on the map and noticed, showing off what they have done here. It's a festival of food, and arts and crafts. Right up your street, Gina. Local businesses and artisans will have the opportunity to show and sell and we will have a great event that guests and the public can come and enjoy. It's a lot of work, but should be good. Perhaps you could get the Harpers out for it. They won't have to go far.'

'I think that sounds great. When is it?'

'It's in a week and by the time it comes around I shall have lost all my hair and probably my mind too.'

I laughed and Lucien smiled a very tired smile before returning to his post.

It was then that Adele walked in and she waved. Before I could look away she was standing in front of me and asking if she could join me.

'Of course,' I said, pushing the book into my bag with a moment of disappointment not to be immersing myself back into Detective Inspector Riley's world. I'd have to wait until later to see if he managed to get the CCTV images he needed.

I chose the bouillabaisse, which when it came I was pleased to see had lovely squid, octopus and saffron potatoes nestled in the delicious broth. Adele had the black truffle risotto and she told me she was a vegetarian.

'My son, Chris, is a vegetarian,' I said. 'But his husband is a big carnivore. Interesting meals in that house. Tell me about your family. Do you have children?'

She choked on her mouthful of food and after a moment of coughing and a sip of water she'd composed herself.

'I think maybe a little too much truffle for me,' she said. 'I have two daughters, Elena and Rebecca. Both grown up and with families of their own.'

'I have a son, Chris, as I said, and a daughter, Alice, and two granddaughters.'

'Girls,' she said with a smile. 'They're not always the easiest, are they.'

'No,' I agreed, thinking about Alice and how fierce she could be. She was an emotional person who adored her father and had found it hard to see us separated. She wasn't happy to see me in Dorothy's boathouse either and wanted me to be able to wave a magic wand and somehow manage to stay in our family home. She constantly overlooked the fact that Douglas had chosen to leave me and instead told me to be patient while her father had his moment and came to his senses. Not very *Girl Power* of her, I thought.

I watched as Adele sipped her wine and wondered how old she was. I supposed about mid-sixties, not quite as old as me, but I was never very good at guessing ages. If I didn't already know and looked at myself in the mirror, I'm sure I'd be hard pushed to speculate at my own age.

'My mother died recently, which was a huge blow as we were very close. The girls miss her terribly. It was breast cancer and she has left us with much to think about.'

She looked as if she was going to say something else, but then seemed to change her mind and she popped another forkful of risotto into her mouth instead. I assumed she must be referring to the possibility of her and her girls developing the same illness. I didn't have a lot of experience with breast cancer, I was extremely lucky to be able to say, but I had read that it could be hereditary and perhaps they would all have to be tested.

'I'm so sorry to hear that,' I said. 'I was very close to my own mother. She's been gone for over forty years now and I still think about her most days.'

I pushed some food into my own mouth then, to stop me talking. I didn't often raise the subject of my mother because it was a painful one. People would ask how she died because she was young and the answer was, house fire, but that's not something I wished to discuss with anyone either. Adele didn't ask, though, and I was grateful.

'How is it going with the old couple?' she asked instead.

'Not sure really. Meredith hasn't settled in and with her daughter away she is obviously feeling a little bit adrift. I'm going to try and orientate her into her new situation.'

'How are you planning on doing that?'

'Honestly, I have no idea,' I said, and Adele laughed. 'I hear there's an art and food festival happening here next week, so I might be able to persuade them to go to that as it will be on their doorstep.'

'What about the memoir?'

'Oh, we haven't started that yet. She wants me to do that in the afternoons. I've just popped in there to confirm arrangements and she says I have most of my mornings free. She'd like me to go in first thing and then I can do what I want to do. It doesn't seem right, though. I'll give it a couple of days and then see how things are. I might be able to do the odd little thing, which might lead to another. I guess it's all about earning their trust.'

Adele just stared at me then, a fork full of ravioli on its way to her mouth. I watched an emotion I couldn't place flicker across her eyes and then it was gone.

'Gina, do you fancy coming into Aix in the morning? I mean, you've got that time to fill and hovering around here annoying Meredith isn't going to help. You could treat it as a sort of recce and find places you think the couple might like to go.'

This was actually not a bad idea and I was happy to use Adele's suggestions as an excuse to be a tourist.

'Okay, will we get a taxi or a bus?'

'That French guy, Lucien, told me they run a shuttle bus from here at nine-thirty in the morning and again at lunchtime, then a last one in the afternoon. So, you could spend the whole day there, or come home for lunch. It's a good arrangement.'

We wandered back through reception after our meal. Adele suggested going to the bar for a nightcap, but I decided to leave her to it and we went our separate ways. She was a nice enough woman, but there was something about her that I couldn't quite get a grasp on. I wasn't sure whether it was just a case of not really knowing her well, or if there was an edge to her. But then I had just agreed to go out with her the following morning, so I could take the opportunity to get to know her better.

Lucien was behind the desk trying to pacify a couple of female guests. They were speaking English, but I could detect a Spanish accent. It was nine o'clock and I wondered if poor Lucien ever took a break. The older woman was talking about some money she had lost and she seemed quite agitated. Lucien had a pacifying hand on her arm, but he looked really tired now and I offered him a sympathetic smile as I walked past. He nodded wearily in response.

The evening was cooling, but still pleasant enough and even though the sun had set a couple of hours ago the grounds of the château were beautifully lit. Perhaps less so as I neared my villa, but I found the switch for an outside light, which showed off the weeds on the patio to perfection. I noticed that my broken chair had been replaced with a new one and decided to have my own nightcap out here, so I made a cup of chamomile tea from the welcome basket and sat on the patio trying not the look at the weeds. I pulled the book out of my bag and onto my lap and as I turned to where I'd marked my page and began to delve back into Riley's world, the black and white cat appeared at my feet.

'Hello again.'

It wound itself around my legs, purring, and I bent to stroke it.

'I might call you Riley,' I said, pulling out my bookmark.

I couldn't get past the first few lines, though. My head was too full of the day and as Riley wandered off into the night I took stock of my situation. I was companion to an elderly couple who didn't really want me and I had a neighbour who seemed more interested in that couple than any usual tourist would be. I had to type the words to a book that sounded as if it shouldn't be written and I had a friend who'd asked me to report on the contents of that book, which meant that I might have to betray the trust of the person who I had yet to earn that trust from.

One thing was for sure, the coming days were likely to be eventful.

8

LUCIEN

The guests in front of Lucien were not as relaxed as the American couple. The Spanish mother was becoming quite animated and even though her daughter looked a little embarrassed, she did nothing to quieten her down.

'And this money wasn't in the safe in your wardrobe?' Lucien asked, although he already knew what she was going to say.

'Should it have been? Is this the sort of hotel where you can't leave anything openly in your *habitación* otherwise it will be stolen?'

She brought her hand down on top of the reception desk and Béatrice jumped back in alarm.

'*Au contraire*,' Lucien said, quickly. 'We are not that hotel at all. Your *habitación* – your room is a very safe space. I'm just trying to understand the situation.'

The woman leaned across the desk towards Lucien and finally lowered her voice. 'Understand this. There were six hundred euros on the table in our room and now they have gone! I expect you to find them!'

The two women walked away, but the daughter looked back

and offered Lucien and Béatrice an apologetic, lopsided attempt at a smile.

'She is too rude,' Béatrice said, after they had disappeared.

'She has lost a lot of money; it is understandable.'

'Two thefts, Lucien. Or do you still think it's more likely misplaced?'

'It does seem like a bit of a coincidence, *non*?'

'I need to go. Cristòu will be waiting for me soon,' she said, looking at her watch.

Béatrice grabbed her bag from the shelf under the desk and Lucien watched as she applied some lipstick and smoothed down her already perfect hair.

'Béatrice, is he good to you? Is he kind?'

Lucien tried to catch her eye as he said this, but she was turning away, pulling the straps of her bag onto her shoulder.

'He adores me,' she said, simply.

'It's not the same as being kind,' he said, but she was already halfway across the reception area, her hand in the air as she wished him a *bon soir*.

Lucien handed over to the night manager and then headed towards the car park. Thoughts of Béatrice began to fade as his mind turned to home. He considered, for just a second, sleeping in his car, but that wouldn't help anyone. He watched as Béatrice and Cristòu came into view. He had his arm draped across her shoulders, but it wasn't protective, she was holding him up. He staggered for a moment, nearly pulling her off her feet, but she steadied him against her car while she opened the passenger door. Lucien remembered the wine he'd had earlier; he must have had a lot more too.

Lucien began to walk towards them, not really sure what he was going to do. Cristòu was a mess and Béatrice shouldn't have to deal with that sort of drunken behaviour.

'Ah, Lucien is here to be a hero,' Cristòu drawled. 'Are you here to save me or her?'

He laughed from his position, slumped against the car, while Béatrice threw her handbag onto the back seat.

'She's not interested in a man like you,' Cristòu continued. 'You live with your mother, for Christ's sake. It's not very sexy for a man of forty to be looking after his mother, you know.'

'Cristòu!' Béatrice said. 'Don't be unkind.'

'You think she is interested in a man who can't even stand up straight?' Lucien said. He took another step closer, wanting to hit the head chef straight in the face and watch him fall to the ground in a heap. He wanted this because of the comment about his mother. Not because it wasn't true, but because he couldn't bear Béatrice's compassion. It made him feel even more of a loser.

'Get in the car,' Béatrice told him and she began to push his huge bulk in a futile attempt to get him to fold himself through the doorway of her tiny Fiat 500.

He resisted, but Lucien noted there was no aggression towards her. His eyes glittered at Lucien in the floodlights of the car park and he looked deranged.

'You love playing the manager, walking around as if you own the hotel. Well, I'm telling you, you don't own a damn thing and when Hugo gets back, it will be me he'll be looking to as his right-hand man. Take a look at yourself, Lucien.' Cristòu blew air from his nostrils like a bull. 'Time has passed you by. We've all left you behind.'

Lucien took another step, his hand curling into a fist by his side, but the moment had gone. Cristòu was already half inside the car and he could hardly punch a man in the back.

'This car is a fucking joke,' Cristòu said as he lifted his leg up and inside.

Béatrice walked around to the driver's door and then caught

Lucien's eye. She attempted a smile that only touched half of her mouth. She was embarrassed and Lucien did nothing as she climbed inside.

He stood and watched as she manoeuvred out of her space and then out of the car park. His hands were now firmly in his pockets as he had a horrible feeling he might wave. Then, he made his way back to his own car with a sour taste in his mouth. This was like being at school, in the playground. Did it never end?

Lucien started the engine and drove away, pushing thoughts of Béatrice from his mind. He had his own mess to deal with.

* * *

He sat in his car outside the apartment in Marseille. The sun had long set over the water and the light from the street lamp above him cast an eerie orange glow through his windscreen. He felt wooden in his seat, unwilling to climb out and walk up the stairs to his front door. He wanted to be in charge in his life. He thought he'd be able to thrive on a challenge. When Hugo had put him in charge on a mad dash to the airport, Lucien had puffed up with pride.

'I will have everything under control, Uncle Hugo,' he had said. 'You don't have to worry about a thing.'

And he was liked by the staff, well, everyone apart from Cristòu of course. He wanted to prove to Hugo that he had what it took to be his right-hand man. It irritated him how Cristòu knew how much he wanted it. Instead he had problems with the building staff not turning up when they should and working later than was scheduled, two potential thefts from guests' rooms, a looming art and food festival and a drunk, obnoxious chef. And that was just the hotel.

He couldn't put it off any longer. He pulled his phone from his pocket as he climbed out of the car and pressed to listen to the voicemail message he'd ignored earlier.

'*Lucien,*' the voice said in an anguished tone, before a long pause and then, '*I'm so sorry.*'

He held his breath for a moment and then sprang into action. He wrenched open the door of the stairwell to the apartment. He sprinted up the steps with his key ready to open the front door, his heart thumping hard against his ribs.

All was quiet inside and he didn't like what that might mean. He checked the bedrooms, the living room and kitchen. Then, when he felt he could, he pushed open the bathroom door, suddenly fearful of what he might find. Nothing.

Slowly, he wandered back to the bedroom and pulled open the wardrobe door. Empty. The hangers were swinging free of the usual assortment of colourful clothing. Like a slowly rising sun, his brain started to grasp all the elements that were beginning to paint a picture of what had happened here and he strode into the kitchen, pulled open the larder door and reached up and to the back where he kept some cash and his emergency credit card in a small box. Empty. Sinking onto a kitchen chair, he rested his head in his hands for a moment while he let his thoughts catch up with themselves. She'd gone and she'd taken his money, not to pay back what she owed, but for herself. Isabel and her crew didn't care who repaid them, as long as someone did, and the small amount he could have raised had just plummeted to zero.

He could cancel the credit card, but she'd need something to feed herself, somewhere to stay. He'd work it out and he still had his other account where he'd been saving up for a deposit on a better place. Then an alarm went off in his brain like a clanging, rusty bell and he reached for his phone and opened his banking app.

Empty.

9

DOROTHY

Dorothy pushed back the covers from her bed and swung her feet over the side. She hovered there for a moment while she mustered up the energy to move herself into an upright position and with some unladylike grunting and momentum, she managed it.

They'd arrived in Barcelona that morning and she needed to get herself moving so she didn't miss the group leaving for the shore. She hadn't realised how energetic you needed to be on a cruise. She'd imagined, when Yvonne had invited her, that it would be a lot of sitting around, watching the sea go by with a cocktail in her hand. In reality it felt a little more like boot camp with the visits to shore starting early and with gusto. Of course there had been cocktails and relaxation and she had enjoyed spending time catching up with one of her oldest friends. But, if she was honest Dorothy was feeling a bit too old for all the antics, despite the onboard aids, the guided scooter tours and the excellent room service.

Dorothy was eighty-nine and fancied a day in bed with a large packet of chocolate biscuits.

There was a tap at her door and Yvonne appeared with a travel guide to the city in her hand.

'All set for today?' she asked as she walked into the room. She was dressed and made up and seemingly ready to go.

'I just need to get myself together. I overslept.'

Dorothy didn't mention the dream she'd had about Gina. How she'd been sailing in a boat down the Hudson River in New York with a ceramic urn in her outstretched hands. Dorothy needed to shake off that image. It was rather too close to the bone. She also wanted to phone Gina and see how she was getting on. Perhaps she'd been too quick to push her into the role. Was it really fair of her to expect her new friend to snoop on her old friend?

Memories of Meredith kept coming to her for the first time in years. Some of them made her smile; some of them made her want to weep.

'I really should phone Gina, see if she's okay,' Dorothy said.

'I think you should just leave her to do her job and stop interfering. We have a city to discover you know, or did you come all this way to sit on a ship and fret?'

Yvonne didn't know Meredith very well. They had moved in different circles and their paths had only crossed a couple of times at Dorothy's house many years ago. She certainly didn't know what they had done, or why they had fallen out. Dorothy had always kept tight-lipped about those events. Now, though, Meredith could be about to blow the lid off the whole thing.

'I'll meet you at the breakfast table in twenty minutes. We can have a quick coffee and a pastry or something,' Dorothy said as she headed towards her bathroom.

Her cabin was not the compact space of her imaginings, but beautifully presented and actually like any other good hotel room she had stayed in. She had a large bed with sumptuous bedding, a sofa and television area and a balcony, which she and Yvonne had claimed as their Cocktail Coven. Despite her worries about Gina, she was enjoying herself.

Yvonne disappeared and Dorothy pulled a shower cap over her newly blow-dried hair before stepping into the shower. Luckily it was a walk-in unit rather than a bath, because the days of being able to lift her leg over the side had long gone. When she was dry, she dressed in comfortable, lightweight trousers and a blouse, slipped her feet into her lace-less trainers – such a joy – picked up her walking stick that leaned against the chest of drawers and then as she closed her door behind her, she reached in her bag for her phone.

Gina answered on the second ring.

'Hello?'

'Gina, it's me!'

'Dorothy, how lovely to hear from you. How's the cruise going?'

'It's been wonderful. We've docked in Barcelona and are heading into the city today. I shall wave at you across the water. You're really not that far from me and will be even closer when we head to Nice for our last stop. I'm flying home from there. It's all gone too quickly, but I have met the most fantastic group of people. They're an art appreciation society and they often travel together to exhibitions. They've asked me if I might like to join them on their next adventure. I'm thinking about it; I really am.'

Dorothy realised she was waffling on and hadn't given Gina the chance to say much.

'How are things in France?'

'Okay, Meredith thinks she doesn't need any help and I am trying to slowly persuade her she does.'

'We can all relate to that,' Dorothy said and Gina laughed.

It was good to hear that sound. Dorothy hadn't realised how much she was missing her friend. It had only been a few weeks since she had moved into Dorothy's boathouse, but it felt as if she had always been there. Gina was fast becoming one of Dorothy's favourite people. And to think that if Lavinia, Dorothy's daughter-in-law, hadn't insisted on a companion for the family wedding, Dorothy might never have met her.

'I'm on my way to hers now, before I head into Aix. I'm going with the English woman in the villa next to mine.'

'That sounds nice. Look at us oldies, out and about. Aren't we well travelled,' Dorothy said. 'Have you found out anything yet?'

'I've only just arrived and certainly haven't been rummaging through her life.'

'Well, you probably should get her onside before you do that, yes.'

'Having met Meredith, I very much doubt I'll get her onside, full stop. Has she always been this brusque? I really don't know whether to run for the hills or offer her a hug.'

'Goodness, I wouldn't do that. She wouldn't like it. For a romantic novelist, she's not remotely tactile or demonstrative.'

'She is with Gerald.'

'Yes, well. How is the old codger?' Dorothy said as her thoughts cast back to an image of Gerald. He had always been a handsome man, tall and with a moustache that Dorothy liked very much. She could never get her Philip to grow one.

'I've only seen him once. He's fairly quiet, understandably. The poor man has dementia, Dorothy.'

'I suppose it would be convenient for him not to remember, really,' Dorothy said.

This was true and also slightly alarming. Was it another indicator of Meredith's intentions? If Gerald didn't know what was going on, perhaps she really was going to tell all.

'In fact, it would be much more convenient if *Meredith* didn't remember,' Dorothy added.

She'd got to the door to the dining room and hesitated outside, wishing to finish this conversation before she joined Yvonne. She heard Gina sigh on the other end of the line.

'I think that maybe I should have got you to explain all when you first suggested this job, Dorothy. I think it would be nice to know what I'm dealing with.'

'Oh, but I would never have told you,' Dorothy said.

'What exactly is it you're asking me to do, then?'

'To see what she writes in her memoir. She might well brush past all the problem areas and keep it simply her love story with Gerald. That would be best for everyone, although perhaps not the most riveting of reads. But, if she does that then, you need never know.'

'Cryptic as ever, Dorothy.'

'Don't overthink it. Just help her out with whatever she will let you do and then let me know if her book takes a turn.'

'And if I don't know what it is I'm supposed to be looking for, how will I know when I read it?'

'Oh, you will know it all right. Sorry, I need to go, Gina. I promised Yvonne I'd get a move on for breakfast.'

'Have fun and take care,' Gina said. 'I miss you.'

She added this in a rush and the effect was quite profound on Dorothy. It took a little of her breath away.

'Do you know, I miss you too. Can't wait to catch up in person,' she said, and then after a simple goodbye, she pushed her phone back into her bag and walked into the dining room.

10

GINA

I held the phone against my chest for a moment while I let the conversation sink in. I was pleased that Dorothy was having a lovely time. I felt as if I had helped her, in a small way, to get closure on what had happened to her husband, Philip. His death in a bungled burglary had been hanging over her for some time, but the person responsible had been brought to justice, so Dorothy could finally begin to move on.

But, hearing she might be going away again threw me for a moment. Part of my justification for living in Dorothy's boathouse was to look after her. It was an unsaid understanding between myself, and Dorothy's son and daughter-in-law. I'd quietly promised Miles and Lavinia that I would be there for her, even though Dorothy always insisted she didn't need any assistance. And perhaps she didn't need much help to be fair, but it suited everyone to play the game. I had a lovely place to live, Miles and Lavinia didn't need to worry so much about Dorothy, and she seemed very happy to have me around as a friend. We got on incredibly well. If she was planning another trip, I would probably have to plan another companion job. This thought made me feel a little uneasy. You never really knew what you were getting yourself into.

I felt more prepared going back to Meredith's villa. My expectations of a warm welcome had vanished and I was just going to help them get their morning going. I didn't need to be friends with this woman; I could just do my job.

It was cloudier today, which was a welcome relief, and I was more comfortable in my habitual long-sleeved top. My right arm had scars from the house fire that had taken my mother's life and I had never really been comfortable showing my skin. Dorothy had been so kind when she had seen the scars back in August. She had asked why I wasn't wearing a strappy top on one of the hottest days of the year and I had decided to confide in her. I hadn't told her all that had happened on that terrible day, though. That was a story too far for most.

I slipped my phone back into my bag, then knocked on the door, took a very deep breath and prepared to see Meredith again.

* * *

Adele was sitting on the back seat of the shuttle bus when I stepped on board and she patted the seat next to her with a grin. I stopped myself before I told her that I'd get travel sick sitting at the back. I realised how that would make me sound and I didn't want to be the woman who said no to everything. Not any more.

The driver dropped us all at the *Fontaine de la Rotonde*—which was, unsurprisingly, a round fountain—and told us to be back here at one if we only planned on a half-day visit or five if we wanted to spend the whole day. It was perfect timing for me to get back to Meredith and Gerald.

Meredith had been reticent while I'd helped her to get dressed and got her and Gerald breakfast. It made the whole thing so much harder than it needed to be. I did manage to help Gerald a little with his outerwear. Meredith had already got him washed and into his underclothes. Then I left them as requested on their patio, with cereals, fruit and toast, orange juice and coffee. It was a start.

'I did try to suggest other things I could help them with,' I told Adele when she asked about the morning routine, 'but she told me she thought she'd been clear that she only wanted me there first thing and then to start on her book in the afternoons. So, that is what I shall do. I can't make her accept help she doesn't want.'

'Right,' Adele said with her phone in her hand open on a maps app. 'I've found an easy walking tour of the city we can follow. Are you up for a wander? I won't take us too far; most of what we'd probably want to see is within a condensed area.'

She looked me up and down then and I felt all of my seventy-one years.

'I'll be fine if we don't speed walk,' I told her.

'This is the *Cours Mirabeau*,' she read from her phone.

We were in a tree-lined boulevard that was almost entirely a pedestrian zone with a few bicycles and mopeds passing by. There were small cafés and shops either side of the street and the buildings were all a rich ochre-coloured stone. The contrast between that and the bright, azure-blue sky was startling. I took out my phone and snapped a couple of pictures. I wanted to send them to my daughter Alice and my son Chris, but I'd wait until we got back to the hotel so I could use the Wi-Fi to send via WhatsApp. We had a group chat that had once included Douglas, but he had left the chat when he left me. I couldn't explain why it had upset me so much to see the words *Douglas has left* on the screen. He'd already flown across the world to Santa Fe to a retreat, leaving me with a Dear John letter explaining his need to find himself without me, so it wasn't as if he hadn't made his intentions perfectly clear. Those words, though... They broke me a little and I think it was because it was on our family chat. It was as if he had left us all.

I knew Alice kept in good contact with her father, but Chris and his dad had a more complicated relationship. When Chris had come out to us all those years ago, I had pulled him into a huge hug and told him that, of course I knew he was gay, and how happy I was that he felt he could tell us. Douglas had stepped back as if he'd been slapped, as if it was an affront to him as a man, as a father. Douglas had never related that easily to his son before that time – Chris didn't like the same sport his father liked, the same music, the same food and now Chris had hammered the final nail in the coffin of their nebulous relationship, by marrying a man.

I had always been the conduit to keeping things as harmonious as they could be, but now Douglas and I weren't together, I really did feel as if that had been broken too.

I took another couple of photos and then slipped my phone back into my pocket.

In the middle of the street there was a large stone fountain with a moss-coloured urn sitting in the middle with pigeons enjoying a dip. A young couple were sitting on one side. They were clearly in love with limbs entwined, heads close together as they whispered into each other's ears. They were animated and laughing. A perfect example of youth and vitality. It was hard not to stare.

Adele nudged me and drew my attention to the couple sitting directly opposite them on the other side of the water feature. They were older, perhaps even older than me, sitting slightly apart, turned away from each other. She was looking down the street towards the shops. Her expression suggested her thoughts were a million miles away from here and he was slumped over, leaning his arms on his knees and staring at the ground. There was something quite sad about the scene. Not so much that they'd just had a disagreement, but more that the energy had gone from their relationship. A quiet resignation seemed to emanate from them both.

'Young love and old love,' Adele said, chuckling and we continued walking.

'Just down there is the *Caumont Centre D'Art*. Used to be a hotel built in 1715 but is now an art centre featuring Cézanne's work, and others,' Adele said, reading from her phone. 'It's fourteen euros fifty entry if you want to go in, but that seems pretty steep to me. I'd rather go to the *Musée Granet* given the choice.'

'I'm very happy to go with the flow,' I said, following her past the entrance to the museum. Given the opportunity, I'd actually like to come back and explore it alone.

Adele took us for a wander through the smaller side streets and we kept over to one side where the imposing buildings shaded us from the sun. They all had shutters and the same black, iron-work railings that ran along the balconies.

'This is the fountain of the four dolphins,' Adele announced as we came to another water feature. 'They do certainly like a fountain around here.'

And there was indeed something resembling stone dolphins; however, they looked more like scary mythical creatures to me. We stopped long enough for me to take another photo and then we continued.

'The church of *St Jean de Malte*,' Adele read as we were standing outside what looked to me like an English Gothic-style building. She must have thought the same because she suggested I put it on my list of places to persuade Meredith and Gerald to come to. 'It could be a little bit of home for them.'

'There's your *Musée Granet*,' I said pointing to the building right next to the church. 'Do you want to go in now?'

'No, let's come back another time. I'd rather go and soak up some café culture.'

I looked at the information on the board pinned to the wall and could see that the museum had ten of Cézanne's works and I was keen to see them, but I had time to come back and maybe I'd combine the two museum visits. Perhaps I wouldn't visit alone and could discover them with Meredith and Gerald instead. Gerald used to be an architect after all, perhaps a trip into Aix and a couple of museum visits would hold his interest. Maybe I should persuade Adele to join us too. There was a feeling of safety in numbers. Adele might be able to soften the edges of Meredith.

We walked towards what Adele told me was the old town, the *Vieille Ville* and I could see the charm with its shuttered buildings, boutiques and cafés. Every corner we turned there would be another fountain, another café with tables and chairs on the pavement, more potted trees and shrubs to shelter customers from passing pedestrians.

We'd reached *Place Richelme,* a lovely large square. The centre was taken up entirely with seating under huge parasols, which in turn was also sheltered under the enormous canopy of trees above. Fractured sunlight dappled the ground below, giving the impression of twinkling fairy lights. Adele suggested we stop for coffee and we picked our way through the occupied tables until we found a nice spot with a free table and a couple of plastic chairs. I was glad of the rest because we'd covered some ground even though we hadn't really set much of a pace. We ordered *café au lait* and *pains aux raisins*, glasses of fresh orange juice and something called *beignets,* which when they came were tiny doughnuts, crispy on the outside and fluffy in the middle. They were covered in icing sugar and neither Adele nor I had any problem getting our fingers covered. It was all delicious and reminded me how hungry I was, as I'd chosen to skip breakfast.

It was the perfect place to people-watch and we were happily quiet for a while as we observed the comings and goings around us. The demographic seemed young, or maybe if not exactly young, then youthful. It was the Mediterranean climate. People who were used to being outside and active, not popping on slippers and sitting down for afternoon television, but out in the sunshine, being sociable. I could see the appeal of living in this environment, however much *I* enjoyed curling up on my own sofa with a book and a cuppa. You would never see this many exposed and tanned limbs in the UK.

'I need to get a few things so I can prepare some light meals to eat in the villa,' I said, thinking about the shops we had passed. 'I don't want to be bothering with an extensive breakfast or lunch every day. I know you're a guest at the hotel and of course you should indulge, that's part of your holiday, but I'm really here to work.'

'So am I, to be fair,' she said, but I wondered when she did her work. I hadn't seen her take a single photo so far and she didn't have a camera with her today, even though she had told me the previous evening she was going into Aix to take photos. Did she only use her phone to take pictures? I knew that phone cameras were very sophisticated now, but surely if you were a professional you'd need a proper camera.

I stretched my legs out in front of me and finished the last of my coffee as Adele excused herself to use the loo. I imagined the lovely things I could buy to sustain me until an evening meal. We'd passed many shops with tempting treats, but I would also need to get some simple food stuff too.

While I was busy making a mental note, Adele's phone pinged from where she had left it on the table. I didn't really mean to be nosy, but it was right in front of me and I only had to lean forward with the tiniest of movements to read the message displayed on the screen.

> What have you found out? We might need to move quickly if he's not in the best of health, so keep digging. Let me know how you get on Jx

I had just leaned back in my seat when Adele hurried across from the café searching in her bag, I assumed for her phone. I didn't mention the message and decided to pretend I hadn't even heard it, let alone read it, but my mind was swirling with thoughts as we left the square and resumed our walk.

We retraced our steps back towards the drop-off point as time was ticking and even though there was more to see, I was keen not to miss the minibus. Adele said she didn't mind at all and was happy to visit the *Atelier de Cézanne* – the studio of Paul Cézanne – another time. It was something I was keen to do too.

We found a small *supermarché* on the way and I filled a basket with cheese and bread, fruit and cereals. I bought milk, wine, biscuits, crisps and nuts, a bag of pasta and a couple of jars of roasted peppers and sun-dried tomatoes. Adele did ask why I didn't want to eat in the restaurant, especially as I didn't have to pay for it, but I told her I expected I would have a lot of work to do on Meredith's memoir and would eat and work at the same time in the villa. She seemed disappointed and I thought of her eating alone. She also renewed her offer to help, but, in truth, I didn't yet know how much work I would really have to do, or how long I'd be here to do it. I assumed that whatever I would be doing would be temporary. Surely I wouldn't be here long enough to type a whole book.

Also, I didn't think it was appropriate for Adele to be reading Meredith's words. I wasn't even sure it was appropriate for me to be reading her words. But I'd be lying if I said I wasn't interested in knowing what or who had broken up Meredith and Dorothy's relationship. I wondered for a moment if it had been a man. I doubted it, though. One thing I had learned in the months I'd known Dorothy and the day and a half I'd known Meredith was that both women had been devoted to their husbands. It had to be something else.

Adele's text message was playing on my mind as the minibus rumbled out of the city and whisked us back to the hotel. I couldn't shake the feeling that the man in question was Gerald.

11

GINA

By one-thirty on the dot I was knocking on Meredith's door, thoughts of Adele pushed to the back of my mind as I tried to focus on what I had to do. *It will be fine,* I had repeatedly told myself. *I just have to listen to Meredith's words and then type them.* I had decided the best thing to do would be to record her talking so I wouldn't need to make extensive notes.

Meredith opened the door abruptly, her face a picture of concern.

'There you are! Where have you been? Gerald is missing!'

Meredith looked frantic, although it didn't escape me that I was being reprimanded for being perfectly on time as per the plan.

'Right, where and when did you last see him?'

'He was resting in the bedroom and I was preparing some things for our writing session. Then I went in to see if he wanted a cup of tea and he was gone. He's only in his pants and a vest.'

'Come on,' I said, taking Meredith's arm and leading her towards the main hotel. 'We should alert Lucien and he can help us look.'

Lucien was in his office looking blankly at his phone when we were ushered in by Béatrice.

'Lucien,' she said, trying to catch his attention. 'Meredith and Gina need your help.'

He looked up and took a moment to orientate himself.

'Lucien?' Béatrice tried again. '*Êtes-vous d'accord?*'

'*Oui*, I'm okay. What can I help you ladies with?' He gulped some water from a glass on his desk and then gave us his attention.

'Meredith's husband, Gerald, has taken himself off for a little wander,' I said gently.

'He's missing,' Meredith said.

'Right, well, let us go and find him. Has he disappeared before?' Lucien said.

'No, not here, but he used to take himself off for walks if I didn't lock the door when we lived in London.'

We all left the office and headed outside.

'I'll go and talk to staff, see if anyone has seen him,' said Lucien. 'Why don't you go and see if he's walking though the gardens. Can he swim?'

We both looked at Meredith then.

'He used to be a strong swimmer, but I don't know if he would remember how to any more.'

'We'll check the pools,' I told Lucien as he turned to leave. 'And, Lucien.' I lowered my voice. 'He's in his pants.'

He looked at me uncomprehending.

'Not his trousers, his underwear.'

'Ah, *d'accord,* I understand,' he said, and then he was gone.

We walked as quickly as we could towards the infinity pool, but he wasn't there and when I asked a couple of the guests if they had seen him, they hadn't.

'Where do you think he might go?' I asked Meredith. 'What

does he like to do around here? Walk in the gardens? Does he go to the gym? What are his interests?'

It was Meredith's turn to look at me blankly then. 'I didn't know they had a gym,' she said.

'No matter, let's just go and see what we can find.'

We walked along the far side of the garden as it was slightly elevated and that gave us a view all the way across the grounds to the other side. We would have seen him if he'd been walking among the trees and shrubs, but there was no sign of him. The château stood magnificently behind us and I paused to admire it from this angle. It was a shame I could only just see the top of one of the towers from my villa.

'He doesn't have access to a car, does he?'

'No,' Meredith said, startled, and I decided to change my tack.

'Am I right in thinking that Gerald was an architect in his working years?'

'Yes, he was. He was a prestigious architect of some repute,' Meredith said in a voice that was in part proud, but somehow also managed to carry an air of indignation with it. She probably thought I should have heard of him. 'He built Charters Place in London and the new library building in Tursbury.'

'Goodness,' I said, although in truth I didn't really know either of those buildings.

'He was responsible for a large shopping complex outside Cambridge, not to mention several of Kevin McCloud's grandest designs.'

'Is it possible he'd be looking at some of the building work around here, then?' I suggested.

'He wasn't a builder, he was an architect,' she snapped.

'It was only a thought. I'm just trying to think of what would interest him within walking distance.'

'He hasn't been around the hotel complex since we've been

here. Other than the day we arrived, we haven't really been further than the main building. He likes it in the villa.'

I thought that the fact he'd gone walk-about might tell a different story, but in truth, I didn't really know that he'd decided he'd like to go for a walk and he could just as easily have been frightened and confused when he opened the door. An elderly man, in his underwear, unsure of his surroundings on what was becoming a hot afternoon. I picked up our pace.

We walked through the back side of the spa and I glanced in through the window to check he wasn't in the pool inside. No one was swimming. I guessed they were all enjoying the outside pool. Weaving our way through the gardens and grounds I could feel Meredith becoming more tense beside me. Her arm gripping mine was vice-like and I thought it was such a shame that her first proper look around the hotel was under such circumstances.

'Let's go back to the villas,' I suggested after a while. 'He may well have found his way back.'

I glanced at my phone, hoping that Lucien might be trying to get hold of me, but then I remembered I hadn't actually given him my number.

Meredith was flagging by the time we reached their villa and I darted inside to see if Gerald had found his way back. He hadn't, but I did fill a glass with some water and handed it to Meredith, who had sat down in the shade on the patio. I could see Riley lurking in the bushes behind her, but the cat didn't come out, which was a sensible move in my opinion.

'We could go and ask Adele if she's seen him,' I suggested and got a blank stare back. 'She's your nearest neighbour; an Englishwoman here to photograph the countryside for her travel vlog.'

Although, I had yet to actually see her photograph anything and Meredith was still looking at me blankly.

'I know. I'm not quite sure what a vlog is either,' I said.

We knocked at Adele's door, but didn't get an answer. I was able to persuade a reluctant Meredith to go further to where the building work was being done and she followed on behind me, no longer holding my arm and obviously revived by the water.

I was surprised to see what a mess it was behind my villa towards the boundary to the hotel grounds. It was a proper building site with piles of materials, small machinery and four incomplete villas with exposed insides where we could see the potential through the gaping holes in the exterior walls. And there, sitting on the grass in front of it all, was Gerald with a pad of paper in his hands and a poised pencil. He wasn't alone – Adele was sitting right next to him and engaging him in conversation, although it was a little one-sided.

'My love!' Meredith called, but only Adele turned her head.

'Thank goodness,' she said. 'I didn't want to leave him to find you, but I couldn't persuade him to come with me either. He just wanted to sit and contemplate. You should see what he's drawn. He's finished the villas off beautifully.'

Despite Adele's kind words, Gerald looked very vulnerable sitting there on the grass in his underwear. I stepped forward and without really thinking about it, I pulled my arms from the sleeves of my summer cardigan and laid it across his lap. Meredith did glance at the scars on my arm, but quickly her eyes found my own and I was rewarded with a small smile. I felt as if I may have chipped away a piece of ice. She was probably just relieved to have her husband back.

Just then, Riley the cat decided to join us. He wandered straight over to Gerald who lifted a hand to stroke it.

'Get that cat away,' Meredith said, her voice raised to an unpleasant pitch, her smile gone. 'Gerald is allergic to pet hair.'

I walked across and scooped it up from the ground and set it down in the shade of the villa where I began to stroke it.

'I'm actually allergic to cat hair too,' Adele said, and then Lucien arrived looking flustered.

'All is well,' I told him. 'Gerald is here. I should have phoned you, but your card is still in my villa and I didn't think to put your number in my phone yet, sorry. Time to exchange numbers properly, I think.'

'*D'accord, bon,* good, Gina, this is good. All is fine.'

Adele got up from the ground and held out her arm to Gerald who took it and allowed himself to be pulled to his feet. She took my cardigan and tied it around his waist from front to back to cover his dignity. In truth, though, he could almost be wearing a pair of swimming shorts as his underpants were quite substantial.

'Let's get you back home, my love,' Meredith said in the most tender of voices as she stepped towards him. Adele still had her hand on his arm and Meredith stared at her.

'This is Adele, your neighbour,' I said to try and dispel the tension that seemed to have descended over the scene. Meredith continued to stare, while Gerald suddenly looked bewildered to find himself in his current situation. Adele, on the other hand, appeared to be ever so slightly defiant in her stance. 'And this is Meredith and Gerald,' I continued.

They both nodded an acknowledgement and the two older people began to walk away. I had no idea what had just happened.

'Are you okay, Lucien?' I asked him. 'You seem to have a lot on your mind.'

'A few minor problems, but nothing I can't handle, *merci.*'

'Are you sure there's nothing I can do to help you?'

'Honestly, thank you, but I just have a family issue that needs my attention. It's really only me who can do this.'

'Can I give you my number in case anything like this happens again with the Harpers?'

'Of course,' he said and we both pretended he hadn't been

looking at the network of scars running the length of my arm while I found my phone in my bag. I unlocked it and handed it to him, then after he had added himself into my contacts and sent himself a message so he'd have my number, he smiled briefly and then strode away.

'Well, that was odd,' I said, turning to speak to Adele, but she too had left and I was completely alone.

12

LUCIEN

'And all is on track? Cristòu has the menu sorted for the canapés we will be offering and you've gone through the wine with him? I want the little tasting cups to be handed out quite liberally. It is not a time to be tight. And get Helena involved; she is an unmined gem in that kitchen. I think she is overlooked. This festival is so important to get our hotel on the map and prove us *compétent* to all those who doubted we could turn it around.'

'*Oui*, of course, Hugo. I know this. You've put in all the work and it's just a few loose ends that need tying up. You shouldn't be worrying about these things; we have everything under control here. How is Oliver doing?'

Lucien walked away from the busy reception area so he could take Hugo's call in the office. He had him on speaker so he could do other things with his hands. He absent-mindedly began to clear some of the mess that had made its way back to the desk while he listened to his uncle. His to-do list had migrated from his phone, back to a piece of paper and he picked up a pen and began scribbling.

- *Make sure each artist has adequate display space*
- *Check the number of gazebos/sunshades*
- *Béatrice to go over the artists' layout*
- *Clear the overflow car park*
- *Find those damn tasting cups*

'I think the euphoria of being alive and leaving the hospital has worn off now. His situation is beginning to sink in.'

I know how he feels, Lucien wanted to say, but managed to keep his thoughts to himself. It wasn't the same. His own problems could be resolved. There would be an answer; he just didn't know what it was currently. He felt like a duck frantically treading water with that serene expression they always seemed to have on their faces. He wasn't sure his own expression was all that serene, though. Gina had noticed he had something on his mind, but then, she did seem like an observant person.

'Oliver has a determination that will see him through; I'm sure of it,' Lucien said, but as the words left his lips he had a moment of sorrow pass through him at a memory of a young Oliver somersaulting in the garden at a family barbecue and saying he wanted to be a stunt man in the movies when he grew up. His mother – Lucien's aunt Rose – would always suggest more gentle careers, saying how she would prefer him in one piece. He changed his mind when he got older. His passion became the ocean, and he was studying to become a marine biologist on a special programme in New Zealand. How horribly ironic that he took his mother's advice and could still end up with life-changing injuries.

Hugo turned the conversation back towards the hotel and in particular the festival. It would mark the end of the renovations on the main hotel and a perfect opportunity to show off all they had achieved. No one would see all that was still to be done with the villas and Lucien was very keen for Hugo not to know how problematic the builders were being.

'I really want you to make sure the set-up is perfect, Lucien. You know how we discussed the food stalls would all be together in the main stretch of the garden with plenty of tables and chairs for the guests and visitors. Please make sure our guests get their vouchers for the stalls offering complimentary goods. The art needs to be prominent and will work best behind the spa where the light is better and away from the trees. Béatrice has my plan and she must stick to it.'

Hugo sounded anxious and Lucien wasn't surprised, what with him being so far away on this very important occasion. It was up to him to pacify Hugo and make sure he knew the festival was in safe hands, but he wasn't really feeling it, if he was honest.

Béatrice arrived in the doorway to the office with an unpleasant expression on her face and she was making slicing motions across her throat with the sharp edge of her hand. Lucien wanted to laugh, she looked so comical. He also wanted to repeatedly kick himself for that time before she committed to Cristòu when Lucien had dithered about and not made his intentions towards her clear. He told Gina that Cristòu was an *imbécile* but it was actually himself – he was the *imbécile*.

'So we're all good then, Hugo. We are all in control, *oui?*'

'I guess so. I just wish I could be there, but that is going to be impossible.'

'*Bon*,' Lucien said, imagining the word had stayed in his head rather than spilled out of his mouth. 'I mean everything is good and I hope for Oliver's speedy recovery.'

Béatrice was looking impatient now, hopping from one foot to another.

'And what about Solène? How is she?' Hugo asked.

Lucien grabbed at the phone on the desk and flipped it off

speaker. Béatrice stopped hopping and instead fixed her penetrating gaze on him.

'Fine,' he said quickly. 'All fine, Hugo. *Non problème.*'

'Because I know she's been having some money issues. So, I just wanted to say, don't be a martyr. If we can help we will. *Nous sommes une famille.*'

'*Merci beaucoup,*' Lucien said quietly. They were family, but he wasn't sure if that was such a great thing.

'*D'accord,* okay, so, Lucien, I have to go, please don't ruin my festival and don't break my château,' Hugo said with a chuckle and then he cut the call.

Lucien turned to Béatrice and forced a smile onto his face.

'I'm all yours.'

She raised her eyebrow at him and then closed the door behind her.

'And Solène? What's going on with your mother?'

'Nothing,' he said.

He couldn't tell her; he couldn't tell anyone. He hadn't even told Hugo what was really going on, yet, and surely if anyone should know it was him. Lucien's mother was the reason he had dithered about and not taken that leap when he first met Béatrice. He realised there had been a spark between them, but his father had just died after a long illness, his mother had sunk into a terrible state and her once-a-week fun night at the casino had become an addiction. She couldn't pay the rent on her place without his father's earnings and he had no choice but to offer her his spare room.

That had been ten years ago when he was just thirty, when he thought he could pull Solène out of her problems and still get the girl, when his compass still held promise. What a joke!

He knew what that decade had done to him. He'd become embittered by his mother's failure to sort herself out. And the truth was, he'd facilitated it all. He'd allowed it to continue, because he wanted her to be happy again and he thought if he just cared for her, all would be well. It turned out he wasn't a carer after all, he was an enabler.

His life was a mess and he came here every day playing the big boss when really he couldn't even keep his home life in order. He sank down into the chair. He might have been able to sweep Béatrice off her feet ten years ago, but now, he had nothing she would want. He used to hold an image of himself as a husband, a father, but not any more.

'So, what's with the...' He slid his hand across his throat, mimicking what Béatrice had done before.

'Oh, that. Basically, there's been another theft.'

'For Christ's sake, what now?'

'A guest, Monsieur Barrent. He has lost a sculpture.'

'A sculpture? Who goes on holiday with a sculpture!'

'An *artiste*, Lucien, an *artiste* of course. Keep up! He is supposed to be displaying his work at the festival and now he is one piece of work down. He says he's not happy; he thought that this hotel was secure.'

'I'm not cut out for this,' he said, resting his head in his hands on top of the desk, scattering papers.

'You are! You have to be. Come on and put your big-boy knickers on. Monsieur Barrent wants to talk to you.'

Lucien lifted his head to see Béatrice grinning at him and God! He wanted her so much it hurt him. He stood up and mimed wriggling into a pair of pants and she laughed.

There was no putting it off; he was going to have to call the police.

13

GINA

It was the summer of 1961 and my twenty-first birthday celebrations were still fresh in my mind. I was at the railway station on a Saturday afternoon to catch the 2.45 to Guildford, but I was running late and arrived in time only to watch its back end sliding out of the station.

I was supposed to be meeting my friend for tea at Woodbridge café and now she would be waiting for someone who would never show up.

What transpired that afternoon was so extraordinary that I have to confess it took me a while after that day to phone my friend and apologise. I was so overtaken by events.

I leaned my back against the wall, not caring that my mother wasn't there to tell me to stand up straight. Deportment was so important to her, but it wasn't to me, not right now, and I slumped down a little further, letting my handbag fall to the ground.

'You missed the train too?'

His voice caught my attention and I looked up into the deep hazel eyes of an attractive man. Right then I wished not to be slumped against a wall with a bag at my feet and I immediately stood up a little straighter, then changed my mind and stooped to reach for my bag, only for my hat to fall from my head and roll along the platform. Even though deportment was my mother's domain, right then I sorely wished I was deploying some of her tactics.

The man picked up my hat and turned to hand it to me, those hazel eyes of his, sparkling.

'Gerald Harper,' he said.

'Meredith Sloan.'

'Look, the next train isn't for another hour. Would you like to get a cup of tea with me while we wait?'

I scanned his face to see if his intentions were good and I only saw kindness in his expression.

'Yes,' I said, without giving it much thought at all. 'I'd like that very much.'

I learned two things over that steaming cup of tea in that crowded station café: that Gerald was also going to be studying at The Royal College of Art come September and that I thought very much I'd just met the love of my existence.

If there was ever a time I'd have liked to be plucked from my life by a handsome stranger then it was at that exact moment. It was serendipity. To outrun my past and fall into a new and exciting future was very welcome. Gerald could indeed be the answer to everything.

'Scrap those last two lines, Gina,' Meredith said.

I pressed pause on the voice recording as Meredith reached for her glass of water and I sat back in my chair. Those were the best lines out of all of it, in my opinion. It would be a shame to delete them.

Gerald was sitting in the other armchair with the newspaper in his lap. It was impossible to tell if he was reading it, and if he was, how much was registering. Either way, it was comfort, it was routine and he didn't seem to be listening to Meredith talking about their past. I had wondered if he might chip in with his thoughts, but so far, he hadn't.

Lucien had delivered the copy of *The Times* earlier when he came to see if Gerald was okay after his unexpected outing. I added 'newspaper round' to the extensive list of jobs Lucien turned his hand to. Once Gerald was dressed again, he seemed quite happy and no worse for his trip around the grounds of the hotel. I was going to suggest to Meredith that we might all go out tomorrow while she still had today in her mind. I would gently remind her how animated Gerald had been.

My thoughts returned to the memoir and I wondered when Dorothy came into her story. Was she the friend waiting in Woodbridge café? I couldn't ask Meredith. I wasn't supposed to mention Dorothy at all. It did make me suddenly realise that this wouldn't be a case of sneaking around and poking into Meredith's affairs; she was actually going to tell me all of them anyway. When she got to the parts that were bothering Dorothy, I could make an executive decision as to whether Dorothy needed to know what was being written about her.

'So,' I started, but Meredith cut me off quickly.

'Is this a question about the process or my story? Because I just want you to write what I tell you to.'

'I was just wondering why you're not starting in your childhood or even as a teenager. Why have you picked that moment to begin your story? I'm just interested, that's all.'

And I was really interested in what she meant by *outrun her past*.

'This is a record of my life with Gerald and our marriage and family. I met him in 1961 and have no interest in dipping back further than that.' She replaced the glass on the table, but I noticed that her hand was now shaking a little.

'You're the boss,' I said and smiled at her, hoping she would return it. She didn't.

'Well, let's leave it at that, then.'

'Can I just ask why you wouldn't get someone at your publishing house to do this for you? Isn't there someone who would type better and faster than me and know about how to put your book together?'

'Because I'm a professional. I don't want my editor to read anything less than perfect and we are a long way from that at the moment. They think this is the ideal time to produce my memoir and, with my inclination for another romantic novel dwindling, I do think they might be right. Perhaps it's important to do this now, to write about my life with Gerald while I can still talk to him. He does remember things from the past. Much more than he remembers things in his present, don't you, darling?'

'I do,' Gerald said without looking up and with no sign he knew what he was agreeing to.

I glanced at the pad of paper on the table where Gerald had done a perfect sketch of the finished villa. It was remarkable. With his slightly shaky hand he'd built the walls and windows, the shutters, the boarding, and the veranda. He'd even potted up some plants to decorate the place. No wonder Adele was impressed.

'I think you have achieved such a lot in your writing life. I spoke to your daughter and she told me how many books you've had published. Very impressive.'

'When did you speak to Rose?' she asked sharply, and I realised I probably shouldn't have told her that. But it seemed dishonest to keep her in the dark.

'Just a quick computer meeting last night that Lucien set up. I think that she just wanted to meet me, make sure I was suitable. You are both obviously very special to her.'

This seemed to be the right answer, as Meredith happily settled back in her chair.

'I can only do this if you simply listen and write what I say. I don't need a critique or an opinion of any sort whatsoever. It's precisely because we don't know each other that I can tell you about my life with Gerald. It wouldn't work if we had a connection or any history. Do you understand?'

I did understand completely, but the fact that we had a mutual acquaintance in Dorothy now sat awkwardly. She mustn't know; it was as simple as that.

Meredith began to talk again so I pressed to record her voice and settled back myself to listen to her words.

* * *

I left the villa with a better sense of Meredith as a person. I could see that she was clinging on to Gerald because of something that had happened to her previously. Gerald was clearly in love with her and obviously they went on to have a very happy marriage. But what had occurred she wasn't going to say. Was that the link to Dorothy? Is that when they fell out? I doubted it, as they were still so young at that point. I got the impression from Dorothy that she had a friendship with Meredith well into adulthood. My mind was a swirling mass of thoughts and I wanted to go back and begin typing straight away.

Once inside my villa, though, the noise coming from the building site was overwhelming and I picked up the laptop, walked back to the garden and found a table in the shade to set myself up. It was much too nice a day to be inside. Despite the number of guests relaxing by the pool, on the terrace café outside the spa and in the garden itself, there was a sense of peace and quiet.

I opened the laptop and was about to start typing when I decided to look up Meredith's books. I found her website and I scrolled through to see all the titles. The covers were pretty, inviting the reader in with clifftop views and sweeping vistas. There were cornfields and mountains, cottages tucked into woodland and large country houses. In each one there was always a woman. She was a small figure looking the other way, giving the impression of a person deep in thought. There was something a little sad about that figure, despite the beautiful backdrop.

I opened a link to read the first chapter of one of her books and found I was immersed in the world she had created very quickly. Her words rang out, drew me in, and I realised she was holding back with her memoir. I closed the link, intending to read again later, for now I had work to do.

I was about to pop in some earbuds so I could concentrate when the conversation between an English couple and a French man caught my attention. He was speaking in English to the couple about his missing sculpture.

'I hope he finds it,' the Frenchman said. 'I worked hard to get this collection together and it feels incomplete without that last piece.'

'Surely the hotel will reimburse you? They must be insured,' the woman said.

'I heard that a gold necklace has gone missing too. That American couple were telling me in the bar the other night. She was really upset about it. But, so far it's not been returned.'

'What is going on here? The manager needs to get his staff under control. It is unacceptable.'

'You think it's the staff?' asked the Englishman.

'Who else could it be?' said the woman Gina assumed was his wife.

'I suppose it could be a guest, but how are they getting into the rooms?'

I slipped my earbuds in then, to begin work, but as I pressed play on the recording and began to type, my head was full of poor Lucien. He really did have a lot on his plate.

14

GINA

The next few days I fell into the rhythm of waking early and having coffee on my patio before the sun worked its way around and the builders began their daily orchestra of bangs and crashes. I then went for a walk around the gardens and discovered some lovely little sunken areas with some unusual planting. There was a shaded garden with old gnarly tree trunks covered in ferns and other woodland plants. I'd even been for a swim, which I hadn't done in years. I was never comfortable in a swimming costume, but here I could go early before anyone was around, before I would go to the Harpers to help them with their morning routine. It was very different from a trip to my local swimming baths. As most of the guests went for breakfast before they ventured outside, it felt as if I had my own private pool.

Béatrice lent me a costume. Not one of her own, of course, but one from the lost property box. She had turned her nose up at the very idea and offered to buy me one from town, but I had reassured her it would be fine and after a quick wash in the kitchen sink it was serviceable. It made me smile thinking back to school days where we would have to raid the lost property box rather than miss PE if we'd forgotten our kit. At that age it was a horrible thing to do and every girl would be ashamed to be wearing someone else's fusty old gym knickers. Now, though, I found I didn't care. Béatrice said it had been in there for a while and was unlikely to be claimed, and I found a few lengths of the outside pool would leave me feeling invigorated.

I was firmly in the love story of Meredith and Gerald now and had followed them from first encounters, to meeting family, to Gerald asking permission for Meredith's hand. The storytelling so far had been insular, though. Meredith was retelling her history as if in a bubble and I was beginning to wonder how much of it was exactly as she said. We all alter our past in the retelling to some degree. Aren't we always suggesting it was raining a little harder than it actually was; we were kinder than we actually were; bolder, funnier, more in love?

It was Meredith's memoir, though, and for her to tell as she saw fit, but at that moment, I wasn't sure who would be interested in reading it. I wanted to suggest she inject some drama. I wouldn't, of course. It wasn't my place.

Then, on the fifth day of my stay at the hotel, she did exactly that.

* * *

I met Lucien as I left my villa, locking the door behind me. He was marching past on his way, I assumed, to the building site. It was midday and there had been no sign of any work going on.

'Is everything okay?' I asked him, but really it was a stupid question because he looked far from okay. He looked tired and drawn. I remembered the conversation I overheard the other day about the missing things. 'Have you found the sculpture?'

He looked surprised for a moment and then his expression softened and he walked over to me.

'*Non*, I haven't. Who have you been talking to, Gina? I thought it was just in-house information at the moment.'

'I overheard a couple talking to the Frenchman whose sculpture is missing. They were suggesting it could be a guest.'

This caught his attention and he seemed to weigh it up.

'That is a thought; to be honest, that hadn't crossed my mind. I've been looking at all my staff with new eyes over the last few days and it's not nice to do that. I've had the police in, but to be honest they have left me with a case number and told me to get in touch with the hotel's insurance company. I don't have the details, though, and I don't want to bother Hugo with it. I thought they might do some actual investigating, but ha! *Non*, they couldn't care less. Have you seen or heard anything else that you think might be suspicious? How about that Englishwoman?'

'Adele? She seems perfectly nice,' I said.

I didn't add that I wasn't sure why she was really here, that she seemed a bit twitchy some of the time and appeared to have an odd interest in the Harpers. I didn't mention the curious text message that arrived on her phone while she was in the loo. Because, yes, that was all a bit strange, but did I think she was a thief? No, no I didn't really.

'Gina, you seem very observant. I would appreciate it if you can keep an eye out for anything odd. The festival is only in a couple of days and it would be good to find out who is responsible before a whole lot more people arrive. I don't mean to put you out, just if you happen to see or hear anything.'

'I can do that,' I said, but unpleasant memories of sneaking around the Norfolk country estate for Dorothy came back to me suddenly. 'If I hear anything, I will certainly let you know.'

'Thank you. I have to go now. I need to track down the

builders. There is going to be trouble there; that is for sure. I don't want them working while the festival is going on. They are not reliable. In fact, I'm very close to telling them to leave, permanently.'

Then he disappeared around the back of my villa and I continued on to Meredith and Gerald's.

Riley followed me as I weaved my way down the shingle path, but he stuck to the cooler shade of the grass and shrubs.

'You can't come,' I told him. 'You'll have poor Gerald sneezing. And keep away from Adele – she's allergic to you too.'

I'd never met someone who was allergic to pet hair before, or certainly no one who had told me they were, and here were two people in the same place with the same allergy in the same hotel at the same time. Another strange thing to add to my list.

I could hear Meredith swearing as I approached their quarters and I knocked gingerly on the door, slightly concerned about what I was going to find on the other side. When she opened the door I could see that her cast had become stuck on the sleeve of her blouse and she had got herself in a bit of a pickle.

'Let me help you,' I said as I slipped into the cool interior of their villa. One thing was for sure: having all the blinds lowered certainly did work to cool the place down. Still, I would have liked to have opened them all and the doors and windows too. Cool it may be, but oppressive it was also.

'This thing is a complete pain,' she said as I began to untangle her.

'How long do you have to wear it?' I asked her. 'How did you do it?'

'The usual way, I fell down to the bottom of few stairs at home. It was just before we moved, so I had that to contend with while I was supposed to be packing. Absolute bloody nightmare! And, of course, it reinforced Rose's point about us moving here. No stairs and her on hand if we needed her.'

I watched her for a moment as her expression changed from irritation to something softer.

'But none of that matters compared with poor Oliver. I am praying he will be okay.'

She suddenly looked very vulnerable.

We settled with some iced apple juice and I readied myself for the next instalment. I had my phone on the table as usual and pressed to record Meredith's voice. She never looked at me when she was dictating. She was always in another world, looking into the middle distance, a bit like the woman on the covers of her books. I wondered if that was because she could immerse herself in the story, or if it was because it was easier to fabricate her perfect past without making eye contact.

Gerald's career really began to take off when we finished our degrees at university. Mine was in fine arts and Gerald's in architecture. He was super ambitious and also he was proud of my achievements academically. Of course he wanted us to get married and he'd already secured my father's permission. Mainly he wanted to start a family, but I...

Meredith stopped here for a moment and sipped her drink before she settled back again and continued talking.

I did want those things, but it was a little more complicated for me and besides, that was the summer I met Dorothy Reed.

Bingo! The word nearly slipped from my lips. And there we were at last: Dorothy Reed was officially in the room.

Dorothy was a breath of fresh air in the stagnant pool of wives and girlfriends I was meeting at the time.

We were young, we were lucky, God we were lucky. Both Gerald and I had parents who supported us and he had started an intense apprenticeship with Sebastian Sinclair, an American architect who had moved to the UK and had brought his passions with him. Gerald was well and truly on his way.

And me? Well, I was invited to the studio of a friend of Sebastian's – an American ceramicist – and I fell instantly in love with the work. I met a woman called Dorothy there who was beginning to experiment with using glass in her ceramics at the time and she offered for me to spend the day with her in her studio and watch her work. I had only been working with clay at Edinburgh, but Dorothy's use of glass really turned my head.

She was unlike anybody I'd ever met before. She didn't care what others thought about her clothes or her hair, what music she listened to. She was passionate about her work and didn't have a lot of time for any nonsense. She was fine-tuning her craft and beginning to create the most fabulous pieces I had ever seen using new techniques of the time. I was in awe of her and incredibly inspired, so I spent as much time as possible in her studio. There were another couple of women artist who worked from the same place and we became quite the group.

Gerald was supportive of my work, but of course marriage was still at the forefront of his mind. We did get married, eventually, but it would be a few long years before I was able to produce the family he wanted so much.

'I'd like to stop there for a bit, Gina.'

'Of course,' I said, desperate for her to continue. 'So, you and your friend Dorothy have been friends for many years, then?'

I was pushing, I knew, but was desperate to find out what actually happened. Meredith had been in awe of this woman. To be honest, I was even more so now. Dorothy had never told me the extent of her career. What had gone wrong between them? To go from awe to never speaking again meant something major must have happened. Just then Gerald folded his newspaper shut and put it on the coffee table. Then he looked to his wife seemingly for instruction, because his expression was one of an entirely lost man.

'Things changed,' Meredith said. 'Sometimes people aren't who you think they are; they do things you don't expect them to do.'

She didn't look angry recalling that time; she looked incredibly sad.

She got up and went over to her husband.

'Have you thought about us going into the city?' I asked her. 'Do you think that Gerald would like to go to the museum? And there's a lovely church that has a garden. We could have lunch in one of the beautiful squares they have. Or we could visit Cézanne's studio.'

She looked at me for a long moment then and I expected her to say no, but she didn't. She seemed to be deep in thought. And then Gerald spoke.

'I do love a museum,' he said and Meredith's expression softened.

It occurred to me, that while Meredith was writing her own love story, she could really still be living it too.

15

DOROTHY

They heard their flight was delayed from Nice as they left the ship to board one of the courtesy buses heading to the airport.

After a bit of a confab, the two women decided to get the bus to drop them off on the way. They had four hours to kill and neither Dorothy nor Yvonne were inclined to spend all that time in the departure lounge.

'And you'll be okay on your own?' the bus driver had asked.

'Perfectly fine, thank you,' Yvonne had said. 'Don't worry, we won't miss the flight. Can you drop us on the front? I think we should soak up the sea for the last time before we leave. Near a restaurant, please.'

He dropped them at the Blue Beach Restaurant off the *Promenade des Anglais* and they crossed the road away from the austere hotels and restaurants that dominated the other side of the dual carriageway. The leafy palms that lined the central reservation were a stark contrast to the bright white of the huge buildings behind them.

'Everything is so clean here,' Dorothy noted.

'Quite lovely,' Yvonne agreed. 'A far cry from the graffiti all over the wall of my local supermarket.'

Dorothy laughed. Yvonne's local shop may well be graffitied, but was not remotely visible from the select development of houses that her friend lived in. They were both privileged old women and she knew it.

They walked down the steps that led to the beach from the promenade and found the restaurant on the sand.

'We've eaten like queens over the last couple of weeks. The most beautifully prepared food, all super healthy, and now all I want is some junk food,' Yvonne said. 'Can we get a burger and chips with a good glass of chilled Chablis?'

Dorothy didn't agree that everything they had consumed had been healthy. One morning Yvonne had talked her into hitting the chocolate fountain for breakfast, for goodness' sake. But, looking at a delay and knowing she would be heading home to eat toast and soup until Gina returned and encouraged Dorothy to make more of an effort, she agreed. Some highly calorific junk food would be welcome.

They were shown to a table with a large blue umbrella above them to protect them from the sun that still shined relentlessly in the cloudless sky. The menu proved fruitful as they did serve burgers and chips, or actually *Burger à L'italienne* because they had inadvertently dropped into an Italian restaurant for their last hours in France.

Dorothy chose the grilled sole at the last minute, deciding that her stomach couldn't cope with anything too heavy before a flight, but she was happy for Yvonne to order a bottle of wine. She scanned the menu for exactly what she wanted. Dorothy didn't care all that much, but Yvonne, she noted, after spending a fortnight together, was now a wine snob. She never used to be. It was just an irritating trait she had managed to pick up with age. She would talk about grape and region, bouquet and nose. She'd not been the same since she'd been on that wine-tasting experience with her husband Bill. She was suddenly an expert. They all had something, though; Dorothy was a self-confessed busybody. She couldn't help but interfere.

Once they had eaten and Dorothy had allowed Yvonne to pour her a second glass, they began to pick apart their holiday.

'I did enjoy myself, but I think the itinerary was perhaps too much for me now, at my age,' Dorothy said.

'I do agree. I think that a beach holiday or lounging by a pool might be more in order next time.'

'I wonder if I might get bored, though,' Dorothy said. 'The truth is, I do like to explore a new place. I could just as easily sit in my garden at home and do nothing if I felt so inclined.'

'In the rain, though. Part of going on holiday is to escape the British climate of cold, damp winters and warm, damp summers.'

'That is true, too. The problem was, we were out almost every day. I need a couple of days in between to recover.'

Dorothy was really feeling the warmth right now, but it wasn't from the temperature of the air around her. She had finished two rather large glasses of wine and her cheeks were on fire. She could also feel her head begin to swim pleasantly.

'What did you think of the art group? Nice bunch of people, I thought,' she said.

'Honestly, I thought they were a bit weird,' said Yvonne.

'Oh? They were so friendly, though.'

'Yes, and weird. You know what you artists are like,' Yvonne said with a chuckle.

'They aren't artists, they're an art appreciation group.'

'Either way, I thought they were odd.'

Dorothy excused herself to go to the loo and wobbled a bit as she got up. She clutched tightly to her stick as she navigated the walk inside the restaurant building. Was she weird? She wondered as she found the ladies'. If she was, she didn't care. As she sat down to relieve herself, her phone began to ring from her handbag she'd hung on the hook from the back of the door. It was Gina, she noted as she fumbled inside for it.

'Gina, I'm on the loo.'

'Well, you didn't need to answer. You could have waited until you'd finished,' Gina said, laughing. Dorothy joined in.

'And, I'm a bit pissed too.'

'Sounds like you're having a great time.'

'Hang on a mo.'

Dorothy placed the phone on the toilet cistern and flushed. Then she opened the door and called out to let Gina know she was just going to wash her hands. She could hear the tell-tale beep of her low battery.

'Right, I'm back,' she said picking the phone up again.

'Honestly, Dorothy, what are you like?'

'Yvonne and I are just having lunch before our flight. It's been delayed by a few hours, so we thought we'd stop off before going to the airport. You know how dreary those places can be. We've found a lovely restaurant on the beach instead. How's things with you?'

'A bit better actually. I've managed to get Meredith to agree to us going into Aix for a day trip. Her daughter was keen for me to get them out, so this is progress.'

'And her book?' Dorothy asked as she made her way back outside.

'Well, you've just turned up. I was keen for her to continue, but I think she was tired. She said she was in awe of you and your talent. How you inspired her.'

Dorothy stopped walking for a moment and leaned against a large pot planted up with a tree.

'She said that about me?'

'Yes, she did and then she began to tell me about another couple of women artists and how you were quite the group.'

Dorothy's walking stick clattered to the ground as she lost her grip on it.

'Dorothy? Are you still there?'

'Yes,' she said, although her breath was shaky and the word seemed to contain several more syllables than it should as it left her lips.

A waiter stepped forward and bent to retrieve her stick. Dorothy smiled and instantly wondered where she had managed to pull it from, because her insides were squirming.

'So, she's really going for it, then,' she said as her phone let out another beep.

'It all seems fairly innocuous to me,' Gina said.

'The group. It begins with the group.'

A belated moment of guilt took Dorothy. Meredith wasn't Gina's problem and yet Dorothy had given her very little information and sent her off to get involved. Classic Dorothy in her busybody mode. Her phone beeped again.

'Gina, I'm sorry, my phone is very low on battery life so I'll have to go for now. I'll phone you later when I've had the chance to recharge it, okay?'

'Okay, Dorothy, safe travels.'

Dorothy made her way back to the table where Yvonne was paying the bill.

'On me,' Yvonne said. 'And, I've managed to get us a taxi that's coming shortly. Are you okay?'

'Yes, yes, I'm fine. I think the wine has got to me a bit, that's all.'

* * *

The airport check-in was busy and Yvonne and Dorothy were fast losing the lovely glow of a boozy lunch in the hectic atmosphere of all these passengers checking in their bags. Yvonne was talking about what she planned to do when she got home, what she'd prepare for dinner for her and Bill, and when she planned to visit her grandchildren at the weekend. Dorothy wasn't listening. All she could think about was Meredith. In fact she was now thinking about one of the other members of the group: Janie. She imagined phoning her old friend to say that fifty-four years after the event, Meredith was about to tell all.

Janie lived in a care home in Carlisle now. Perhaps it wouldn't matter to her, maybe she wouldn't have to know. Aoife had sadly passed away many years previously. The four of them had kept their collective secret for all this time and it sounded as if Meredith was about to let it all go.

Dorothy was the chair of the Hampton Heights Art Committee for goodness' sake. They'd chuck her off. What an embarrassment. Really, that was the least of her worries, though. Daniel Williamson wasn't the hopeful young artist he'd been back then. He may now be ancient, but he was huge. Dorothy had followed his career over the years. It was easy to follow; he was everywhere.

'Yvonne?' she said, her heart beginning to hammer in her chest. 'How would you feel about flying home alone?'

16

LUCIEN

Lucien's finger hovered over the screen of his phone as he urged himself to press the call button, but no sooner had he touched it, than he ended it before it connected. He couldn't trust himself to say the right thing if Solène answered. He hadn't decided if he would beg her to come home or to never bother showing her face again.

He'd been walking the grounds of the hotel since he'd arrived this morning, ostensibly to organise exactly where the stalls should be placed, as the marquee people had arrived and some of the stallholders were setting up their own spaces ready for the festival tomorrow, but really he was avoiding guests and staff.

He wasn't needed in the hotel gardens, though, as Hugo had left a detailed plan they were following and Béatrice was really the one in charge. She'd been out here earlier to make sure all was in order and now Lucien was just getting in their way. Not for the first time since his uncle and aunt had left, he felt out of control and being in reception had given him an almighty headache. Everyone seemed to have a question for him and most of them, ones he couldn't answer: Where is my necklace? Where is my money? Where is my sculpture? And a new entry, where is my watch? This was from an elderly man staying on the first floor in one of the small suites. It was a Rolex that was missing and even Lucien had to agree with Béatrice that it was probably time to call the police again. Except he hadn't, not yet. It was the festival tomorrow and he didn't want the place crawling with police. They hadn't taken it very seriously when they came before, but they might come back with renewed vigour now there had been another theft. He had reassured the guests that the hotel was fully insured, although he hadn't checked this with Hugo. He'd be very surprised if it wasn't. He just wanted to get through the festival without any issues.

He had asked Béatrice to search the staff lockers while they were all outside during the event and she had reluctantly agreed. He knew he would be betraying everyone's trust, but it was a compromise he was prepared to make. A compromise Béatrice was prepared to make. It had to be a staff member, someone with access to the rooms. He doubted she would find the actual items – no one would be stupid enough to leave stolen goods in the hotel – but he hoped they would find something.

Eventually he gave up the pretence of doing anything useful in the gardens and headed back inside. He felt bad for Béatrice holding the fort alone in there too.

Reception was a heaving mass of people. Guests were arriving for the festival and the whole place was so noisy it was making his blooming headache bloom even more.

Béatrice looked harassed and when she caught his eye, she looked annoyed too.

'*Je suis là maintenant,*' he told her, forgetting his English for a moment as he walked behind the desk to join her.

'I can see you're here now,' she said. 'But are you here to help or hinder?'

Lucien needed to shake off his despondency and snap to it. He turned to a couple who were checking in and took their details while the brooding presence of Béatrice busied away next to him.

He managed to mess up the booking and had put them in an already occupied room and activated them a key to another room entirely. A porter waited with their cases while Béatrice corrected his mistake.

'*Je suis désolé*,' she told them, quickly.

The couple seemed amused until Lucien suggested they use the safe in their wardrobe to store any valuable items and then they just looked worried.

'No problem at all,' he soothed them. 'It's just something I tell all of our guests.'

Béatrice rolled her eyes at him as they left.

'What is going on with you? You are not your usual self. It's not just these thefts, is it? It's Solène. You know you can tell me; maybe I can help?'

She rested her hand on his arm.

'No one can help, Béatrice,' Lucien said, staring down at her hand. Any other time he would be delighted at the contact, but right now he just wanted Isabel to phone him so he could be angry with somebody. She seemed to have gone quiet on him and that bothered him more than the increasingly demanding phone calls.

Gina appeared in front of them then and Béatrice withdrew her arm and smiled warmly at the older woman. Lucien was, as always, amazed at her professionalism.

He remembered the first time he had seen Béatrice. It had been in a bar in Marseille. A group of them had been out one Friday night and she was just standing there at the bar ordering drinks for her friends. When she had looked at him it was as if something exploded in his chest. It sounded mawkish, but he had felt it. In that moment he thought, *I'm going to marry that girl.* He pictured their kids, their house, their life together. But he had dithered, thinking he had lots of time, feeling all those thoughts about her, but not ever telling her. Firstly in case of rejection and then bit by bit all the elements of his life began to disintegrate and he couldn't tell her at all. Who could blame her for finding someone who hadn't offered out his spare room to a problematic, grieving mother, who couldn't meet her for a drink because he'd have to talk his mother down from a huge gambling or drinking binge, who couldn't invite her back for a coffee in case his mother was on her knees with her hands down the back of the sofa looking for coins.

'*Bonjour,*' Gina said and then blushed.

Lucien wanted to tell her that he appreciated her attempt at his language. Not everyone bothered when they heard the staff speaking English.

'I realise you're busy,' she continued, 'but amazingly, the Harpers have agreed to a trip into the city.'

'That is great news,' Lucien said. 'How did you manage it?'

'I don't know, lucky timing I guess. I wanted to take them to the *Atelier de Cézanne,* but I know it's a little walk from the city centre and perhaps too much for Meredith and Gerald. Do you think you could arrange a taxi to take us there and to wait for us, please?'

'Of course. I can do that for you now.'

'How about if you take them, Lucien?'

Béatrice had her hand back on his arm again and she was looking at him with her kind, blue eyes.

'But there is so much to do here,' he said.

'The stallholders are organising themselves and the last time I looked it was under control. Rachel is on shift in ten minutes and can help me here and so, we are all fine. You could do with a little time away, don't you think?'

'But, the guests... things,' he said, glancing at Gina.

'You know you won't be questioning staff until after the festival tomorrow, so you don't need to pretend with me. Just go, Lucien, and come back refreshed.'

'I certainly don't want to be a bother – a taxi will be fine,' Gina said.

'*Non,* Lucien will take you. It is no problem at all. See you later, Lucien.' Béatrice began to push him towards the edge of the desk and Gina laughed.

'I feel terrible for asking now,' she said.

'It's fine,' said Lucien. 'If you are sure, Béatrice.'

'You are no use to me as you are, so go,' Béatrice said, not unkindly. 'You can come back with a spring in your step this afternoon. You've been working a lot of hours lately and a break is a good idea for you.'

'I will get myself together and meet you in the car park at ten, if that is okay?'

'That will be wonderful, *merci,*' Gina said to them both and then she left.

'I will book some tickets,' Béatrice said. 'I think you have forty-five-minute slots and it can get busy. My friend works in the gift shop; she will make sure they can visit.'

Lucien turned back to her and a myriad of thoughts went through his head before he simply said, '*Merci, mon cher.*'

* * *

Lucien had the car running and the air con was on by the time Gina reappeared with the Harpers. The last time Lucien had seen Gerald had been when he'd gone missing a few days back and it was good to see him looking less confused and with his clothes on. He thought about how pleased Rose would be when she knew Gina had got her parents out of the villa and out of the hotel.

He glanced at his phone one last time before sliding it into his trousers pocket. He wouldn't phone Solène, he'd wait for her to contact him. He'd also lost the wish to speak to Isabel. He wasn't angry any more, he was surprisingly happy about the prospect of a morning with three pensioners.

17

GINA

I saw Adele briefly just before I rounded up Meredith and Gerald. She was sitting on her patio with her phone in her hand and looking a little nervous. When I told her that I'd managed to get the Harpers out, she seemed genuinely pleased for them – or for me, I wasn't sure – but she perked up a bit with the news. I had just said goodbye when I turned back to her and thought how forlorn she looked by herself. I nearly invited her to join us, but decided that the Harpers' first visit out shouldn't be with a stranger in tow. Other than myself of course.

'If you're free, we could get a drink later or tomorrow at the festival perhaps.'

'Thanks, Gina, I'd like that.'

I phoned Dorothy, assuming she had managed to charge her phone, as I walked round to villa number one, but it went to voicemail and I left her a message saying I hoped she had got home safely and to phone me back.

We left the hotel and travelled back down the windy lanes to the main road into Aix. Gerald sat in the front with Lucien, and Meredith and I squeezed ourselves into the back.

'You're never very far from home, are you?' Meredith suddenly said, and I looked out to see what had prompted her words. A Lidl supermarket was just off the main roundabout and I laughed.

'Aix has some lovely shops, so you won't be hankering for supermarkets from home,' I said.

'Believe me, I wasn't,' said Meredith in a clipped tone, reminding me that she hadn't completely thawed and I should tread carefully.

Lucien took us off the dual carriageway and down towards the city, navigating a few busy roundabouts at some speed. Admittedly not as fast as he had when he'd picked me up from the airport, but still fast enough.

'I don't know how you do it,' Meredith said.

'Do what exactly?' Lucien asked.

'Drive on the wrong side of the road.'

'It's the correct side to me, but I did okay when I lived in the UK for a few years. You get used to it.'

'Well, I know I wouldn't,' she said and drew her handbag closer to her as if it could somehow protect her.

The main road to the east of the city was lined with trees and there was that wonderful dappled sunlight coming through them that I remembered from my trip with Adele.

'The light here is impressive,' Meredith said. 'It's no wonder Cézanne was so inspired.'

She had loosened her grip on her bag and was leaning forward now and peering out of the window. I noticed Gerald doing the same.

'Do you see the light, Gerald?' she said.

'Indeed I do,' he replied.

I was glad that Lucien had given us a lift, because as we turned onto *Avenue Paul Cézanne* I could see it would have been too far and too steep a walk for both Meredith and Gerald.

Probably too much for me, if I was honest. Especially in this heat.

'At least it's quite cool today,' Lucien said, with comedic timing that only I appreciated.

'Spoken like a true *Provençal*,' said Meredith. 'Us Brits are used to a more damp and chilly climate.'

Lucien drove past the entrance to Cézanne's studio and pulled up outside a hair salon a couple of hundred yards up the road. A woman inside who was cutting someone's hair waved to him as we all climbed out of the car and then she blew him a kiss.

'Véronique is a good friend and happy for me to park here,' Lucien said.

We walked the short distance back down the hill and through the unassuming red gates and into Cézanne's garden. The studio was larger than I was expecting and Lucien corrected me when I assumed that Cézanne had lived here too. It was painted in the yellow ochre colour I remembered from the stone buildings in the centre of Aix and it had muted-red doors and shutters that were shaded under the canopy of trees from the garden. Where there was light it was bright, though, and the shadows from all the different species of tree were cast across the façade of the building. Cicadas droned all around us in that unmistakably Mediterranean chorus and I suddenly wanted to just sit in the gardens and soak it all up.

'Would it be okay if I just sat outside while you went in?' I asked Meredith. 'I have a yearning for the garden at the moment.'

'Won't you miss seeing the studio, though?'

'No, I'll leave you and Gerald to explore it together. And I'll be just out here if you need me.'

I didn't add that I was suddenly feeling a little overwhelmed and also if I did see the studio, I would really like to see it alone without the need for conversation.

Lucien made sure they went in the right door and then he disappeared into another.

I sat down on the wall with the garden behind me and looked up at Paul Cézanne's studio. I didn't really know where this feeling had come from, but I just concentrated on breathing and trying very hard to be in the moment. Lucien reappeared with a couple of cans of cold drink and he handed me one.

'Are you okay?'

'Yes,' I said. 'Just having a moment.'

I flipped up the ring pull and pushed it back, then sipped at the cool, fizzy orange drink as I tried to quell my thoughts. I was in the South of France at Paul Cézanne's studio, sipping a cold drink, talking to a nice Frenchman, but I'm not quite sure how I got here. I mean, I know I flew here on a Ryanair flight, but...

'Only four months ago I was living in our family home in Oxfordshire with my husband, Douglas, with a clear, daily routine and a vision for the last couple of decades of my life. And then he left and now everything feels a bit transient,' I told Lucien.

'It's better, though, *non*? Opening up your life to possibilities is no bad thing.'

'I feel lost, though, Lucien,' I said, and as the words came out I realised how true they were. 'I'm seventy-one and it's not easy to restart your life. I've had some nice things happen to me, granted, but I'm just not sure where I belong.'

'And what wonderful thing is your husband doing that meant he had to give up on his marriage?'

'Finding himself with another woman, I think. I expect she's younger, more exciting. It's an age-old thing – I'm not the only one.'

At that moment my phone started ringing and I pulled it from my handbag and laid it on the wall next to me. Douglas's name was flashing on the screen.

'How odd that he should phone now,' I said. 'I guess his ears were burning, as we say in the UK.'

Before I could stop him, Lucien reached for it and tapped the screen.

'Gina's phone, who is this?' he said in a deeply husky voice and I couldn't help but smile.

'It's her husband!' said a very indignant Douglas. Lucien had switched it to speaker phone so not only I could hear the conversation, but so could the couple sitting at a table next to us.

'I'm so sorry, but Gina can't come to the phone right now; she is tied up,' he said simply and I could only imagine what Douglas was thinking.

'I beg your pardon,' my husband said, in the most British voice I had ever heard him use, and I put my hand over my mouth to stop myself from laughing out loud.

Lucien held the phone away from him and said one last thing before he ended the call.

'Gina, darling, I'm coming.'

He handed the phone back to me with a sheepish grin.

'Sorry, I probably shouldn't have done that. I'm in an odd mood today.'

'No, it was very funny and has cheered me up no end.'

'I think that if you want your husband back, then he sounds pissed off at me, so that is a great start. And if you don't want him back, then it will sound very much to him as if you have moved on, so that is also good, *non*? Do you agree?'

Did I want Douglas back? The thought hadn't really crossed my mind. I had just been going through the motions assuming there was no other option. Did I want Douglas back? The truth was, I just didn't know.

'I'm a bit too old for games, to be honest, Lucien, but I hear what you're saying.'

My phone pinged with an incoming message and Lucien smiled.

'That will be him.'

I read the words on the screen.

'He wants to know who the hell you are, why there's an international ringtone as I hadn't told him I was going anywhere and can I please phone him back to discuss our house sale.'

'What an arse. Are you going to respond?'

I tapped out a quick response and pressed send.

'I have told him to mind his own business and I'm very busy with my young, French friend.'

'You see, Gina,' Lucien said with a grin. 'You are never too old to play games.'

18

GINA

We left Cézanne's place and Lucien drove us back into the centre of Aix. Meredith told us how Gerald seemed to enjoy seeing the artist's studio and how the audio guide really brought it all to life. She said it was a humbling experience and she was so glad she'd seen it. I had bought a tea towel from the gift shop with my favourite of his works printed onto it. I knew that once I was home, it would look like a very cheap keepsake, but somehow, here in his garden as I held it up to the light, it looked perfect. *L'Estaque, Melting Snow.*

Lucien, it turned out, had another friend with a great little parking space and we left the car tucked behind some shops.

'You have girls stashed everywhere,' I teased him.

'That's me, always the bridesmaid, never the bride.'

'That's a very English saying,' I said.

'I'm becoming more and more English I think.'

'I've yet to see you queue, drink tea or complain about the weather. You have a long way to go,' I said and we grinned at each other.

We walked into the *Cours Mirabeau*, which was now transformed into a bustling market. Gone was the wide expanse of boulevard and in its place were a sea of stalls. There were clothes and handbags, baskets, food and as we walked a little further it became more of a flea market with trinkets and collectables. Gerald was very animated all of a sudden and went off to look at what was on offer, Meredith at his side. Lucien and I followed on behind them and I was so taken with a small silver photo frame that I decided to buy it as a gift for Dorothy. Lucien insisted on bartering with the seller and I was very happy to only pay half of what he was originally asking. Gerald bought a couple of books, which looked to be written in French, and Meredith smiled and shrugged as he handed over some cash.

Lucien guided us into a stone passageway that led away from the street and brought us out onto a pretty tree-covered square with cafés and restaurants. We found a table and sat down while Gerald opened his newly purchased books and looked very much as if he was reading them.

'Gerald doesn't read or speak French,' Meredith said quietly to me and Lucien.

I was about to make some comment about how it was keeping him happy or quiet, but I stopped myself. Gerald was not a child and he didn't need to be kept quiet or happy. It made me realise how easy it is to dismiss someone when they lose their sense of self and cease to communicate as they once did.

'Tell me, which of Gerald's buildings was he most proud of?' I asked, as Gerald closed his book in favour of the plastic menu propped up on the table.

'Our own home on the outskirts of London,' Meredith said. 'We bought some land and Gerald created our very own grand design. The neighbours were not keen to start with. They complained that it was too modern and wouldn't fit with the other houses around the area, but we were granted planning permission and once it was built, most agreed that it was a triumph. We won them over in the end with a large open-house party.'

'And is that where you left to come here?'

'Yes, we sold it when it was clear Gerald was struggling and I suppose I was as well. Rose wanted us close to her, but we won't always be in the villa; we are going to buy a property when the right one comes available. Something on one level, close to the hotel.'

The waiter arrived then and we ordered coffees and pastries, then whiled away a lovely half an hour, not really talking, but just soaking up the atmosphere. Gerald returned to his books and Lucien spent most of the time staring at his phone.

* * *

Meredith actually thanked me for encouraging them to go out and before we sat down to continue her memoir we had a plan to go into Marseille after the festival. I was pretty sure that Lucien would take us, but if he couldn't afford the time I would organise us a taxi. I didn't think the Harpers would be up for hanging around bus or train stations.

Gerald had taken his books into the bedroom and left us to it. He'd actually said those words before he left.

'I'll leave you ladies to it.'

It had made Meredith smile momentarily before a look of sadness washed over her face.

'It's so hard to have him for only snippets of time,' she said. 'And I never know when those will be. It's why I can't bear to be apart from him in case I miss one of his lucid moments.'

I poured us both a glass of water and then I placed my phone onto the table and, when Meredith was ready, I pressed to record.

Dorothy and I began to exhibit together in a small way. She

was much more experienced than me and knew so many people in the art world. I knew I was hanging off her coattails, but I was happy to be doing so. We spent a lot of time together and became very close.

'Gina,' she said, interrupting my thoughts about Dorothy. 'I'm quite tired, so if you would consider leaving your phone for a while, I can go and lie on the bed and record. You really don't need to be listening to me here and then have to go and listen again. It's a waste of your time.'

'But what should I do then? I'm being paid to look after you,' I said, actually desperate to listen to her continue.

'Well...' Meredith looked around the room as if trying to conjure up a job. 'There are some dishes in the sink if you wouldn't mind washing them, and then do you think you could go to the spa and make an appointment for Gerald to have a neck and shoulder massage? I think he'd really like that. And could you make a hair appointment for me?'

I left their villa after I'd cleaned the kitchen and I wandered down to the spa to make the appointments, which took all of thirty-five seconds. Then, feeling a bit like a spare part I walked back towards my villa with my head full of Dorothy and Meredith. As interesting as Meredith's memories were, they didn't stack up to a book. Surely she could see this herself as a successfully published writer. I wondered what her true motivation was for this memoir. I assumed it all wrapped itself around Gerald's dementia and her need to remember for him. She was holding something back, though. I could feel it in the way that she spoke. I wasn't sure if it was her holding back generally, as a stranger would when telling a story, or whether it was the event Dorothy was worried about that she was keeping to herself. As much as I wanted her to skip forward so I could find out what had ended her friendship with Dorothy, I also willed her to go back as well, back to when she was younger. What was it she had said? *To outrun her past.* The words she'd asked me to scrap. That was what I wanted to hear about and I imagined that her readers would too. Maybe she might open up more without me sitting and listening.

I could see that the door to my villa was open. I was convinced that I had closed and locked it before I went to Meredith's. Cautiously I approached, hoping that it was just an oversight and not another theft to add to the list. I thought about those few precious things of my mother's that I always carried with me and picked up my pace. But, surely a thief wouldn't be interested in an old birthday card, a photograph and a set of car keys.

Adele was standing in the middle of my living space when I walked through the door. She looked surprised to see me and then quickly started speaking.

'Oh, Gina, I saw your door was open and I wanted to check everything was okay. I knew you were at Meredith's and couldn't understand why you would have left your villa open. I don't think anything has been taken, though.'

'Good,' I said. 'I thought I'd locked up. My mistake.'

'How was your morning?' she asked.

'We had a lovely time, thank you. I think the Harpers were both pleased to get out. I suggested Marseille next time and Meredith seems keen. If I can leave one legacy for Rose, I hope it will be a happier father who is enjoying what he can while he still can and a mother who hasn't given up on life.'

And then, quite suddenly Adele started crying.

'Goodness,' I said stepping forward and reaching out for her, but she took a step back from me.

'Sorry,' she said, dabbing at her eyes. 'I'm just being silly.'

'Are you thinking about your mother? It can hit you suddenly like that. What about your father? Is he still alive?'

'My father was a married man,' she said. 'My mother told me a few truths before she died and has left me with a lot of questions that I wish I didn't have in my head.'

'I'm so sorry; that's tough. Deathbed confessions don't always help the living, but maybe she needed to lift it from herself.'

'It was selfish of her. She could have told me all the truths many years ago, but decided instead to load them all onto me just as she was dying, just when I couldn't ask her not to. I was happier not knowing. I'll get out of your way,' she said and then walked past me and out of the villa. I noticed two things as she left. One was the glittering of that gold necklace she wore all the time and the other was that the laptop was open on the table. I was pretty sure that I had shut my front door before I left, even if I didn't lock it, but I was convinced I'd closed the lid of the laptop.

19

LUCIEN

'What do you mean she's gone? Jesus, Lucien, have you spoken to her? Where has she gone? Is she coming back? I actually hope she doesn't; she's toxic. You will be better off without her in your life. But, do you need to tell someone she's missing?' Béatrice said.

'I haven't spoken to her and she's not missing; she's left. They are two completely different things. It's not only that, she's cleaned me out, too. Taken my credit card, cash and she got into my account and took my savings.'

'*Non!*' Béatrice gasped theatrically and her hand flew to her mouth. 'She took your money? What are you going to do? Are you going to call the police?'

Lucien sighed. He could call the police and they could solve all of the crimes at the same time. A buy one get one free. Find the hotel thief and put his mother behind bars. Uncle Hugo would be delighted to come home to news of his sister's incarceration.

'*Non*, no police for *ma mère*. Anyway, they will say I'm an idiot for allowing it to happen and they'd be right. Also, I think we have established that they aren't all that useful.'

'But, you've cancelled the credit card, *oui*?'

'I haven't, but I will. She hasn't used it yet, because she transferred eight thousand euros from my account to hers, so she has quite enough to be getting on with.'

'But, Lucien, this is terrible. She cannot be allowed to do this.'

'Too late – she has already done it. I think she took my phone when I was asleep and she's already set up as a payee, so it was easy for her.'

'You should never had given her your passwords.'

'I stupidly trusted her. I thought it would be okay. I expect quite a lot from my mother, but I didn't expect this.'

Béatrice stepped forward then and pulled him into a hug. Lucien allowed himself to be held for a moment and then broke away. He had a sudden urge to get drunk.

'Let's talk again after the festival; we will have a plan. It all looks amazing, by the way. I think it's going to be a great success.'

'I agree. Everyone has worked hard.'

'Go and relax now. Get some dinner, get some sleep. Once tomorrow is out of the way, things will be easier.'

Lucien was about to leave the reception desk when an elderly woman walked into the foyer. She looked as tired as Lucien felt as she pulled her case with one hand and gripped her walking stick with the other.

'Good evening,' he said as she got to the desk. 'Welcome to *Hôtel and Spa du Cézanne.*'

'*Bonsoir,*' the woman said as she rested her stick against the counter. 'I have a booking.'

Béatrice clicked the mouse to invite her computer screen back to life and Lucien walked around to the front of the desk to help the woman into a comfortable chair.

'Have you had a long journey?' he asked her.

'Not in miles, but, in a sense it has been a journey: over forty years in the making and then a snap decision.'

'How interesting,' said Lucien.

'Do you think it's possible someone could get a phone to me, please? Just an inexpensive device I can message and call on.'

'*Non* problem. Did you leave yours at home?'

'No, this silly old fool left it on charge in my hotel room.'

'Will you be wanting a meal?' Lucien asked. 'We're just at the end of dinner service, but perhaps some room service?'

'Thank you, but no. I am going to drag myself to bed and sleep until breakfast.'

'What name do you have?' Béatrice asked her from the other side of the desk.

'Reed,' she said. 'Dorothy Reed.'

* * *

Lucien lifted a bottle of wine from the counter and poured a small amount into two glasses. Cristòu glowered at him as he took the glass Lucien offered and knocked back the contents.

Lucien wanted to laugh at him. He really was the picture of the surly French chef as depicted in many books and films. He wondered if Cristòu knew what a cliché he actually was.

Cristòu had been making sure the wine was ready for the following day and Lucien had insisted on getting involved. He hadn't really needed to – the head chef was perfectly capable of doing it by himself – but part of him really did want to tick all the boxes Hugo would have done if he was here. The other part, the masochistic part, wanted to front up to the man. Although, Cristòu was probably the wrong person to be picking a fight with – a fight Lucien seemed to be spoiling for.

He had opened a couple of bottles and said he wasn't sure it was quite right for the guests. Did Cristòu think it was a bit heavy for tasting? Were they really sure it was the right wine to be promoting? Was the white a bit too sweet or not sweet enough?

'Why don't you just let me do my job!' Cristòu had shouted and Helena, who had been cleaning down the surfaces, had jumped.

Lucien was reminded that he hadn't done anything about her complaint about Cristòu and she wasn't the only member of staff who had told of his vicious outbursts. He smiled across the kitchen, now, holding her eye in the hope that his face conveyed authority and leadership. That he would deal with the complaint and hopefully persuade Hugo to get rid of Cristòu when he got back. Helena just sighed and left the room.

'This seems to only be your job when you choose it to be and I want tomorrow to be perfect,' Lucien said, turning back to the wine.

'Yes, and that is why you need to let me do it.'

Cristòu poured from three more bottles and Lucien had a line of drinks in front of him.

'Just drink those, say you like them and then get out. I have things to do.'

Lucien tipped one after the other down his throat without really tasting them. It was pointless trying to do anything with this man. Cristòu had his own agenda and Lucien couldn't objectively work with him, because he despised him.

Lucien felt light-headed. He didn't usually drink that much. He told Cristòu to do as he saw fit and then as the other man turned his back, Lucien swiped a bottle from the counter. He felt he had a taste for it now.

He headed for the office and closed the door behind him. He filled the mug that earlier had been full of coffee and drank it down in one. He turned the bottle to see what he was drinking and it was a Syrah from the *Château Richeaume* estate.

The Old Girls' Chateau Escape

Béatrice had started another to-do list and he had just refilled his mug and settled down to read it when his phone began buzzing.

'Isabel! How delightful to hear from you. To what do I owe the pleasure?'

He didn't bother to speak her Italian or his French, but instead chose to use the English he'd been speaking all day. He had no idea if she would understand him, but he needn't have worried because when she spoke in that sultry voice of hers, her English was impeccable.

'Enough of this nonsense now, Lucien. I will come to you and we can get this sorted once and for all.'

'I'm not at home,' he said, filling his glass again and drinking it down like it was water.

'I'm sure you're not; you have a festival at your hotel tomorrow. I do my research. I know where to find you whether you're at home or at work.'

'This stays away from work!' he said. 'I will meet you somewhere.'

'No, Lucien. You are not in a position to tell me what to do. I will come and find you and we will put this to bed.'

Lucien was supposed to feel threatened, he realised, but a combination of her voice, the word *bed* and now two large glasses of wine in his system were making him feel otherwise. She ended the call and he poured the remainder of the wine into his mouth.

In the bar, Lucien collided with a stool as he went to lift another bottle of wine. Their Australian barman, Simon, was working his shift and he stepped over to where Lucien was fumbling.

'Can I help you?'

'Can I have a bottle of wine? Actually can I have some whisky?'

Simon turned round, pulled two bottles from the shelf and put them on the bar in front of him.

'Eighty euros and one hundred and twenty euros. Which one do you want?'

Lucien licked his lips and tried not to seem as drunk as he knew he was. The only thing he'd eaten today was a pastry in Aix.

'That one,' he said, pointing to the cheaper bottle. 'Make a note. Oh, and charge me for this too.'

He handed over the empty bottle of red wine. Even drunk, he still had some integrity and wasn't about to steal from his employer. Despite the fact that his employer's sister had stolen from him.

He used the mug that still had the residue of red wine in it and sloshed some whisky in. Then he propped himself up on the stool he'd nearly toppled and resumed his drinking while Simon tactfully looked away. If it was all going to shit, Lucien felt he might as well be numb for the experience.

He looked around at the guests enjoying their evening and the room seemed to sway and shimmer in front of his eyes. He thought it best if he found somewhere quieter to be. Somewhere less conspicuous. When he tried to climb down off the stool, though, he stumbled, grabbed at the bar and nearly knocked his drink out of his own hand. Simon glanced over at him, but Lucien raised a hand to prove he was fine.

He took his mug and weaved his way across the room with the bottle in his other hand until he found a little corner to sink down into. Then when he was settled onto the far edge of the bench seat he took out his phone and tried his mother's number. She needed to come home and sort out her mess. He no longer wanted to entertain the idea of bailing her out. It was not his problem.

The call went to voicemail as it had done the last time he had tried and he decided in his drunken state to choose this moment to leave her a message.

'Solène,' he slurred, not wishing to call her anything as sentimental as *Mère* or *Maman*. 'You have left a big mess here and I don't have the time and I now no longer – thanks to you – have the money to sort it out. I wash my hands of it and you. Don't bother coming back. I don't need such a toxic figure in my life. I'm better off without you!'

He jabbed at his phone to end the call and immediately felt terrible. Did he just wash his hands of his own mother? She needed help and support, didn't she? Too late, though. The final straw had been the clearing of his bank account. That was the limit.

20

GINA

I closed the lid of the laptop, although I could barely tear myself away from the story unfolding in front of me. Meredith's tone of voice had changed this afternoon. I was right that without me sitting in front of her she sounded more relaxed, more natural. I had an unpleasant feeling about what might be coming next, though. It all seemed to be going along so perfectly, but in every novel I had ever read, it was at that moment in the story that things began to fall apart.

I decided on a cup of tea and filled the kettle, then I remembered I didn't have any milk left. I could drink it black or have a herbal tea, but I really did fancy a cup of Earl Grey and I'd definitely need a coffee in the morning, so I thought I'd head to the hotel to find some.

There wasn't anybody on reception and I wondered if I could go to the restaurant. Perhaps I could just help myself. That was when I saw Lucien. He was stumbling towards the door that led out to the overflow car park. He had a bottle of whisky clutched in his hand. He put his other hand out for the handle and then with a sharp yank he opened the door into his head.

'Lucien, are you okay?' I asked him.

He looked round and it took a second for him to focus on me, but when he did, he smiled.

'I'm a bit drunk,' he said and his words slurred together.

'Are you planning on going home tonight? You're not going to drive, are you?'

'No, not going there – it's dangerous. Do you know I'm not safe in my own home any more? Can you imagine that, Gina?'

I ignored that comment because I knew he didn't really require a response and also because I knew exactly what it was to feel unsafe in your own home.

Lucien couldn't possibly drive and I knew he did do exactly that each night because he'd told me.

'I'm going to sleep in my car,' he said.

I really didn't want him to do that, either. If he had the keys he might take a stupid chance.

'Come back to mine for a bit,' I said. 'We can have a hot drink and you can think about what you'd like to do.'

In any other scenario this would have sounded a bit weird, but luckily Lucien was too drunk to make a joke about it and seemed happy to follow me out of the hotel and into the grounds with only the raised eyebrows of the night manager who had appeared behind the desk. I decided that a black coffee was in order for Lucien and I would just drink herbal tea. I could worry about milk in the morning.

Lucien stumbled through the gardens behind me until I stopped, worried he was going to end up in a bush. I linked my arm through his and held him up as we carried on. The lights in villa number one were all out, unsurprisingly, but there was a faint glow from Adele's place. Was she reading, talking to someone on the phone, looking through her non-existent photos, or remembering what she had read on my laptop this afternoon?

Tomorrow at the festival I was going to ask her what she was really doing here. I was beginning to see that her interest in the Harpers was more than simply neighbourly. I had a sinking feeling that Gerald may be at the heart of whatever was going on with her.

My father was a married man, she had said and I just couldn't get that out of my head.

Or maybe the sensible thing would be not to get involved and perhaps I should mind my own business.

Riley sprung out from a bush and began to follow us back to my villa. When I opened the door he walked right in as if he lived there.

'Who owns this cat?' I asked Lucien as he sunk down onto the sofa, still clutching the bottle of whisky.

'Hotel cat, just turned up one day and gets fed from the kind hearts of the kitchen staff, not Cristòu obviously.'

'I call him Riley.'

'It's a good name. No one has bothered to name him before. That name might stick.'

'Do you know that Gerald and Adele, the English guest, are both allergic to cat fur?'

'No,' he said, bemused. 'Should I?'

'Not really, just an observation.'

I had turned on the lamp in the living room rather than the overhead light. I didn't want to scare him half to death. I popped the kettle on and made us both a black coffee. I'd have the herbal tea for breakfast.

'Thanks again for the chair outside,' I said as I put the mugs down on the table. 'It's nice sitting out there in the morning for breakfast.'

'The least I could do, honestly. It's pretty poor in here.'

'It's fine, truly, perfect for what I need.'

Sitting down opposite him in the armchair I curled my feet up underneath me and then immediately put them back down on the floor. The temporary comfort wasn't worth the dead legs I'd get in no time and I didn't fancy fending off the cramp. Riley stalked over to me and, without even asking, he jumped up onto my lap, turned around three times and then settled.

'So, you've had a bit of a night then?' I said and he laughed.

'Not intentionally. Cristòu and I did a bit of impromptu wine tasting and he can handle it more than me.'

'Were you trying to impress Béatrice?' I teased.

'*Non*, I don't think she is impressed with drunk men, which is a bit of a problem because Cristòu is often drunk these days. He's going to fu—' he started, then stopped himself. 'He's going to mess up his chances of that Michelin star. *Imbécile.*'

'That's on him, though. It's not a reflection on you. Anyone who knows you in this hotel seems to like and respect you. I've seen it. What Cristòu does is his own lookout. It's not really your problem, is it? If Hugo doesn't like the way Cristòu is behaving he will get rid of him when he gets back.'

'It very much feels like my problem at the moment. I'm supposed to be in charge and it's all going to shit around me. There is a thief in this hotel somewhere and I need to find who, but am I to line up all the staff? I will lose their trust if I do that, but who has done it and how am I to catch them? I'm not even giving it the attention it deserves. But, maybe if I'm patient, they might reveal themselves.'

'It isn't easy, but I think you probably need to be more proactive. I found a stolen painting once,' I said, immediately wondering why I told him.

'I'm not surprised. I think you could do anything you set your mind to. Look how you've brought Meredith out of her shell.'

'Barely, but I'm glad she agreed to go into Aix with Gerald.

And she's thinking about Marseille after the festival in a few days' time. I suppose that is progress.'

'That is wonderful, Gina. It has not been an easy time for them, moving here, dealing with Gerald's illness and then poor Oliver too.'

With those words he looked despondent again.

'Is this just about the hotel? Or is there more going on, Lucien? You don't seem like the happy man who picked me up from the airport last week. But if you don't want to talk about it, I understand.'

He had his head back on the sofa now and his eyes were closing. The coffee wasn't doing its job, but at least he wasn't trying to do something stupid like drive home. Then they snapped open and he leaned forward. For a second I thought he was going to be sick, but luckily he just wanted to speak.

'My *mère*, my mother,' he said and then stopped.

I drank some of my coffee to fill the silence and he began again.

'She has a gambling problem.'

'Ah, that's not good. Can you get her some help? Would she be receptive to that?'

He laughed then and it was disconcerting for a moment. This near stranger sitting on my sofa, drunk and maudlin.

'I don't know where she is. She left my apartment the other night with every euro I had. And do you know what's great about it all? She owes a lot of money to some not very nice people who want it back. It could have gone some way to helping her, but she took everything I had. What kind of parent does something so despicable?'

'I'm so sorry to hear that, Lucien. Some people are just not good at being parents.'

'Was your mother the same – a disappointment?'

The Old Girls' Chateau Escape

'No, quite the opposite. It was my father who was the problem. I adored my mother.'

'What did you adore about her?'

'She was good, kind and funny.'

'What specifically? I'm interested in how good people operate,' Lucien said.

'You're a good person, Lucien. Don't forget that.'

'I hope I am, I try to be, but tell me about your mother.'

'She kept me safe, I suppose. She knew what a difficult situation we were in with my father and she still managed to make my childhood as good as it could be. And then later, when it was just the two of us, it was wonderful. She was an art historian.'

'Like you,' Lucien said, remembering what I'd told him when he picked me up from the airport.

'Yes, we worked together at a National Trust property in London. She was the head of collections and I assisted her. Before that, after I graduated from university, we spent a summer in Venice together. We travelled the canals and explored the centuries-old architecture, the tucked-away churches and cobblestoned side streets. We visited the island of Murano – the home of hand-blown glass – and Burano with its colourful houses and intricate lace. That was when I saw the person she really was. She was free and so happy. That time and the years after were blissful.'

'And what about your father? Why was he a problem?'

I put my mug down on the table and licked my lips. It was hard enough conjuring up happy memories of my mother, but talking about my father was something else. Lucien wasn't really looking for answers: he was drunk and probably feeling sorry for himself and I wanted desperately to tell him he wasn't alone, that other parents did despicable things.

'My father was a controlling man and it took a long time for my mother to leave him. We were living in America for a time – he was American – and she flew me and her all the way back to England to escape him, but it was never going to be far enough; he was always going to try and find her because he assumed he owned her. We were so happy for those few years. For quite a few years he stayed away, or he couldn't find us, but then he tracked her down through her work. He found us and he stalked us for a long time until one night while we were sleeping...'

I stopped speaking because I wasn't sure I could get the words out, but actually it didn't matter because Lucien, I realised, had fallen asleep. His head had collapsed onto the cushion behind him. I picked Riley up from my lap and let him out of the door. I didn't want to risk him waking Lucien up. I still had a horrible thought that he might drive home. I took the cup from Lucien's hand and left him a large glass of water on the table. I considered laying a blanket over him, but really, it was too hot, then I turned out the light and took myself off to bed.

21

GINA

The grounds looked spectacular on the morning of the festival. They had all worked their magic the previous day and now it was set as if the circus had come to town. With the backdrop of the château there was a theatrical vibe. It really did have a welcome feel with the way the marquees had been placed in the gardens. Fairy lights and bunting, clever signs and enticing displays. I had imagined once everything was in place the gardens would be completely obscured, but actually, it had all been arranged to show off the careful planting as much as possible. Food vans and vendors had arrived with what Lucien called the best the area could offer. The smell of coffee and pastries filled the morning air and the sun was already climbing to accommodate. There were a few welcome clouds around to take the edge off the rays, but rain wasn't forecast.

Lucien had arranged a magician to circulate among the crowds and keep people entertained, and there was a children's play area set up in the far corner of the main lawn. The hotel didn't really accommodate young children usually. The place was mainly aimed at adult guests, but this was very different. They knew this festival would appeal to families and it seemed as if they had thought of everything. I hadn't actually met Hugo on the call the other night, but I could only assume he'd be thrilled with it all.

That was when I saw Lucien stalking around the area and recording the scene with his phone. He was talking into the camera and even from this distance I could hear the tell-tale croak of a voice that had had a late night and a lot to drink. He'd gone when I woke at six-thirty. His coffee mug was washed and upturned on the draining board proving that he hadn't just stumbled out, but had at least been properly awake. He had the world on his shoulders and his mother ideally needed to come back and sort out her own mess.

He hadn't been clear who these people were she owed money to, but whoever heard of a friendly loan shark? He could be in real trouble. I wondered if when he was back, his uncle Hugo would help his sister out. It was none of my business, but when someone comes and tells you about their biggest problems, don't they in fact make it partly yours too?

I was happier now I had seen him. He'd been in quite a state the previous night and I was surprised to see him up so early. Youth: don't they say it's wasted on the young? But it always seemed to me that they were using it for all it was worth.

I suddenly had an urge to talk to my children and hear a bit about what was going on at home. I didn't get an answer from either Alice or Chris, so I logged onto our WhatsApp group chat and uploaded a couple of pictures of Aix then typed out a message.

GINA

It's beautiful here in the south of France and the weather is perfect. I hope all is well at home.
Mum x

The Old Girls' Chateau Escape

The trouble with a mobile phone was that it lulled you into thinking you were part of something, that you always had friends at the end of your fingertips. Then you would look up from the screen and find yourself completely alone.

I'd been into the hotel and Béatrice had kindly gone and fetched me a carton of milk. I decided to disappear back to my villa for breakfast, keen to type up some more of Meredith's words and listen to the rest of the recording she had done without me yesterday. The festival officially started at ten-thirty and I'd leave Lucien to it. He was fine, he was up, and he was back in charge.

I set up the laptop on the table and pulled up a chair, then with a coffee, my cereals and a glass of orange juice to hand, I replayed Meredith's last recording.

Dorothy came to see me and offered her condolences. It was the night of my fifth miscarriage and I could barely speak to her, I was so beside myself with grief.

She said all of the right things of course and wouldn't entertain the idea that it was actually my own fault. I withdrew from everyone around me, consumed as I was, and even Gerald couldn't bring me out of my despair. I could hear him and Dorothy talking, trying to find a solution, but what could be done? I wasn't going to be a mother and would have to live with the consequences.

I paused the recording for a moment and finished my cereal while my brain whirred. Meredith was in a dark place back then, but she had a loving husband, a good friend and a wonderful career in the arts. What she wanted, though, was a child and I could hear the grief in her voice as she spoke. She did go on to have Rose, but remembering that time was clearly painful to her. I wondered why she felt the need to blame herself. There was so much sadness in her voice. Much more than I would expect of someone looking back from the position of achieving the motherhood she seemed to crave so much. I put my empty bowl in the sink and pressed play.

It was another year until I found out I was pregnant again and everything had changed. Dorothy had moved away and we had lost contact, which made Gerald and I much closer finally. I had given up my part of the studio and put art to one side in favour of nurturing the baby I had growing inside me. It was the furthest I had managed to get in pregnancy and I wasn't about to do anything to jeopardise it.

It was a wonderful time. I really did feel that at last I was my own person, living my best life and with the very best man beside me. As I got bigger and more confident that everything would work out, Gerald and I became even closer. For a while I thought he'd never come back to me, but he did. He was back by my side and fully committed to us and our baby.

Where had Gerald gone? Had he just been metaphorically or emotionally missing, or had he actually gone somewhere? Why had she lost contact with Dorothy just because she moved? That made no sense to me. Dorothy had said they had fallen out, though, that she had done something she wasn't very proud of. Was that what she had said? I squinted my eyes as if that would help me to remember that conversation back in the boathouse when Dorothy had first mentioned Meredith to me, but it wasn't really helping.

And then two light bulbs went off in my head. Did Dorothy and Gerald have an affair? Meredith and Dorothy fell out, Dorothy said she'd done something she wasn't proud of and moved house, Meredith said she lost Gerald for a while.

No, surely not. I just couldn't square that scenario.

Plus there was the other light bulb – the one that had me thinking about Adele and Gerald, Gerald and Adele. Her mother told Adele her father was a married man. They both had allergies to pet hair. Adele seemed to have an odd interest in the Harpers and she was not here to take photographs, whatever she said. There was that text message too, about moving quickly as he wasn't well and to keep digging. I told Adele I was writing Meredith's memoir and I'm convinced she had looked at my laptop. Had she been searching for evidence?

Where did Dorothy fit into this, though? Did she find out and tell Meredith? It wouldn't have been welcome news. Did she try and get Meredith to leave him? Did Meredith keep the husband, ditch the friend? After all, Meredith was pregnant at that point.

I felt like I was picking through a badly written mystery story that the writer hadn't given me all the clues to and those I did have were out of order. It seemed to me that Meredith had skipped a whole chapter.

I was more and more convinced that Gerald was Adele's father and I decided I would go and talk to her before I picked up the Harpers for the festival. As I made my way to her place my phone pinged with a message.

It was from Chris, saying how much he liked the photos and hoped I was having a lovely time.

I thought that he'd probably forgotten I wasn't actually on holiday, even though, right now it felt like I was. A moment later Alice messaged too, although her message didn't have the same tone as her brother's. Alice had obviously been speaking to Douglas, because she wanted to know who the French man was that had answered my phone. I smiled to myself, thinking how silly it was for her to be asking and I did consider replying in an ambiguous tone, but changed my mind.

GINA

> His name is Lucien, he's 40 and kindly drove me and the couple I'm looking after into town. Your father has the wrong end of the stick. Mum. x

CHRIS

None of Dad's business. Go for it, Mum!

ALICE

Chris! That is disgusting!

CHRIS

Keep your wig on, Alice, I'm only joking. When are you back, Mum? Thought Gav and I could pop over to your boathouse, bring the dog and a bottle, crash on your sofa?

How lovely that sounded. Chris and his husband, and Kenny the dog complete with his waggy tail. A bottle of wine, a good meal, and I could tell them all about this trip. I told them it was bit open-ended, but I'd message them as soon as I knew for sure. I suggested Alice might bring the girls over at some point, as she had said she would, and typed that I loved them.

* * *

I could see that Adele's door was wide open, so she must be around. My plan of knocking on her door and asking questions had vanished on the short walk from my villa. How on earth would I word it? I did realise that none of this really had anything to do with me, but I still wanted to talk to her, to find out if I should be preparing the Harpers for something big. I felt responsible for them. I was supposed to be their companion, after all.

I knocked on the doorframe and called Adele's name, but there was no answer, so I did the very same thing that Adele had done to me: I stepped inside.

I thought back to the conversation I'd had with Lucien when he had asked me what I thought of Adele and whether she could be the hotel thief. I didn't think she was, but I was keen to get a better sense of the woman.

I didn't exactly poke about through her things, but just planted my feet in the middle of the room and slowly rotated to take everything in. It was a nice villa, decorated in a similar style to the Harpers' with cool and neutral tones, but this place was a lot smaller, more like mine, and it didn't have all the colourful artwork of Meredith's.

Did I expect to see a sculpture, a pile of cash and a gold necklace? Honestly, no I didn't. Surely Adele couldn't be both the hotel thief and Gerald's illegitimate child as well. My mind was moving at a million miles an hour and not making an awful lot of sense.

On my third rotation I stopped. This was most definitely an invasion of Adele's privacy. I walked back to the door and closed it behind me as I left.

* * *

I called for Meredith and Gerald. They both seemed keen to visit the festival and it wasn't long before they were sampling the cheeses on offer, the wine and beer and some delicious *Calissons*, which were sweet little pastries with candid fruit and sugar paste.

The place was buzzing with people and the children were running wild in the play area. Someone had rigged up speakers and music was in the air around us. The sweet aroma of roasted vegetables circulated and invaded my senses and mixed with the richness of barbecued meats it was making me realise it was a long time since that small bowl of cereal. I suggested we buy some proper lunch and found somewhere to sit and eat.

'This is very good,' Gerald said between mouthfuls of his barbecued beef sandwich. He was particularly animated today in contrast to Meredith's quiet demeanour.

'What do you think of Adele?' she asked me, which took me by surprise after all that had been in my head earlier.

I had a bowl of seafood salad in front of me and put down my fork while I considered my response.

'I think she seems very nice, but I'm not quite sure why she's here. She says she's writing and photographing for a new travel vlog she's doing, but I've not seen her do any writing and I've yet to see her take a single photograph. Why do you ask?'

'I don't know. There is something about her, something I can't quite put my finger on, but I'm sure we've never met and she certainly hasn't said she knows me or Gerald from the past, but she does seem quite familiar with him and it just made me wonder.'

'Made you wonder what?'

Meredith stared at her platter of cheese and meats she hadn't touched.

'About something I haven't thought about for a long time. I think it's just all this talking about my life, bringing up memories, that's all.'

She picked up some brie and nibbled on the edge before putting it back on the wooden board and I thought in that moment that she looked immensely sad.

'I think you are telling a wonderful story, Meredith. Your life with Gerald is an inspiration for us all.'

She laughed then. It was a proper bark of laughter that seemed to erupt out of her and it took me by surprise. It was the first time I had heard her laugh and it wasn't exactly natural.

'My wonderful story – yes, Gina – I imagine that is how it comes across. Do you mind sitting with Gerald while I excuse myself for a few minutes?'

'Of course, no problem. He seems happy enough with his lunch.'

In fact he'd almost finished his and was now leaning across the table to pinch some of Meredith's cheese. She smiled indulgently at him and then took herself off in the direction of their villa.

'Are you enjoying yourself?' I asked Gerald, who'd stopped eating for a moment and really looked as if he was thinking about the question. Then he continued to take chunks of cheese from Meredith's platter, but with a contented smile on his face.

'Can I take your photograph?' I asked him. 'We could send it to your daughter.'

He nodded a response and smiled broadly. I took out my phone and snapped a photo of him with the backdrop of the festival and the château behind him. I would, of course, check with Meredith first, but it would be a nice one to send to Rose. She would love to see her father out and about in the sunshine, eating a lovely lunch and looking so happy. It would also prove that I was doing my job.

I watched across the garden and could see Lucien busy with stallholders and talking to the people looking at the art. I would encourage Meredith and Gerald to walk across that way after lunch. We could all have a closer look at what was on display. Maybe they might like to buy something for their villa, if they could find somewhere to put it, that was.

A woman caught my eye for a moment. She stood out because she had a deep shade of crimson painted across her lips, which contrasted with her ebony-coloured hair swept up on top of her head. She wore a dark grey trouser suit and had heels – the same shade as her mouth – that were not working well on the grass. She didn't look as if she was here to buy art or eat cheese; she looked like a woman on a mission, someone heading into a situation. Douglas would have called her a ballbreaker. I let my eyes follow her line of trajectory and I could see Lucien standing in her path.

I immediately thought back to what he had told me last night: how his mother owed money to bad people. Was she bad people? Was she here to shake up his work event and demand he pay back his mother's debt?

I couldn't leave Gerald and intervene. Instead, I just sat and watched her circle around the group of people Lucien was talking to until she caught his attention. It didn't take long – how could it with someone who looked as striking as her?

Was she going to shoot him? Stab him? Get him in a headlock?

Instead, she held out her hand to him and smiled.

22

LUCIEN

'Isabel,' she said. 'Lucien, I suppose?'

Lucien took a moment to process all that was going through his head with this woman in front of him. This woman who sounded like the chain-smoking Isabel he'd imagined on the end of the phone, but actually looked like a goddess. After all the alcohol he'd consumed the previous night everything was taking longer to process in his head. He felt that his brain was a bit fluffy this morning.

'I would like to talk to you,' she said in her seductive voice, with her Italian words singing in his ears.

'*Mi scusi,*' he said to the customers he'd been talking to, who all looked bemused. '*Pardon, excusez-moi,*' he said again, but this time in his own language. And then: 'Excuse me.'

Isabel turned on her heel and Lucien dutifully followed her away from the festival, across the lawn towards the privacy of the sunken garden on the edge of the hotel's border.

Everything was going to plan, the stallholders were reporting good trade, guests looked entertained, impressed and sated. He could afford a few minutes away. He wasn't at all sure whether he had any choice anyway. He didn't want her to create a scene.

His head was still thumping and he was keen to speak to Gina, find out how much of an arse he had made of himself last night. He remembered the whisky, after twice cleaning his teeth he was sure he could still taste it. The bottle had been half empty when he had picked it up from Gina's coffee table that morning.

He tried to keep his eyes on the back of Isabel's head, on her silken, black hair that was wound around an elegant clip, but he couldn't help his gaze from dipping lower to the smooth skin of her neck, the line of her shoulders, the swaying of her hips and further down the length of her legs to those red heels. He was mesmerised.

He hadn't been to this part of the hotel garden in ages. It was an undeveloped opportunity that Hugo would have plans for, but which he so far hadn't shared with Lucien. It was only as she stepped off the shingle path and walked down the steps and out of sight that he realised how stupid he was being. Did she have someone down here waiting for him, someone who wanted the money his mother owed him, or did Isabel herself hold all the threat? An attractive face and shapely legs and he was being an idiot.

'Lucien!' she called to him. 'Get down here before you're seen.'

He hesitated at the top of the steps and wondered at these words coming from a woman who had walked across the hotel gardens with all eyes on her. He didn't believe anyone was looking at him for one moment. He took a leap of faith or stupidity and followed her down the steps and under the ivy-covered arch to the bench at the end of the sunken garden.

She was standing with her hands on her hips, her lips puckered into a perfect pout and she suddenly didn't look intimidating at all.

'We need the money, Lucien. We won't wait any longer. Things are going to get serious if you don't pay up.'

'Who is we? I don't see anyone else. Who is too gutless to come and talk to me themselves?'

'What, you don't think a woman can be intimidating? We are dangerous people, Lucien.'

'And also how do I know what is owed? No one has ever told me.'

'Those are just details,' she said, waving his question away as if he was an annoying fly.

He looked at her then, really looked at her, and he saw a nervous woman with a whole lot of false bravado. Someone was pulling her strings and that suddenly really bothered him.

'If I saw you in a bar, I don't think I'd feel in danger; I think I'd like to ask you to have a drink with me.'

He tried to inject some humour into the situation, but knew it was probably going to fall flat. He smiled a slow smile and tried to win her around. She was trying to look furious, but then her whole demeanour changed and she blew a lungful of air out through barely parted lips.

'These shoes are killing me,' she said and bent to slip them off before sitting down on the bench to massage her feet, letting them fall to the ground beside her.

'It's my brother; it is him who wants the money back. Solène paid him some, but not all. She still owes him five and a half thousand euros.'

'Is that it? The silent calls, the demands, the intimidation for less than six thousand!'

He sank down beside her on the bench. Then he remembered the money his mother had stolen from him. It could have paid them back. She could be clear now, which went to show Lucien that she had no intention of stopping.

'My brother is a wannabe mafioso. He's a bit of a fool, to be honest. I didn't mind doing the calls for him, but this is something else.'

'Why *are* you doing it? Why don't you let him chase his own money?'

'Because he's my little brother and he asked me. It seemed harmless to start with. "Just phone this number and remind this woman she owes me money."'

'That's not harmless, Isabel; there is always going to be a vulnerable human on the other end of the phone.'

'I know, but he borrowed the money himself and now he's in some deep shit. He's a fool, but I don't want him to get hurt or worse.'

Lucien sighed. He really didn't need to inherit someone else's problem too.

'Well, it's a shame you weren't more up front to start with, before Solène stole from the one person who could have cleared this debt. Me.'

'You don't have the money?'

'*Non*. I did, but she took it when she left. She is a lost cause.'

'Don't say that; she is your mother!'

'Would your mother steal from you?'

'No, of course not. My mother is a *bibliotecaria*.'

Lucien laughed then. He laughed so hard, tears began spilling from his eyes. His hangover had well and truly kicked in.

'Your *madre* is a librarian?' he asked, wiping his face with the back of his hand.

'What is wrong with that? We are a family of big readers.'

'You have a wannabe mafioso brother and a librarian mother and you are the go-between. They could make a movie out of that, a terrible movie,' he said and then started laughing again.

Isabel's serious face dissolved and she began to laugh too. 'It does sound pretty lame when you put it like that.'

'Look, there will be an answer to this and it won't involve mysterious phone calls. I want to meet your brother and I want proof of my mother's debt and then I will see what I can do.'

'That is fair, Lucien, thank you. I will arrange it.'

'We could have done this over the phone,' he said.

'Where's the fun in that?' she said and offered him an amazing smile.

'Now, can I interest you in some of the finest food, drink and art in the area? Or do you intend to sneak around in the shadows?'

'I like good food, drink and art, but I will only come if I don't have to wear these damn shoes,' Isabel said.

23

GINA

Meredith returned looking a bit less peaky and told me she'd taken some tablets for a headache. I couldn't stop thinking about her suffering five miscarriages and wanted to lean across the table and take her hand. Of course I didn't, but instead I suggested we go and see the art.

I got up from the bench and helped Gerald to his feet; then, just as we were about to set off towards the marquee I noticed something from the corner of my eye. A woman was madly waving her hand as if she was trying to catch someone's attention. It was then that I realised two things: the person she was trying to catch the attention of was me and the woman was Dorothy Reed.

Several questions flooded my mind; the hows and the whys and the wherefores as my stomach turned over in an unpleasant rolling action as if I was guilty of something and had just been caught out. But it wasn't me who was guilty of something, it was probably Dorothy.

'Why don't you both go on ahead?' I quickly said to Meredith. 'I've got to pop back for something, but I'll catch you up.'

I waited until they were out of sight and then turned to my friend who was grinning at me from the door to the château.

'What on earth are you doing here?' I said as she pulled me into a hug.

'Let's go and find somewhere to sit,' she said 'and I can tell you.'

'We can go to my villa. It's tucked away enough.'

I poured us both a fruit juice and I dragged a chair from inside so we could both sit out on my weedy patio.

'You can tell they haven't got to finishing this end of the hotel. My room is lovely,' Dorothy said as she took her seat.

'Never mind that, why are you here?'

'I realised after talking to you that I should never have sent you off unarmed as I did. I didn't really think it through, but I had a feeling at the airport that I needed to be here. Actually, the feeling was borne from two large glasses of wine, if I'm honest. So, I changed my ticket, sent Yvonne off home and spent a night at the airport waiting for my flight. I got in last night. The lovely staff have got me a phone because I managed to leave mine at the hotel. That chap, Lucien, even phoned the hotel in Nice and they've posted my phone back to me at home. What a thoughtful thing to do. He said this could be my burner phone, whatever that is.'

'It's a secret phone criminals or people having affairs use,' I said. 'You must have seen them on television.'

'Oh, I see, he thinks I'm a criminal. How thrilling.'

'Or he thinks you're having an affair. Did you have an affair with Gerald? Is that why you and Meredith parted ways?'

'Are you insane? Of course I didn't have an affair with Gerald. What on earth made you think that?'

'I don't know, Dorothy,' I said, somewhat sarcastically. 'All these little hints I'm getting from Meredith's memoir, you not quite telling me why you fell out and there's an Englishwoman staying in the villa next door.'

'What's she got to do with anything?'

'She's taken an interest in the Harpers and told me her mother had said on her deathbed that her father was a married man. She and Gerald both have an allergy to pet hair. I have a feeling that if you didn't have an affair with him, then she's here to tell Gerald she's his love child.'

Dorothy's eyes had grown larger as I spoke and then she opened her mouth and roared with laughter.

'Well,' she said, 'at this rate, Meredith's memoir will be a corker of a read.'

'I've got to go,' I said. 'I told her I was popping back and would join them in the marquee. Will you stay here until I get back and we can talk properly?'

'Okay,' she said. 'I will.'

I took a step away from her and then turned back and reached out for her hand.

'I am very glad you're here,' I said with a quick smile and then I left her to it.

* * *

The mix of media in the art marquee was overwhelming. There was lace, glass, ceramics, paper-craft, woodwork, knitted work and weaving with the artists showing their skills. Someone was printmaking, a few people were painting, of course, and someone was even bookbinding. There was a woman making pictures from pressed flowers, leaves and grasses overlaid on a painted board. The effect was stunning. The place was busy and bustling, colourful and fascinating, and Meredith and Gerald were in their element. She looked so animated talking to the artists, and

Gerald was even having a go on the huge loom that had been set up.

Lucien, I noticed, was walking and talking with the woman I had seen him with earlier, but now her shoes were dangling elegantly from her fingers as if they were walking home after a big night out. I'd seen Béatrice watching them too, and she didn't look all that happy. The despair and delight of young love. I was not downhearted to know I'd not have to worry about that pain again.

After an hour and with a couple of purchases under our belts, the Harpers were flagging and I wasn't sorry to be walking them back to their villa so they could have a rest. I really wanted to talk to Dorothy.

'Thank you, Gina,' Meredith said as we walked inside. 'I think we've both enjoyed today. If Rose and Hugo plan on doing this sort of thing again, then I think they will be most successful.'

Gerald laid out the painting he'd bought of *Mont Sainte-Victoire*. It wasn't up to Cézanne's standards but the artist had certainly captured something in the landscape. Meredith had bought a small glass bowl. It was pale pink and green and had a beautifully milky quality to it. I recognised it as *pâte-de-verre*, which was a clever technique using glass powders.

Gerald stood for a moment to admire his painting and then wandered back out of the door to sit on the patio. Meredith took her bowl and shuffled her other artworks around on the already heaving shelves to accommodate it.

'Do you want to record again later?' I asked her.

'No,' she said, after a moment's thought. 'I'm beginning to think it might all be a bit too much and listening back to some of my earlier recordings yesterday when I still had your phone, I realise that it isn't really a truth of my life at all, just some of the prettier bits. Who on earth is going to want to read that?'

I didn't answer for a moment, because she had a point.

'I suppose if you're writing your memoir, then it's probably important to write your truth,' I said. And then, because her last recording had been on my mind all day, I felt I should say something else. 'May I just say how sorry I was to hear about your miscarriages. That must have been a terrible time for you.'

She looked up at me then as if she'd forgotten she'd recorded the not so pretty bits too.

'Thank you,' she said, quietly. 'Let me have a think about the book. It's a lot harder than I thought it would be. If you come back tomorrow afternoon, I'll let you know what I'm going to do.'

'I suppose it was always going to have an end point. Your daughter will be back and then perhaps she will help you.'

Meredith looked surprised for a moment and then seemed to understand. Maybe she thought I'd moved in forever.

'If I do write this story, then it won't be about Rose,' she said.

I left them then and walked back to my own villa thinking about what Meredith had said. Surely her daughter featured in her memoir and besides, she could still type it couldn't she?

Now that Dorothy was here I walked that bit quicker, keen to hear what she had come to say. It would be good to get *some* answers.

She was just where I had left her, except now she was reading my book and drinking a cup of coffee. The way the villas were positioned, you couldn't see the patios until you were right up at the door and the fact that my hedge was so overgrown meant it was all the more secluded. Dorothy seemed quite happy tucked away behind the laurel.

'Everything okay?' she asked me, closing the book.

'Yes, Meredith and Gerald had a lovely time and are back at home.'

'She looks quite different,' Dorothy said.

'I expect she does. It's been years since you've seen her, hasn't it?'

'Well, yes, but that wasn't exactly what I meant. I've read all of her books and her author photo is in the back. I think whoever must have taken the picture had a remarkable camera.'

'Are you being unkind, Dorothy?'

'No, not at all. I just think she looks so sad.'

'She's moved hundreds of miles from home, has broken her arm, her husband has dementia, her grandson has had a serious accident and her daughter is away from home. She's not cock-a-hoop, no.'

'Fair enough,' she said. 'What's in the bag?'

'I bought gifts for my grandchildren.'

I opened the bag and tipped the contents onto the table.

'I bought a flower press for the youngest, Meg. She loves pressing flowers and leaves, but usually uses a couple of sheets of paper and some of her dad's hardback books.'

This was actually the perfect gift for her and I bought the largest one the artist had for sale. 'For Lou I found a cheese-making kit. She isn't interested in art particularly, but she loves cooking and baking.'

'Splendid.'

I quickly popped the food gifts I'd bought for Dorothy and Erik back into the bag and then the girls' presents.

'Right,' I said, 'time to talk.' I sat down opposite Dorothy and pushed aside any thoughts of making a cup of tea. I didn't want any more interruptions. 'What broke up your friendship?'

Dorothy looked at me for a long time before she spoke.

'I'm not starting with that,' she finally said.

'But, Dorothy, what's the point of you being here if you're not going to play the game? To be honest, Meredith is now saying she's not sure about the memoir; it's all a bit too much for her. So, perhaps this whole thing has just been a waste of time.'

I sat back in my chair feeling a bit like a petulant child, or certainly a frustrated one. Meredith's memoir had Dorothy getting *me* over here to investigate, and she'd now got herself over here – although I think that was from a bout of drunken guilt more than anything else – and now, Meredith had said she wasn't sure anyway.

'Well, I got them into Aix if nothing else and they still want to go to Marseille,' I said shaking off my frustration. I was not a child and would not behave like one.

'I want to tell you what I was worried that Meredith might write.'

'But you just said you didn't want to.'

'The reason Meredith and I went our separate ways is extremely personal and not something I would share in a gossipy way. That's not what I was worried about her writing. If she wants to talk about that terrible and painful time in her life, then I would completely respect her for it. I want to tell you about what we did in 1970. Something entirely different.'

I sat forward in my chair all petulance gone. I was primed and interested.

'Shall I open some wine?' I asked her.

'Yes, I think we're going to need it.'

24

DOROTHY

Gina came out with a bottle of rosé and two glasses, and Dorothy took a large gulp before she began to speak.

'Just so you know, before I begin, a pact was made back then, that we would never talk about this.'

'So, why do you think Meredith might write about it, then?'

'I don't know. I just felt very twitchy after Barbara told me Meredith was writing her memoir. Barbara called it a *tell-all story* and it got me thinking.'

'Well, I can tell you that what I've been privy to so far, has been far from *tell-all*. It's more like *tell-very-little-at-all*.'

'Hopefully I'm worrying about nothing, then.'

'A lot of trouble for hopefully nothing.'

'Gina! Do you want to hear this story or not?'

'Sorry, go on.'

'Who is the most famous ceramist you've heard of?' Dorothy asked her and Gina looked thoughtful for a moment.

'I suppose Bernard Leach. The Leach Pottery in St Ives is considered the birthplace of British studio pottery, isn't it?'

'Well, yes, but I was thinking about somebody still alive today.'

'Then, Betty Woodman, Grayson Perry, Ron Nagle?'

'Betty Woodman died in 2018.'

'Oh, right. Erm, Daniel Williamson? He made vessels didn't he? Big pieces?'

'Yes, Daniel Williamson,' Dorothy said in a voice worthy of a bit part in a TV drama.

'He was pretty big in the States wasn't he?' said Gina. 'Do you know him, personally? I've read somewhere that he was a bit of an arse.'

'Yes, that's him and he was a huge arse.'

'So, what's the story?'

Dorothy put her glass on the table, surprised to find it empty. Then she took her mind back to the autumn of 1970 when she, Meredith, and two other artist friends, Janie and Aoife, made the decision to fly to New York to the art exhibition of Daniel Williamson.

'We had created a studio in London that we all worked out of. There was some serious work being produced. Aoife in particular was making strides in the feminist art movement that began to erupt at that time. She was a painter, Janie was a painter, but also a silversmith, and Meredith and I were working with ceramics. But, that year we started to collaborate and mix our media. To be honest, Aoife led us all in that. She really got us to see that we couldn't just be painting pretty pictures, making delicate silverware or creating nice tableware, but really making a point. We wanted to influence cultural attitudes and transform stereotypes. It was an exciting time to be producing art. What eluded us, though, was proper recognition.'

Dorothy had loved that point in her history. She still thought of it as one of the best times of her life. She loved her family, but she knew she was privileged to able to follow her passion too.

She had met Daniel Williamson at his first exhibition.

The Old Girls' Chateau Escape

Dorothy was intrigued by his work, because she had heard a lot about him. Janie already knew him from what she described as a collaboration of ideas on a project with others a couple of years previously, but what Dorothy took to mean they had a fling. One thing was indisputable about Daniel Williamson – he was an incredibly attractive and eligible man and there was an ever-increasing list of women who had been seduced and then discarded by him. It was hard to open an art magazine or talk to a fellow artist without his name coming up at that time. But, what she saw on his opening night wasn't what she had heard about. His ceramics were quite minimalist, and had interesting forms and lines, but nothing to get excited about and she assumed his PR machine was doing a lot of the heavy lifting.

It was a big night, though, a big deal and despite Meredith leaning in and quietly saying *Emperor's New Clothes* in her ear, most of the assembled party were pulling out all their most complimentary conversation. Janie was enthusing, but Aoife didn't hide the fact that she thought it was, in her words, a load of shite. Dorothy honestly thought they wouldn't see his work again, but that wasn't the case.

While she and the girls were desperately trying to get their own exhibition space somewhere that people would want to be seen, Daniel Williamson was everywhere. And then it was announced that he would have his new collection at a private exhibition in New York at the Metropolitan. The word was that it was innovative, pushed boundaries and would blow everyone's minds.

'It was quite a big deal for us to go,' Dorothy said. 'But after a lot of discussion we decided, as a group, we should be there. After all, Gina, *everyone* was going to be there and if we wanted to talk about our work we needed to be talking to *everyone*.'

Gina refilled both of their glasses and Dorothy could see she was rapt. There was something quite liberating about telling this story after all this time. She trusted Gina; she knew she wouldn't repeat it to another soul. Would Meredith? That was the question. The truth was that now Dorothy was in touching distance of her old friend, she felt more comfortable. If there was even a whiff of the story going into her memoir, then Dorothy could act to try to stop it, persuade Meredith to omit it from her work. As for their other shared history, well, that was just too heartbreaking to think about.

Dorothy had thought about Meredith a lot over the years. She'd read all of her books, was sorry to see she had given up her art, but delighted to hear she finally had the child she so wanted.

'I'd love to see some of this feminist art,' Gina said.

'Aoife produced most of it, but we all had our little moment before we moved off in different directions. Aoife was always keen to get a vagina on a canvas – I can tell you that. Most of what we produced together was mixed media, a series of painted sculptures that were, basically, us flipping the bird to the patriarchy.'

Gina spluttered some of her wine as she laughed.

'Dorothy Reed, flipping the bird,' she said. 'What a thought.'

'Don't be fooled. Inside this ancient shell is a woman who will always go up against the patriarchy. They should be grateful we only want equality and not revenge. I read that somewhere – good isn't it.'

'It is. So, back to flying to New York...'

'Yes, so we all left our various family situations for a weekend in the Big Apple. None of us had been before and we were trying to be cool about it, but we weren't really; we were very excited. I'm not going to bother recounting all the fun we had that weekend before the big night at the Metropolitan Museum. We took in the sights; that will suffice. To be honest, after the night at the Met, all of the rest of it was forgotten.'

The Old Girls' Chateau Escape

'Hold that thought for a moment. I need a wee and I think some crisps and nuts if we're going to keep drinking wine. We could treat ourselves to room service in a while,' Gina said looking at her watch. 'Goodness it's already six-thirty.'

Gina disappeared inside and Dorothy pushed herself up from her chair. It wasn't all that comfortable and her backside had become numb. She took the few steps out onto the path that led down to the other villas and could just catch a glimpse of the edge of Meredith's place. To think she was so close to her friend after all this time was both heartening and alarming. She could just walk up and tap on her door.

'Here we go,' Gina said and Dorothy retraced her steps.

Gina opened crisps, nuts and a jar of olives. She had also placed a cushion on each of the chairs, thank goodness.

'Right, back to the story,' Gina said and Dorothy took a breath and a sip of her rosé before she began again.

'The exhibition was pretty amazing. The people we got to talk to and make connections with were brilliant: top artists, journalists and collectors. We really felt seen at last in the company of those who could help us to further our careers. But that was before the unveiling of Daniel Williamson's work. It was indeed, innovative, would push boundaries and blow everyone's minds. The only trouble was, it was Janie's work.'

'He stole her work?'

'He stole her ideas. It had come from sketches she had drawn, ideas she had told him about when they had their brief fling. She hadn't taken her ideas through to finished pieces, but her passion project was laid out before her in a startlingly good exhibition. It was such a departure from his previous works, that I was surprised no one was questioning him about it. He made all the right noises. Listening to him pontificate, I believed it was all of his own work, but when an ashen-faced Janie told the three of us the awful truth, I could suddenly see it was all hers. The shapes and colours of the pieces, the metalwork inclusions, it was all her. Aoife went mad and we had to drag her from the room.

'Janie chose a quieter moment to congratulate Daniel and try to draw him out, to get some sort of apology without directly confronting him. He said she had inspired him without an ounce of honesty. He showed her and others his sketches and they weren't hers, of course, but they may as well have been.'

'That's terrible, Dorothy. Janie must have been so upset.'

'She was – she was very quiet. She said she should have just made the pieces at the time and that it was her own fault she didn't. And she didn't because she had been so wrapped up in our group and our ideas. Meredith just wanted to leave. Aoife wanted to cut off a part of Daniel's anatomy. I wanted to do something less gruesome, but I wanted to do something all the same.

'We left the party for a while and talked. Everyone had differing ideas, but one thing we agreed on was confronting him with an audience would be a mistake. We would have just sounded like a group of embittered harpies. He had the big boys' club around him, his family were wealthy and had contacts, there was no way we could really prove he had taken Janie's ideas and she wasn't sure she still had her sketches after a couple of house moves. She continued to say it was her own fault and that if she had been serious about it she would have made them. Then she cried about her signature silver work he had imbedded into his pieces. Aoife was clearly still thinking about finding a knife and she disappeared while we continued to console Janie.

'What happened next was not discussed as such, but rather it was a moment of madness that we all, somehow, silently agreed too. When I say silently, I don't really mean that, because at this point Aoife had pulled the fire alarm.'

Gina was on the edge of her seat, wine glass in one hand and a fistful of peanuts in the other. Dorothy hoped she wasn't going to put them in her mouth or she might choke.

'If I'm honest,' Gina said, 'this is exactly the injection of drama that Meredith's memoir needs. But, please continue.'

'Everyone was making a move for the exit, of course. There had been a lot of champagne consumed, so, in the furore, no one really noticed us four slipping back into the exhibition space. Of course there were security staff rounding up the guests, but we were careful. Aoife had found a museum trolley from somewhere and pulled it into the room, where we loaded up the pieces. There were ten in total and it took some lifting, I can tell you. They weren't huge pieces, but it became apparent very quickly that we didn't really have a plan of what we were going to do with them. Meredith kept saying that she wanted no part in it, but she helped all the same. Aoife repeatedly reminded us that Daniel had stolen from Janie, and what we were doing was justified. Janie was still silent and I felt as if we had all lost our minds in some collective, unhinged way and wondered if we could render that feeling in our art. I had had some champagne, don't forget.'

'What did you do, Dorothy?' Gina whispered out the words.

'In short, because I have gone on a bit, it involved a heavy implement, ten minutes in the ladies' lavatory and the pouring of pieces into carrier bags. By the time security moved us out of the building, Daniel Williamson's plagiarised work had been reduced to shrapnel and we walked out with it, without anyone giving us a second glance.'

'Oh, my God! You destroyed them!'

There was nothing quiet about Gina's voice now. Dorothy could see she was shocked.

25

LUCIEN

Isabel and her brother arrived the following morning and Lucien managed to get the office cleared, have coffee for three laid out on the desk, and Béatrice well and truly out of the way.

Isabel looked very different this time. She didn't have that hard edge she'd been sporting at the festival. The look that was supposed to intimidate him, but actually had the opposite effect. Now she was wearing a simple pale-blue summer dress with gold, flat sandals. Her hair was down from its clip and curled around her bare shoulders, little flicks around the straps of her dress. *Now* he felt a little intimidated because she was really quite beautiful.

Her brother looked exactly as she had described him: a wannabe mafioso with a stupidly sharp suit that he must be sweltering under on this warm morning.

'Lucien DuBois,' he said as confidently as he could, holding out his hand.

'Lucien, this is Dino.'

Dino nodded and took Lucien's hand. It was sweaty and Lucien resisted the urge to wipe his own on his trousers.

'Take a seat, *per favore*.'

Dino sat down, but Isabel didn't. She hovered behind his chair with her hands on the back like a queen behind her king. Except that analogy didn't really work, because they were siblings. Isabel looked to be in her thirties; her brother was closer to early twenties. Not for the first time, Lucien wondered what it would be like to have a brother or a sister, someone to share all this with. Then again, why on earth would he want to share all of this with anyone? He should be glad there wasn't another soul to have to worry about Solène DuBois.

Isabel, he could tell, was nervous. He was left not sure whether to sit or stand, so he chose to perch on the edge of the desk.

'Right,' he said, feeling like a teacher about to dish out detention. 'I understand you think my *mère* owes you money. Exactly how much and please show me proof. I cannot find a scrap of evidence in what she left behind to prove she owed anything.'

'But, she stole from you,' Isabel said and Lucien cut her a look before remembering she wasn't actually on his side.

'Well, that proves she's a thief and nothing more.'

'I have proof,' Dino chirped up. 'You think I'd come here asking for money without evidence?'

'Honestly, yes! You got your sister to make threatening calls.'

'I'm sorry, I was getting desperate after I wasn't getting anything further from Solène. I like my limbs where they are.'

'Maybe you shouldn't play with the big boys then. How do you know my mother, anyway?'

'I work at the casino she likes to play at.'

Lucien knew the place Dino was talking about. He'd seen his mother leaving on many occasions when he was driving around trying to find her. She'd stumble out with one drinking buddy or another, her pockets empty and her mind already on her next visit once she had sobered up.

Dino got his phone out of his pocket and, after tapping on the screen, he turned it to show Lucien. It took him a moment to take in what he was looking at. It was a banking app of all things. There was a transaction showing eight thousand euros from this account to Solène DuBois on a date back in August.

'You set her up as a payee and transferred her money?' Lucien wanted to laugh at the absurdity of it. Where was the dodgy handing over of cash in a grimy car park scenario? 'How was it you had this money in your account in the first place? I was led to believe you borrowed from some not good people and passed it on to my mother. Is that right?'

'Yes, they gave me cash and I paid it in to my account. I wanted it to be traceable.'

Lucien did laugh then. 'How old are you? Oh, Dino, you have a lot to learn.'

'I'm nineteen. So, we are clear? You can see me paying her and her paying me some back and this is what's left. Five thousand three hundred.'

Lucien sighed. He wanted to kick this stupid little man-child out of his office, but it wasn't his office, not really, and wasn't he playing at being one of the big boys too? His mother's debt was not his, but he would like to get things back to normal and he had a mad idea that he'd like to ask Isabel out for a drink, but then, if this little twerp of a brother was only nineteen, maybe she wasn't that much older.

He thought about his uncle and what he'd said about family and if he could help. He thought about the hotel and the money his aunt and uncle had spent on it, but also what it was bringing in now. He thought about the money taken daily in the spa, in the restaurant and he thought about all that wine in the cellar. He licked his lips and then he knew what he should do.

'Solène cleaned me out before she left, so I don't have any ready money. But I would like to get this situation finished and I can think of one possible option,' he said.

* * *

Lucien was leaving the restaurant when he bumped into Béatrice. He had done what he needed to do to pay back the money and was feeling quite gutted. He channelled all his annoyance at his mother. It was her fault he had to stoop as low as this. Now, he really had nothing, not even his self-respect. But it was done and he could turn his attention to another pressing matter. The hotel thief.

'Come and sit outside with me, Lucien,' Béatrice said. 'I'm taking a break.'

He followed her out to a secluded staff seating area and watched as she picked apart a croissant and licked her buttery fingers.

'The last of the marquees are being cleared away and the word is that it has been a huge success. You should be proud, Lucien. Hugo will be, for sure.'

'I am happy it was well received,' he said.

'You don't look happy; you look a bit down, to say the least.'

'Just sorting through some problems, but it's okay.'

'Have you spoken to your mother?'

'*Non,* and I have no wish to. So, tell me. I know it was big ask, but did you find anything in the staff lockers? Or anywhere, or anything you think will help?' Lucien asked her.

'*Non*, I'm sorry, but everyone seems squeaky clean. Well, there's... no, it's not relevant.'

'Are you sure?' he asked.

She nodded.

'I'm at a loss and we will have to get the police back to show we are doing something. The festival is done. It is time now.'

26

GINA

Dorothy and I decided to get the minibus into Aix. Neither of us wanted to hang around the hotel in case Dorothy bumped into Meredith. Now the couple were being a little more adventurous it wasn't unlikely they might all meet. This may well still happen of course, but hopefully under more organised terms. Besides, we were both keen to go and see Paul Cézanne's work.

I didn't honestly know what to think after Dorothy's revelation the previous evening. I was shocked for sure and an image I had conjured up in my mind of them smashing up the pieces kept popping into my head so I could be shocked all over again. I was also appalled at the blatant plagiarising, of course, but as a former museum curator, the very idea of destroying pieces of art didn't sit easily with me, either.

I'd popped in to help Meredith and Gerald get their day going while Dorothy got herself ready. We had a routine now that involved Meredith doing the intimate tasks for both herself and Gerald and me helping with dressing, breakfasting and a little clearing and tidying. I didn't really need to do the last job as hotel staff came to clean, but it made me feel better about my role as companion. Meredith said she'd make a decision about the book and would let me know when I returned to her at lunchtime. Once I'd made their breakfast and cleared away the dishes, they were both off to the spa and I wasn't needed further. Even though I didn't know them that well, I still felt a small sense of achievement at getting them out of the villa. We made a plan to go into Marseille in a couple of days and I noticed that Meredith had opened the blinds in the living room to halfway up the window, which seemed like extra progress. I didn't tell her I could see Riley sitting on the windowsill.

When I was outside I called him away and he jumped down and followed me. When we were a safe distance I crouched down in the grass with him while he rolled onto his back as if to have his tummy stroked. I didn't fall for it, though – cats could be contrary like that. I just petted his head and back before he let me know he'd had enough and wandered off.

I found I was struggling to get up from my crouch. I often forgot how my limbs didn't bend and stretch as they once did. I was just about to get on my hands and knees and help myself up that way, no matter how undignified it looked, when Adele walked around the corner. I could only imagine how ridiculous I appeared now that Riley had wandered off.

'Gina, are you okay? Do you need a hand up?'

I looked up to her gratefully and nodded.

'Yes please. I forget I'm not middle-aged any more.'

'What are you doing down there anyway? You didn't have a fall, did you?'

I laughed then and wondered what was the exact age that you stopped *falling over* and instead *had a fall*. I'd read that middle age was considered to be from forty-five to sixty-five, but it seemed absurd to think of someone in their late sixties as elderly. What came next? Older age I guessed, but what did that really mean?

Had it? Past it? Even as Adele helped me up from the ground, I thought: *No bloody way am I past it*, and then rubbed at the grumble beginning in my lower back.

'Thank you,' I said. 'Did you get to the festival yesterday? I didn't see you.'

'I popped in briefly but didn't stay long. I saw you with the Harpers. They seem quite content, don't they? I'm thinking of heading home early, actually. I think I have what I need for now.'

'Oh, that seems a shame to cut your holiday short, but if you got what you needed...' I trailed off, not sure what to say, then added, 'yes, the Harpers are fairly content.'

I tried to inject meaning into my voice, but wasn't sure I succeeded.

'I think the problem is that I don't know what it is I'm really looking for,' she said. 'I thought I did, but when it comes down to it, it's harder than you think it might be to make that leap of faith and jump into something new.'

'With your travel vlog?' I said and Adele gave me a lopsided smile. 'I'm taking Meredith and Gerald into Marseille in a couple of days. If you're still here, you could join us if you'd like to.'

This time I felt I had managed to get some meaning into my words and she said that yes, if she was still here, she would like that.

* * *

'You're very quiet with me today,' Dorothy said as the minibus pulled out of the hotel driveway. 'Are you very scandalised after what I told you?'

'I will be honest and say that, yes, I was, I suppose, scandalised. To destroy artwork like that is shocking.'

'I know, and perhaps you can see why I wouldn't have wanted

Meredith to have a moment of self-revelation and write about it. I'm not proud of what we did and if this gets out, my days as chair of the Hampton Heights Art Committee are finished. I sometimes think it was all a dream and it didn't happen at all.'

'What did you do with all the... bits?' I said, thinking that losing her position on the committee was the least of her problems. This was criminal damage, surely.

'Well, nothing that night. Everyone dispersed, because it was the end of the evening anyway. We didn't hear about the theft of the pieces until the following morning when we had a call at our hotel from another artist we knew. There was a big scandal about it, of course, but we weren't implicated. There was no way us four could have carried all the pieces out of the hotel and no one see us doing so. I have to be honest, it was a long time until I could breathe freely when answering the phone, or the door, or opening a newspaper. Daniel did call Janie, to ask her if she had any idea or if she knew anything about it, but she very sweetly told him how shocked she was that someone could have taken them. I remember her telling us he said, "*It wasn't you, was it, Janie? Because they were a little like the ones you had talked about and those sketches you did.*"

'She told him not to be silly, of course she didn't take them, and besides they weren't anything like her designs; she would never have put in all those gaudy inclusions. She never spoke to him again.'

'So, what *did* you do with the bits?'

'On our last night, we walked from our hotel down to the Hudson River and out along Pier 1. Each of us had a bag and when we got to the end we took it in turns to drop the contents into the river. And yes, I do realise that we added polluting to our list of misdemeanours. Janie kept a small silver disc as a memento. Nothing that could be incriminating, though. We stood there for a while and talked about what we had done, tried to justify it, and then agreed we would never talk about it again.'

'Goodness,' I said. 'It was almost like the scattering of ashes.'

'In a way it was, because it was the end of us as a group, really. We strung it out for a while longer, but only in our shared studio space. We never collaborated again and eventually Janie went off into teaching and Aoife went back to Ireland. Meredith and I carried on for a few more years, but I moved into glass and she would come in and potter about, chat while I worked. It wasn't that often anyway, because I did have my family. Sophie was still quite young then, although Miles was in grammar school. Philip was great at co-parenting before that was really a thing. Meredith's dream was to be a mother, though; her focus was on that.'

* * *

We stepped through into the cool interior of the *Musée Granet* and it was welcome after the warmth of the street outside. I couldn't remember the last time I had been in an art gallery or museum. It was a shocking number of years, I realised.

We breezed past a lot of the ancient Egyptian collection, because Dorothy said it always made her feel as if she was on a school trip. I told her she should broaden her mind, but I wasn't all that bothered. It was really Paul Cézanne's paintings I was keen to see, but I couldn't possibly walk past the fourteenth-to-eighteenth-century paintings – the detailed cityscapes of Caspar Van Wittel and the highly charged compositions of Peter Paul Rubens.

The museum had a major collection of nineteenth-century works, most notably the famous large-format work by Ingres. Unsurprisingly, as the namesake of the museum, there was an entire room devoted to the Aix-born painter, Granet, and it was organised around a portrait of the painter by his friend, Ingres.

It was fitting to see Cézanne's work in the place it was painted. It was easy to understand his use of the light here in Aix in his brushstrokes on the canvas. We spent a while just looking and contemplating and of course I began to think about my mother and her passion for her work, how we complemented each other when we worked together. I imagined a life for her that hadn't been cut short by the vicious and unnecessary actions of one man. I wondered where we both might have been if she hadn't died in the fire. And then I stopped because those thoughts would only go so far and could actually be destructive. There was the potential to lose yourself in the *what-ifs* in life.

I left Dorothy to ponder and I walked over to Cézanne's portrait of Émile Zola and I sat down on the bench. There was an elderly man sitting there staring at it too. He had a walking stick that had slipped to the floor and both of his legs were stretched out in front of him, crossed at the ankles of his baggy blue cords. I picked up his stick and leaned it against the seat.

'Hello,' I said not wishing to be rude.

'Hello,' he responded. 'What do think of Cézanne's paintings?'

His English was perfect in his gruff French accent.

'I don't have anything clever to say about them, but they appeal to my eyes,' I said and he laughed.

'That is the truest and the best compliment. No further analysis required. Did you know that Cézanne and Zola were childhood friends?'

'I don't think I did know that, actually,' I said as I tried, unsuccessfully, to find that information in my brain.

'They lived here and went to school together and passed their formative years in this countryside. It fuelled their creativity. The hills of *Saint Marc* and *Sainte Baume* and *Mont Sainte-Victoire.* They swam in the river Arc in the summer and spent hours lying on their backs, discussing their dreams.'

'It sounds beautifully idyllic. Were they friends for years?'

'As they got older they became quite different. Zola was political and Cézanne was incurably bohemian. What finished it, though, was Zola's book *The Masterpiece*. He used Cézanne as the model for his unhinged artist, who becomes increasingly disturbed and then commits suicide. Cézanne wrote to thank him for his copy and then never spoke to him again.'

'Goodness, all that friendship disappeared.'

We both sat for a little longer looking at the painting and then I got up and thanked the man for the interesting information he had shared. Once I was a few steps away I turned back to see that a teenage boy had sat down next to him.

'What do you think of Cézanne's paintings?' he asked the lad and I smiled to myself as I walked back to Dorothy.

'Shall we go and get a coffee?' I asked her. I didn't want to sit in silence looking at paintings with my friend any more. I wanted to talk to her.

We left the museum and walked back towards the *Cours Mirabeau*, taking our time. Dorothy didn't walk very quickly, unsurprisingly at eighty-nine years of age. She was determined, though; she always kept going. It didn't matter what the challenge was, she would take it at her own pace. Now that I had lived with her for a few weeks, I noticed this was her approach to most things. She would say yes to opportunities and then work out how she could manage them. I wanted that attitude to rub off on me. I thought that maybe it was beginning to; after all, I was here in the south of France.

We found a café and took a table outside under a canopy. The market wasn't here today, but there were still plenty of people about. Dorothy ordered a coffee and some sort of almond cake and I decided on a glass of sparkling water and a scoop of blueberry ice cream in a waffle cone. With the first lick I felt as if I was on holiday.

'You know I won't ever repeat what you told me, to anyone,' I said to Dorothy.

'I know,' she said. 'That's why I told you.'

'Douglas phoned the other day,' I said feeling that Dorothy probably thought we'd said enough on the subject.

'Oh, what did *he* want?'

'I don't actually know, because I didn't answer.'

Dorothy chuckled as she stuck her fork into her cake and lifted a slice to her lips.

'Well done, you,' she said before popping the slice into her mouth.

'Lucien answered it. We were at Cézanne's studio, in the garden while Meredith and Gerald were inside. He did it for fun, because I told him that Douglas had left me. He gave Douglas the distinct impression that he was more than a friend.'

'Lovely,' Dorothy said and she wasn't talking about the cake.

'Lucien said that if I wanted him back then it could be a possibility because of how annoyed Douglas sounded.'

'What! You don't want him back, do you?'

Dorothy looked horrified for a moment and I assured her that, no, I didn't think I did.

'You are worth so much more than that,' she said. 'Douglas said he needed to find himself when he left, didn't he?'

'Yes, that's what he said.'

'Well, it seems to me, that he *has* found himself. He's found himself very much without you.'

27

GINA

'I've made a decision about the book,' Meredith told me, no sooner than I had knocked on their door.

Dorothy had gone back to her room to let her family know where she was. I reminded her that they wouldn't have the number of her new burner phone. I also wondered if they might think she'd rushed to be by my side and didn't want to be accused of being a needy companion. I hoped she'd be clear on that score. I was still feeling my way with Dorothy's family. I wanted to justify the reasons for staying in her boathouse. I wanted it to be that Dorothy needed me more than I needed her, but at the moment I wasn't sure if that was the case.

Gerald had taken to having his afternoon naps on the sun lounger, which was fully in the shade by this time in the day. He was fast asleep with his hands across his body in an unnerving corpse pose, but the rise and fall of his chest and the slight whistle coming from his barely parted lips was enough to stop me reaching to check for a pulse.

Meredith seemed animated and invited me to join her at the table on the other end of the patio. I had brought over some of the

Calissons I bought at the festival and after making us both a coffee I sat down with her, quite eager to hear her plan.

'I have had a long conversation with my editor and we're both now on the same page, so to speak. Talking to you, Gina, and recording my history has been difficult for me.'

'Revisiting your past is always going to be difficult – it's bound to be,' I interrupted.

'No, you misunderstand me. It's difficult precisely because I've haven't been revisiting the past; not properly. I've been plucking out some nice memories, like I said the other day. If I'm doing this, then I need to *really* do it, not half-arse it.'

I suppressed a giggle at her choice of words and nodded instead. It sounded like Meredith was on the right track, but what that meant for the New York debacle I didn't yet know.

'I don't know how long I have you before you have to leave, but I'd like to get a good, three opening chapters to this book down for now. That way I can send it to my editor to show her where I want to go with it and, hopefully, they'll decide whether it's worth continuing. As they've published all of my romances, they should, but the publishing industry can be a tricky beast at times. Then I can employ someone to take over the typing. I'm determined to write it now. I think it's time. What you said before about writing my truth has really resonated with me. I didn't know how I wanted to approach it before, but now I do. I have things from my past that have been hanging over my head for many years. I live with a lot of guilt, Gina, and it's time to be open and honest about it all.'

Oh, shit.

'Okay, then, let's get cracking,' I said, in as steady a voice as I could. I was already imagining the conversation I'd have with Dorothy later.

I took my phone out and laid it on the table, but Meredith placed her hand over mine.

'Do you mind leaving that here for a while and I can get started alone? I think it will help me, to be honest.'

'Of course, I completely understand.'

Meredith picked at the cuff of her blouse then. She awkwardly used her fingers exposed from the end of her cast to try and pull the sleeve back.

'Do you want me to turn that back for you?' I asked her.

'Umm, no, it's just that I'm not quite sure where my watch is,' she said.

'Do you remember when you last had it on?'

'I think it must have been at the spa earlier. While Gerald had a lovely head and shoulder massage I was offered a manicure and they took it off for me then.'

'I expect you left it on the table and they will have it in their lost property. I'll go and get it for you. What sort of watch?'

'It has a gold face and a bracelet strap. I think it might be by the pool, though. We both laid out on the loungers for a while and I think my watch was with my bag that I put down on the floor.'

Once Meredith had double-checked her handbag and her jewellery box I left her with my phone and set off for the spa with an unpleasant feeling that she might have been the victim of another theft.

* * *

There wasn't anyone on the reception desk when I pushed open the door to the spa. Both treatment room doors were closed and it looked like everyone was busy.

There wasn't anyone in or by the indoor pool either. The place was deathly quiet. It was such a lovely afternoon outside. Why would anybody be in here? I realised I was going to have to acclimatise myself to going back home to a British autumn when I returned and oddly I was looking forward to it. I loved this time of year in the UK. The days could still be warm, but the nights came quicker and cooler and it was perfect for curling up with a book and a hot drink earlier than you would do if it was still light outside.

I ducked down behind the sun loungers along the side of the pool to see if I could find Meredith's watch and I really hoped it had just been left behind as she thought; misplaced rather than deliberately taken.

It was while I was on my hands and knees, feeling along the tiled edge near the plants, that I heard the door open and the sound of footsteps flip-flopping across the room. I was about to shout out a hello so it didn't look too odd when I popped back up, but the next words stopped me.

'This is the last one and then that's it. I'm done. You said a couple of things, a few days, but it's gone on too long this time. The necklace was a mistake. And so was the Rolex. A few euros and the odd misplaced watch from the spa is one thing, but those two, there were *précieux* – valuable and too noticeable.'

His voice was deep, commanding and French, although he was speaking mostly English.

'Oh, come on, think about what you're getting out of it.'

I tried to turn my body without giving myself away, but it wasn't easy from my position. I couldn't see the man, but the woman was clearer to me. I wished I had my phone to take a photo of them or record their voices.

When I met Dorothy at her family's wedding, her granddaughter, Juliet, did that. She recorded people's conversations and that was how she found out what Dorothy and I were up to. Now I would gladly be able to do the same.

I could see she had blonde hair, cut into a sharp bob, a slim body in a floral dress pulled in sharply at her waist with a wide belt and sparkly flip-flops. I couldn't see her face, but she had an English accent with a tiny hint of the North East, perhaps.

I couldn't stay in this position for much longer; my knees were beginning to scream at me. I couldn't give myself away now, either. Cornering two thieves was not something I was prepared to do.

'Have you seen that woman with the toy boy? She's got some good jewellery. Get me into her room and then we'll call it a day, job done. Then, tomorrow I'm checking out.'

The man laughed then, a deep sound from the back of his throat.

'You were never booked in,' he said and then there was the most awful, sloppy sound of them kissing and she was up on her tiptoes.

Thankfully it was brief, although I still looked away and then I heard her flip-flops slapping across the tiled floor and the sound of the door to the changing rooms swinging shut behind them.

My heart was racing, and I pushed myself up to standing with some considerable effort, holding on to the sun lounger for support. I didn't hesitate to catch my breath; I set off immediately, my own soft trainers silent on the floor. I had to find Lucien and tell him what I had heard.

I bumped into Dorothy outside the spa, almost literally as I let the door swing shut behind me.

'Gina, there you are. Where are you off to in such a rush?'

'No time to explain – come with me if you want to,' I said turning round to face her.

'Not at that speed I won't be,' she said, although she certainly gave it her best shot. Manners slowed me down in the end as I stood holding the door to reception open for her. I just didn't have it in me to let it close in her face.

Once she was through it, though she stopped.

'Where are you actually going?' she asked. 'I wanted to see if I could hang out at your villa. My room doesn't have a balcony.'

'Of course,' I said, rummaging for my key and handing it to her. 'I have an errand to run and then I'll meet you back there after. I'm sure I won't be long.'

She turned to walk away, but I called after her before she got too far.

'Don't run into Meredith, will you. We need to talk about her memoir when I get back. Try and stay out of sight.'

'Of course,' she said and then I watched her walk back through the door before I went to find Lucien.

28

DOROTHY

Dorothy walked back outside into the sunshine and closed her eyes as she leaned her head back. She wanted to soak up as much of the Mediterranean warmth as she could before she found herself back home in the chill and the drizzle of the coming months.

She'd phoned her daughter, but didn't get a reply, so she'd phoned her daughter-in-law, Lavinia, to let her know where she was and what she was doing.

'And what *are* you doing there?' Lavinia had asked, to which Dorothy realised she didn't really have an acceptable answer. Certainly not a truthful one.

'Just thought as I was so close, I'd join Gina for a few days in France.'

She felt it had sounded reasonable enough, but she was also aware she was treading a thin line. On the one hand she wanted her family to think she was able to live alone and look after herself, but on the other, she wanted them to accept Gina as a new friend and someone Dorothy could rely on. She knew her son and daughter discussed her future, who might have to move in with her, who she might have to move in with, because she'd heard them. They forgot she was just old and not deaf.

She took the path now, away from the hotel and decided to walk back through the sculpted gardens and try to avoid Meredith and Gerald's villa. It really wouldn't do to accidentally bump into her old friend. She couldn't even imagine how that might be for Gina. It could easily be taken as an invasion of her privacy or certainly a misuse of her trust.

Dorothy's stick pressed down into the grass as she navigated her way around the flower beds and cypress trees. She could see the Harpers' villa over to the right, but she would kept to the left until she was just past it before she cut back in to the path leading to Gina's.

Just as she was level with it she noticed a figure walking out from the front door and she knew immediately it had to be Gerald. Her heart leapt at the sight of him. It brought back memories of their shared history and she clutched her stick a little tighter. She thought he was going to sit down on the patio, but instead he left the little garden surrounding the villa and looked to be setting off towards the hotel. Dorothy was pretty sure from what Gina had said, he didn't walk out alone. What should she do? Her instinct was to follow him, but should she get Gina? Should she get Meredith?

While she pondered, she could see he was getting further away and there was no sign of Meredith, so she followed after him. His safety came above everything else. He had always been a tall and strong man, but now he was little stooped. His hair, once dark, was now entirely white and he no longer had his dashing moustache.

He'd reached the door to reception and Dorothy was struggling to keep up with him. He might be stooped, but he was six years younger than her and a lot quicker. He had disappeared

The Old Girls' Chateau Escape

inside the building and she decided she would go and find Gina and she could get him back home, but as she got to the door and opened it, he was walking back through it and there they were face to face for the first time in forty-eight years.

'Gerald,' she said as he stared at her. 'You won't remember me.'

'No,' he said, but his eyes roamed over her face as if he might.

'Gerald,' said a woman and Dorothy's heart leapt into her mouth as they both turned to the voice. It wasn't Meredith, it was a woman with curly chestnut hair pulled up into a clip on top of her head. She wore a summer dress and had flat leather sandals on her feet. She had hold of whatever was hanging from the gold chain around her neck and then she tucked it down inside her dress.

'I'll walk you back to your villa,' she said. 'I'm Adele, your neighbour. Do you remember?'

'Yes,' he said, not showing any sign that he actually did, but he allowed himself to be taken by the arm. Adele gave Dorothy a brief smile as if she was of no consequence, which of course Dorothy wasn't, but was Adele? Had Gerald really had a fling as Gina suggested? Was Adele the result and had she tracked him down? It seemed so preposterous. It was as likely as... Dorothy paused her thought for a moment, but no, that wasn't preposterous, that was entirely impossible.

After they had left, Dorothy walked to Gina's villa by the other path, the one that didn't go past Meredith's door, and once she was inside she poured herself a cold glass of water from the tap and drank it down until her throat protested against the chill.

She sat down on the sofa and closed her eyes for a moment as her thoughts went back to the last time she ever saw Meredith. That horrible look on her face before she slammed the door with the words: *I know what you did and I will never forgive you.*

Dorothy, of course, knew what she had done, even if it had

been with the best of intentions. She should never have interfered, but Meredith had been so low after the miscarriages, Dorothy had wanted to help her, to get her to see that all was not lost. There was hope out there if only Meredith would reach out.

Dorothy had gone over her head, though, only to find out that devastating news. She knew she would have willingly stood in front of Daniel Williamson with a handful of his broken sculpture and a confession any day than to have to hear those words again.

She wiped tears from her eyes and considered ignoring the phone ringing from inside her handbag, but then changed her mind and reached for it.

'Hello, Sophie,' she said.

'Mum, I'm returning your call, but I would have liked to have heard from *you* about your change of holiday plans not from Lavinia. I am your daughter after all.'

'I did phone you first, you know, but you weren't available. It's no matter.'

'Well, you say that, but she's organised a shop for your return and I've just had to listen to the whole list, as if I've nothing better to do.'

Dorothy sighed. She was firmly back in the here and now.

'Look, darling, I'll be home in a few days. I don't know how long Gina will be here and I really have only popped in for a flying visit. I've never been to Aix and it's lovely.'

'I don't begrudge you a holiday, you know. And I hope you're having a nice time and, most importantly, being looked after. It's just Lavinia – she's irritatingly organised.'

'She is and, do you know, we are incredibly lucky to have her,' Dorothy said.

Her daughter was silent for a moment and then sighed. 'I know, I know.'

There was a knock at the door and Dorothy gently got rid of

her daughter before she peeped out of the window to make sure it wasn't Meredith. It was Adele.

'Oh, hello, I was expecting Gina. Is she here?' Adele asked as Dorothy opened the door.

'No, no she's not. I'm her friend, Dorothy. Do you want to come in? There's actually something I'd like to ask you.'

Adele hesitated on the doorstep for a moment and then stepped inside. Dorothy closed the door behind her.

29

LUCIEN

Lucien was in the office talking to Béatrice. They had been discussing next steps with the thefts, but they were no closer to working out what to do. The staff lockers held no clues, there hadn't been any reports of further thefts over the last couple of days and Lucien wondered if the person responsible had left when the festival did. Perhaps all they could really do was make a claim on Hugo's insurance. That was not a conversation Lucien was looking forward to having with his uncle. Perhaps he should have phoned him at the start; he might have a procedure Lucien should have followed. Well, it was too late now.

There was a knock at the door and Béatrice opened it to find Gina waiting on the other side. It was the first time Lucien had seen her since he'd been drunk. A wave of shame took him for a moment as he remembered how terrible he'd felt waking up on her sofa and then another wave as he recalled how kind she had been.

'Have a seat, Gina,' he said. 'I won't keep you a moment.'

'So, one last thing,' Béatrice said as Gina sat down. 'Do you think that we should leave the main suite for the honeymooners on Friday and put Charles and his wife in the corner room with the bigger balcony? I know it's not his usual room, but I'll put a fruit basket and champagne in to soften the change in bookings. I'm sure they will be fine.'

'We can give them the discounted price that we offered to the festival bookings. I hope they'll be happy with that. It's my mistake, I know. I should stay away from the reception desk,' Lucien said.

'Yes,' said Béatrice, not unkindly. 'Perhaps you should.'

'Let me know if there are any problems.'

'If you stay away, there won't be,' she said and Lucien laughed.

'Sounds complicated. Not sure I'd be up to running a hotel,' said Gina.

'Not sure that I am,' Lucien said, pointedly. 'Come back, Uncle Hugo, please!'

He laughed again, but Béatrice just shook her head indulgently.

'Away from the desk, you are more than capable. Oh, and Cristòu said something about there being some wine missing from the cellar. Do you know anything about that?'

'No, there is no missing wine. Cristòu doesn't know what he's talking about and he has no business being in the cellar. No business at all.'

'Okay,' Béatrice said, looking unconvinced. 'I will see you later, Gina.'

She left then and Lucien turned his attention to the older woman.

'I wanted to say thank you for the other night. I was an embarrassing mess and you were very kind to me. I should never have got so drunk.'

'It's no problem. You had a lot on your shoulders and needed a prop, that's all. It's understandable,' she said.

'Anyway, I have solved the issue with my mother, now. So that can be put to bed at least.'

'Oh? Has she come home?'

'*Non,* not like that. But I have resolved her financial issue, so she has no reason to come home, which is good.'

'I'm sorry, it's never easy when it's a problem with a parent. They are supposed to be the ones who care for you.'

'And you are someone who would know.'

'I thought you'd slept through me wittering on the other night,' she said.

'Not through all of it. I'm sorry, Gina, you have had a lot to deal with. A lot more than me. My mother is selfish, but your father was something else. I assume *was*. Is he still alive?'

'I don't know,' she said simply. 'I very much doubt it. My brother is, though. He still lives in America. I don't talk to him enough. I must make more of an effort.'

Lucien felt it was time to move the conversation on. Gina had been very open and he didn't think she wanted to rake over it all again. Besides, she had come to see him for some reason. He jumped up and out of his chair.

'And to what do I owe the pleasure?' he said, picking up the pot of coffee Béatrice had left him on the table.

'I overheard some people in the spa talking about the thefts. About how they would just do one more.'

'Really? That's amazing,' Lucien said, putting the pot down and discarding any thoughts of a drink. 'I said you were observant and I was right!'

'Yes, but the only trouble is, I don't know who they are. There was a Frenchman who I couldn't see and a woman. I saw the back of her. She was English, perhaps from the north of the country, but that probably doesn't help you, and she had short blonde hair, maybe in her thirties. She said something about him getting her into the room, so I assume he works here and she might be a guest. Sorry, it's not much.'

'It's lots. So, tell me what else they said.'

Gina told him everything she could remember while he made notes.

'So, we have time to catch them. Right, wow, okay, thank you, Gina. You were in the right place at the right time it seems.'

Lucien lifted the phone from his desk and began to tap in a number.

'I wouldn't phone the police just yet,' Gina said. 'In my experience they can be slow and clumsy.'

Lucien's mind flicked back to Gina telling him about the house fire that took her mother's life and he replaced the receiver.

'We phoned them before the festival and they didn't seem that interested, to be honest. Suggested insurance and gave us a case number.'

'So, when you phone them again they may take you more seriously, but do you want them here now? It sounded like the couple were planning one last theft and then stopping. If they get one whiff of the police, they'll be long gone. I can tell them what I overheard in the spa, but I'm not sure it will be enough. If we knew for sure that she was a guest and the police could search her room immediately, that would be one thing, but honestly, by the time you'd get them to do that, she'd have the lot out. It's not like it is in the movies. No crack team are going to bust in here with guns.'

They both smiled at that image.

'It's all about evidence, Lucien. What do you want most from this?' she asked him.

'I really just want to be able to give the guests back their things,' he said. He didn't add that if it was Cristòu involved he would be delighted to see him taken away by the police.

'You need to add Meredith's gold watch to your list. She left it in the spa and it's gone. The couple mentioned a watch from the spa.'

'Right, *d'accord*. So, what do we do?'

'I think you need to find out who this woman is and ideally catch her in the act,' Gina said.

'And how do I do that?'

'You use your biggest asset of course.'

* * *

Lucien went to reception to find Béatrice.

He explained what Gina had told him and asked if she had seen a male member of staff with keycards they shouldn't have or anywhere near the machine they used to activate them.

'There are people here, there and everywhere in this hotel, Lucien. I haven't seen anything suspicious,' Béatrice said, but as she did, Lucien noticed her eyes shift in their focus on him to somewhere else, as if she was trying to remember something.

'What is it? What are you thinking about?'

'I'm thinking about Cristòu,' she said.

'What about him?' Lucien asked, darkly.

'He's been a bit weird lately.'

'How could you tell the difference?' Lucien said.

Béatrice didn't laugh, but he didn't expect her to.

'Did Gina say if the woman was pretty?' Béatrice asked, a frown descending across her features.

'*Non.*'

'I thought he had gone off me a few weeks back, but then he changed and he was all sweetness and light, like he wanted something. I wondered if he was going to propose. Do you think he's been using me to get information about the guests?'

'Or to get close to the machine to activate certain key cards?' Lucien suggested.

'Damn! I've been such a fool,' she said. 'And, you know, when I checked the lockers I nearly didn't check his, because I thought there was no need, but I did check it and I found a ring.'

'What sort of ring?'

'A simple gold band with a princess-cut emerald, about two-thirds of a carat.'

'Oh, so you only gave it a cursory glance then,' Lucien said and Béatrice shrugged, missing the joke in his words.

'I thought it might be for me.'

Lucien looked at her then, at the sadness and worry in her eyes.

'Look, as much as it pains me to say,' said Lucien, 'we don't know yet if it's him. Gina said a Frenchman with a deep voice. It could be any number of people. Maybe Cristòu does have a ring for you. No one is missing an emerald yet.'

He pushed aside his own sadness and worry for a moment as he said this. He hated to see Béatrice unhappy. And then, because he did actually have an ego and he was still a man, he added, 'And, of course, maybe he's a thief.'

'I think that is supposed to reassure me, somehow,' she said, sceptically. 'Right, we need to be cool. We don't want to alert anyone that we know what they're planning.'

'I haven't seen this woman with blonde hair like Gina described. Have you?' Lucien asked.

'I'm wondering now if I have. I think I might have seen her last week talking to the American couple whose necklace was taken, but I can't be sure it's the same woman. I didn't think anything about it at the time. I assumed they were talking to a friend of theirs or something. I definitely didn't check her in as guest. I don't keep tabs on everybody,' she said, as she began to go through the system, cross-referencing room numbers with guests.

You do, though, Lucien thought. Béatrice was on top of everything usually, but if Cristòu was using her, being overly attentive and keeping her mind occupied on other things away from the hotel, Lucien could see how she could have been blinkered to what might be going on. Gina had told him the couple in the spa had kissed; that was why she referred to them as a couple. He was glad now that he hadn't told Béatrice that part.

'We need to find out when the woman and her young friend are not in their room. They seem to be the next target,' Lucien said. He couldn't bring himself to use the term *toy boy*. 'And then we act.'

'Well, that's easy – they have just left. They took one of our maps and are planning a walk this afternoon.'

'Was she wearing her jewellery?'

'I don't know, Lucien. I didn't really look. I think she was dressed simply in shorts and T-shirt.'

'In which case you might well have noticed if she was dazzling in jewels.'

'I don't know what's wrong with me. I've lost my touch.'

'You haven't lost anything,' Lucien said. 'Right, let's keep cool like you said, but also stay vigilant. If you see anyone behaving suspiciously, you message me. I'm going to hang around. I won't be far away. You know, Gina said you were my biggest asset.'

'You do what you like; I've changed my mind, I'm not going to be cool, I'm going to find Cristòu and kick his arse,' Béatrice said.

30

GINA

It was the summer of 1959 and my eighteenth birthday celebrations were still fresh in my mind. I had woken with a terrible headache from the champagne I'd drunk at the party and yet, as I lay in my bed staring at the ceiling, I felt nothing other than sheer delight. I was a delicate rose that had been plucked from the bush and been stripped of its thorns. I was laid bare and beautiful.

Was I in love? I had a deep-seated feeling that it was far worse than that; I was infatuated. And now there was only one thing to be done. I had to convince Frank Batchelor that he was equally infatuated with me.

We met at the second home of my friend's mother – a London flat she had vacated in favour of her house in the country. Unoccupied and on the market, we would meet in secret, avoiding estate agents, which was wonderfully exciting to begin with. But, as the weeks wore on and Frank became increasingly absent in our affair, it began to feel more than a little seedy.

Eventually the house sold and it was time to make decisions about our future, but my fate had already been served to me, because it seemed I had laid myself bare and beautiful too many times and Frank Batchelor, I was to discover, was already married.

I paused the recording and sat back in my chair. Frank Batchelor – the man who came before. I had an immediate wish to talk to Dorothy about it, but she had left me a note to say she was going to her room and I realised I didn't have the number for her burner phone. I don't know why she had changed her mind. Perhaps she was tired and wanted to sleep. I should probably check on her in a bit.

Opening my laptop I began to type Meredith's words. This might not be stretching back to her childhood, but it certainly made me want to turn the page.

Of course Frank didn't want to know about our baby when I told him. He said that he'd not signed up for that nonsense and we should call it a day. I followed him when he left me, all the way to a small terrace house in a side street I had never seen before. It was funny how we'd been cocooned in such a bubble of bliss, we hadn't had any real conversations. We had never wanted to bring the outside world into our joyful but insular situation. We'd not discussed our future, but I had quietly assumed there would be one.

The door was opened by a small blonde woman with a chubby baby on her hip and even from across the street I could see the child had Frank's chestnut curls. I didn't even bother to delude myself with thoughts about this woman possibly being his sister. Frank already had a family; he wouldn't be wanting another one.

I'd been such a fool and now had a big problem, which started with having to tell my mother. Her reaction came as no surprise to me. She was furious. A woman who had spent so much time instilling the importance of deportment hadn't taken the trouble to instil the importance of contraception, although it would be a few years until women could really take that into their own hands. I couldn't really blame my mother; the fault lay with me. I believed Frank when he said he'd take care of it, make sure there would be no baby.

He had failed, though, so it was up to me to make sure there would be no baby and that decision would have far-reaching consequences.

I felt unnerved as I finished typing what Meredith had given me so far. Now, I was really feeling dishonest about Dorothy. This was bigger than a love story between Meredith and Gerald; there was going to be real heartbreak here. It was already simmering on the page. The question was, did I tell Meredith I knew Dorothy or not and was Dorothy planning a reunion? Meredith had named Frank Batchelor – if indeed that was his real name – was there any reason to think she wouldn't name Daniel Williamson? For the first time I felt Dorothy had every reason to think their New York story would come out.

* * *

Riley was outside on the path by my villa. I made a clicking sound with my tongue to encourage him over, but when I looked a little closer I saw he had a small rodent in his mouth. He stared at me, but didn't move in my direction.

'You know, you can really go off some people,' I called out to him and watched as he slunk away with his prey.

'I hope that's not aimed at me.'

It was Adele, sitting on her patio with a glass of wine. She wasn't being serious; I could see she was smiling.

'The cat,' I said. 'He'd caught a mouse.'

'I hope he takes it far away then. I don't want to find a furry surprise on my doormat.'

I took a couple of steps towards her.

'Have you decided whether or not you're coming into Marseille tomorrow?' I asked her.

'I have and I will if I'm still welcome.'

'You're very welcome.'

'I had a chat with your friend and now I feel it's quite necessary for me to come. I think it's time to speak to them.'

'You talked to Dorothy?' I asked, trying to keep the surprise from my voice. I really hoped Dorothy's interference was going to be helpful.

'Yes, lovely woman. She really held the key to unlock my fears. It's fortuitous that she's here really.'

'And will what you tell the Harpers be welcome, or could it be difficult to hear?'

'I hope it won't be difficult and I hope it will be welcome, but of course, I won't know until it's too late. But I've reached the stage where I'm going to do it anyway. If I can spend a little time with them first, I think it might help to prepare them. I do know Meredith isn't aware that Dorothy's here yet. I won't let on.'

I don't know why that jabbed at my heart a little. Well, I did know really. I was pretty upset that Dorothy had confided all in this complete stranger.

* * *

Reception was completely empty. There wasn't anyone manning the desk and the phone was ringing without an audience. I did consider answering it, but decided that was one thing in this hotel I wouldn't get involved with. I hoped that Lucien was busy apprehending his thief.

As I was walking over to the lift, a large, bald-headed man with chef whites and a goatee beard strode past me with his head down and a holdall in his hand. He pushed open the main door and let it slam behind him. It was as if he'd just been fired.

I hovered for a moment to see if Lucien or Béatrice would appear, but they didn't, so I got in the lift and within a couple of minutes I was knocking on Dorothy's door.

'Gina,' she said, when she opened it. 'Come in.'

I wasn't sure if she was just a bit tired or if she might have been crying, but when I was in the room and the door was closed, she walked over to her bed and climbed on top of the covers. She stretched out and propped herself up on her pillows. She patted the space beside her and I climbed on and stretched myself out too.

'Are you okay?' I asked.

'I am,' she said. 'I have just heard the most amazing news and it really has been like a punch in the guts.'

'A nice punch in the guts? I'm not sure there is such a thing.'

'Believe me, there is. I've been winded in the most splendid way.'

'This is about Adele, isn't it?'

She looked at me for a long moment then. 'Would you understand if I said I couldn't tell you? Not yet. This really isn't my story to tell. I expect you will find out soon enough. That's if you haven't worked it out already.'

I thought about Meredith's recording and decided that, yes, I probably did know what was coming.

'Meredith has given me a much more frank recording to type. She's really going to tell her story now.'

'Oh?'

'When you first asked me to take on this companion job, you said that you wanted to know where she would start her story. I know now that you were worried about the New York story, but she's gone back to when she was eighteen and mentioned a man by name. Someone she had a relationship with, before she met Gerald.'

'Frank Batchelor.'

'So, she is using his actual name?'

'It would seem so.'

'And you knew about him? Because it was a few years before you met her.'

'She told me about him.'

'He was married.'

'Yes.'

I drew my knees up and turned so I could look her properly in the eye. 'If she's happy to mention Frank by name, then I wonder if Daniel Williamson is next.'

'So be it,' Dorothy said, simply.

'So be it? I thought it was imperative this didn't come out? What about your position on the Art committee?'

'I'm not sure I care much any more, not after today's news. I thought something terrible had happened many years ago, but now I find out I was wrong.'

'That feeling might wear off, though, Dorothy – and then you'll be in the spotlight. It was a pretty serious thing you did. Criminal damage or something like that, not to mention the headlines in the press. I know Daniel Williamson doesn't produce art any more, but he's still a big name. His son has taken up the baton and is often exhibiting. This wouldn't be laughed off, you know.'

She seemed to consider this for a while and then sighed in one long resigned breath. 'I think that after you've been to Marseille, it might be time for me to see Meredith. Perhaps you can warn her I'm here so it won't be a huge shock for her.'

'When do you want me to do that?'

'You'll know when,' she said.

31

GINA

Lucien was standing behind the reception desk, looking apprehensive when I came back out of the lift.

'Lucien,' I said. 'What's happening?'

'Ah, Gina, we have caught her, the blonde woman, the thief. Béatrice has locked her in the office.'

'Oh my God, is that wise? She might be dangerous.'

'*Non*, she isn't as dangerous as Béatrice. It was Béatrice's boyfriend who was letting her in. The man she was kissing in the spa was Cristòu.'

'Poor Béatrice. Have you phoned the police?'

'Yes, they are on their way, but Cristòu has gone.'

'Is he a big man with a bald head?'

'*Oui*, that's him.'

'I was in reception when he walked out. He had a holdall in his hand and was in quite a rush.'

'Yes, it's a shame really that Béatrice decided to confront him when she did. It gave him the heads-up and he was able to run. She couldn't stop him, but she did manage to give him a whack in the face before he left. If it hadn't been her it could easily have been me.'

'No wonder he had his head down.'

'The police can deal with him when they find him. It seems to me from what this woman has said, that she was manipulating him. I hope that the police will be issued with a warrant and they can search her place.'

'How did you get her?'

'It was Helena in the end. She is one of the other chefs in the kitchen. She'd been watching Cristòu for a while and thought he was behaving oddly. Then she saw this other woman and was going to tell Béatrice. She thought it was just sex, but then she caught them interacting and saw Cristòu hand over the key. Helena told me and I caught the blonde woman as she was going into the room. You were right, Gina, if I had called the police then and waited for them, she would have been long gone.'

'Glad to have helped and I'm so happy you have your thief. I think your uncle will be so proud of you.'

'Thank you and for your help too.'

'Is it okay if I get you to arrange a taxi into Marseille for tomorrow morning? The Harpers are up for another trip.'

'Of course. I'm only sorry not to be able to take you myself, but I no longer have a car.'

'What's happened to your car?'

'I have paid my mother's debt by handing over the keys to it. I'd not long had it, and I won't lie, I feel a bit bereft, but it is done and now my mother and I are done, also.'

'Oh, Lucien, I'm so glad it's your car you've sold. When I overheard you talking to Béatrice I did wonder for a moment if... well, it doesn't matter now.'

'What did you wonder?' he asked a little bemused.

'I wondered if you'd pinched some wine from the cellar.'

'Pinched?'

'Stole,' I said, feeling an immediate heat in my cheeks. 'Sorry, I should have had more faith.'

'Oh, I see.' He laughed. 'Well, the wine is worth a lot collectively to be fair, but you know, it's easier to sell a car, Gina. It didn't stop Cristòu, though. It was him who took the wine, apparently. Béatrice was right about that.'

'What will you do in the kitchen without him?'

'We have Helena. She did a lot of the work apparently, perhaps more so than Cristòu was honest about. I hear it should be her quietly getting the Michelin star, not that big, cheating oaf!'

'Another problem resolved then. We are really getting through this list,' I said and he smiled. 'I'm sorry I thought you'd taken the wine.'

'It's no problem. The other day when I was looking at it and thinking about my uncle offering to help, the thought may have floated past my mind briefly, but, of course he was really offering a loan, I guess. I did consider a loan, but then I thought, this borrowing has got to stop.'

'I'm so proud of you,' I said and that blush reappeared.

'And me of you. Super sleuth Gina Knight.'

'I am in the middle of orchestrating another mystery in Marseille. Honestly, that flight home cannot come soon enough.'

'You will miss us,' he said. 'When you are back home in England, in the rain with the clouds and *le froid* – the cold – you will wish you were here. You wait and see.'

I stepped forward then and gave him a hug without giving it much thought. He pulled me close and patted my back.

'Don't worry about your mother; concentrate on you,' I said when I stepped back. 'I think we need to not always assume that family is the best thing for us, because sometimes they are the worst. And maybe, now Cristòu has gone, you could think about Béatrice too.'

'I'm always thinking about Béatrice,' he said.

'I can see that. I did wonder if your head had been turned, by the Italian woman.'

'Maybe it was, a little. And I was considering asking her out, but really I don't want to get mixed up with people like that. I don't think they are bad people, just misguided and a bit full of drama. I like my life to be quieter.'

'You might want to consider another hotel, then!'

Lucien chuckled. 'I'm sorry I can't take you tomorrow. I would have liked to have shown you around.'

He gave me a map, then and pointed out a couple of things that he felt Meredith and Gerald would like to see.

'And maybe get the taxi to drop you off in the *vieux-port*, the old port. I think that Gerald would like to see the boats, but don't bother trying to get a coffee down there, because there are a lot of Irish pubs and MacDonald's and Burger King, you know, all that rubbish. You can get the tourist train up to the basilica and when you come back down there are many other good places to drink and eat. Here.'

He took a pen and circled a couple of points on the map before handing it back to me.

'Don't try and do it all in a day,' he said. 'There is too much. The Harpers live here now and can go again easily when Rose is home. Make sure you see what you want to and then think about coming back sometime and I will give you a proper tour, show you the best food, the best bars and the best art.'

'I'd like that,' I said and I meant it, but really I knew the truth was that Lucien's city wasn't my city and I'd probably never come back.

32

GINA

Meredith didn't seem too worried when I told her that Adele would be coming to Marseille with us. It might be because I suggested she was sharing the taxi rather than joining us on the visit, but I decided that we could work out the particulars when we got there.

I still wasn't sure I was doing the right thing, but Adele was going to drop her bomb regardless and I really didn't want Meredith cornered in her own villa if the news was unwelcome.

When we were all strapped in and the taxi left the hotel grounds, an uncomfortableness settled over me about what was to come. How I wish Dorothy was here with us and she and Meredith had already had their reunion. When was I supposed to tell her? Dorothy said I would know, but I wasn't so sure. I decided to just sit back for now and see what unfolded. I racked my brains for something to say, for some way of starting an innocuous conversation. I couldn't think of anything, so instead, we sat in silence.

I glanced at Adele who was staring out of the window and when I looked at Meredith she was doing the same. Gerald looked comfortable enough in the front seat and the driver was chatting away to him in French, which had Gerald nodding, smiling and joining in with the odd word like, *absolutely, you're right* and *I didn't know that*. The driver chuckled as he took us into the city.

I honestly did feel quite excited about the prospect of visiting Lucien's home, as I remembered back to his passion and enthusiasm for his city when I first arrived. It was a shame not to be doing this with him, but quite apart from the car, he still had a hotel to run.

We were dropped off at the Old Port and I dug out the map to orientate us.

'Lucien suggests enjoying the view of the boats for a moment before we head up to the *Basilique Notre-Dame de la Garde*,' I said, and all three of them looked up towards the church perched high on the hill.

'And how are we getting up there?' Meredith asked me with a very pointed look.

'I thought we'd use our broomsticks,' I said, and she surprised me by laughing. It was due to her change of heart about her book, I realised. The more she disclosed the more comfortable she seemed to become.

Adele had drifted over to Gerald who was closer to the water and she was pointing out a couple of yachts in the harbour that seemed to hold his interest. Meredith watched them for a moment and then turned to me.

'Is Adele sightseeing with us too?' she asked me, quietly.

'I think so, if that's okay with you.'

'I don't mind,' she said. 'She seems very nice.'

I breathed a silent sigh of relief and left the three of them for a moment to go and buy tickets for the tourist train.

* * *

Le Petit Train was really just an electric vehicle pulling several open carriages behind it. We had our tickets and we found our seats. Meredith chose to sit next to me, behind Adele and Gerald in the next carriage. Adele was getting him talking a little, which seemed to please Meredith. I thought she might be resentful that he wasn't talking to her, but she appeared quite content listening to them chatting.

'He's having a good, lucid day today,' she said and we settled back to listen to the audio guide as the train set off along the coast road. I did try and concentrate, but I felt on edge, waiting for the moment that Adele might reveal herself. At the moment, though, she seemed content to just be in Gerald's company.

I looked out to the small island the audio was telling me was *François I's* sixteenth-century island castle and former prison. It was the setting for *The Count of Monte Cristo*. I would imagine a boat trip out to visit it would be an interesting way to spend an afternoon, but I remembered what Lucien had said about not doing too much. Thinking about how much rest Gerald usually had, *Notre-Dame de la Garde* and some lunch might well be enough after this train trip. At some point I needed to continue typing Meredith's memoir too. Right now, though, this seemed more important. The one thing that Rose asked me to try and do was to get them out of the hotel and here we were.

The train weaved its way around the side streets of Marseille and we got to see a little more of the everyday city and less of the busy tourist spots. The climb became steeper as we got closer to the church. If you chose to walk, it would be quite the trek from the waterfront. There was no way any of us could have done it. When the train stopped in the car park, though, I could see a lot of steps leading up to the front door of the building, so we weren't quite there yet.

Once we were up the first set of steps there was the entrance to a museum, so I left the others to see if I could get an English guide to read. It would be useful if we weren't all just wandering around aimlessly.

Once I had one in my hands, we set off up the next steps, spurred on by some of the facts and figures of the building and its elevated position in the city and how beautiful it was inside. Adele had her arm crooked through Gerald's and Meredith had hold of mine. With the extra effort of helping Meredith and giving a running commentary, by the time my feet found that last step, I was quite out of puff. We all took a moment to orientate ourselves and then turned around.

The view from the top was spectacular. There was a terrace that wrapped itself around the basilica and offered a 360-degree view. You could see how big the city of Marseille actually was from this height. A panorama of red rooftops and white buildings spread out below us interspersed with the odd concrete high-rise. The vista was huge, beginning at the old port where our journey had started and all the way around to the distant mountains. It was clear then what I had seen as we had come into land at the beginning of the previous week. The mountains seeming to rise up to surround and protect the city. I glanced over to where Gerald and Adele were standing together, arms still linked and then I turned to Meredith.

'I have to tell you that I know Dorothy Reed,' I said.

Meredith's head snapped round from the view and her eyes focused on mine.

'Dorothy? How do you know her?'

She didn't seem as angry as I thought she'd be. She looked surprised and interested.

'She was my last companion job,' I said. 'I looked after her in Norfolk a couple of months ago during a family wedding.'

'I hadn't thought about Dorothy for a number of years until I

The Old Girls' Chateau Escape

started this memoir. I know it sounds strange, but I had somehow erased her from my mind. How is it you've come from being companion to her, to companion to me? It's not a mad coincidence, is it?'

'Not really, she was the person who suggested I could be a good fit for you and Gerald. The recommendation came through your friend Barbara, I think.'

'Ah, that makes sense. Barbara is a mutual if a little distant friend of ours.'

'I'm sorry not to have been honest before. Dorothy did say that you had fallen out and it might be best to keep the connection to myself, but now it feels dishonest, especially with me being privy to your story. It's so very personal and I don't want to know anything that you wouldn't be happy a friend of Dorothy's knowing. I hope that makes sense.'

Meredith seemed to contemplate all that I had said.

'Why did she think you'd be a good fit?' she asked, of all the questions she could have asked.

'Because she says I'm a problem solver and quite useful,' I said with a shrug.

'Yes, I can see that you are. But, the thing is Dorothy is right, we did fall out years ago. She had an affair with Gerald.'

Now I was in tricky territory. How could I say I'd already accused Dorothy of the very same thing without it being obvious I'd been talking to her? Quite simply, I couldn't.

'But, I think you must be wrong; Dorothy would never do that,' I said, instead. 'What did Gerald say?'

'I never confronted him about it. I was terrified of losing him. So much had happened before and I wasn't prepared to risk it. He could have his secret and I could have mine. I did confront her, though. I shouted at her, which was something I never thought I would be able to do to my old friend. I told her that I knew what she had done and that I would never forgive her. She said she was so sorry and she did look pretty devastated to be honest, but then I shut the door in her face and I never saw her again. I think you must see why I wasn't being true in retelling my story. I feel differently now, though. I feel it's time to tell it, warts and all.'

It suddenly occurred to me that Meredith could write this truthfully now, because Gerald would probably never know. It wasn't about telling their story any more; it was about Meredith telling hers. Adele and Gerald joined us at the foot of the last set of steps that led up to the main door.

'Tradition has it that true pilgrims would crawl up the steps on their knees,' I read. 'Even more interesting is that able-bodied pilgrims would put pebbles in their shoes to make the climb challenging. Can you imagine?'

Meredith looked up the steps and took a breath. 'Yes, I can,' she said as we began to climb.

'Construction of the basilica began in 1853 and lasted for over forty years.' I carried on reading from the booklet as we stepped inside. 'It is known by the locals as *La Bonne Mère* – The Good Mother.'

I snapped the book shut as both Adele and Meredith turned to look at me. And it was really then that it all began to fall into place.

33

LUCIEN

When the police had arrived the previous day, they spent a fair amount of time reprimanding Lucien for locking the woman in his office. They didn't check for fingerprints in the cellar, although as soon as Lucien had suggested it he realised there would be plenty of Cristòu's prints down there anyway, so it would be pointless. They said they would look into Cristòu and his dealings with this woman and get back to Lucien with any questions they might have for him. Gina was right again, it seemed; they were being clumsy. Or certainly that was how it appeared to Lucien. He wanted action, a car arriving in a spray of gravel at the very least, maybe even a gunfight and a standoff in reception that they'd talk about for years. Instead, they *invited* the woman down to the station for a chat. And Lucien had to remind himself that he didn't really like a big drama anyway.

He was now stuck on reception, double-checking some bookings for the coming weekend and sending out welcome emails to the guests. He was on his own as Béatrice had gone to help a female guest with an intimate issue that he had no wish to guess at, although that hadn't stopped his thoughts running away with him.

His mobile rang then and it was his Uncle Hugo.

'Lucien, Hugo here with some good news at last.'

'Uncle Hugo, good news is welcome.'

'Oliver has made a wonderful improvement and we can make a flight tomorrow. It will be pretty epic for him as we have to make a couple of connections, but at least we will be coming home.'

'He's walking?' Lucien said, his voice raised in excitement.

'*Non!* Lucien, it is not that wonderful. He is just well enough now, for the journey, that is all. Which is pretty damn good.'

It was those words that made it clear just how bad Oliver was and Lucien took a breath.

'That is fantastic news. You must all be so pleased to be coming home. What do you want me to do?' he asked.

'I have ordered a hospital-style bed with winches and all that, which will be arriving later today. I need you to clear a villa and see if you can get it ready enough for his return. I know that will be tricky as the builders haven't finished yet, but see what you can do.'

What Lucien could do was to have not fired the builders the other day, although they were never going to be finished in time for the Guérins' return. The best bet was Gina's place as it was at least clean and tidy enough. It's not like Oliver was going to need a fully fitted kitchen at the moment.

He checked the current situation of the rooms in the hotel and decided to see if Gina wouldn't mind spending a night or two in there. She'd told him she'd stay until Rose returned, so she'd probably be keen to get flights booked herself. He was pretty sure she would be amenable about the room.

'It's not a problem. I will get on it now,' he told Hugo.

'Also, Rose has been ringing the phone in Meredith's villa but

The Old Girls' Chateau Escape

there is no response. Is everything okay? We don't need more illness right now.'

'They are out with Gina in Marseille for a day trip. All is well. No drama at all.'

'That's amazing, Rose will be so happy. Thank you, Lucien. I can't tell you how good it is to know you are there when I am not.'

'There is a way you can tell me,' he said.

'Oh, and what is that, dare I ask?'

'A deserved pay rise,' Lucien said and he could hear his uncle laughing as the call disconnected.

Béatrice appeared then, back from her mission and he was determined not to ask her for details.

'We are going to have to move ourselves,' he said and filled her in on Hugo's call.

'Did you tell him about what's been going on?'

'*Non*, he doesn't need that nonsense in his head until he's back.'

'That's good. He's going to be pissed off about his wine and his head chef, but you know, I've been talking to the kitchen staff and Helena really is the quiet star of the show. Cristòu was just the big mouth while she did all the work. She's been stepping up today and everyone is so much happier. The restaurant is no different, either. It's all been her work, I think. I'm glad he has gone.'

'Are you? Are you really?' Lucien asked her.

'Yes, I can see now how stupid I was. I won't make that mistake again.'

Lucien looked at her and wondered how long to leave it before he made his move. He wouldn't leave it as long as he did before, but maybe it was too soon right now.

'So, what do you want me to do?' she asked him.

'I think we should get the big suite ready.'

'For whom?'

'For the person who keeps their cool no matter what is thrown at them,' he said.

'*D'accord*,' Béatrice said. 'For Gina, *oui*? I can arrange that.'

She took out her phone to call the cleaning staff and then slipped it back in her pocket.

'I will do it myself,' she said. 'It's because of Gina that Cristòu is gone. And let's be honest, she did me a favour.'

She turned to leave, but Lucien caught her arm.

'She did me a favour also. Is it too soon to ask you if you'll have dinner with me?'

She turned back to him, a smile beginning on her lips. 'I'd say it's better late than never,' she said.

When she had gone, Lucien took out his phone and tapped out a message.

> LUCIEN
>
> Gina, Oliver is well enough to come home, so they'll be on a flight tomorrow. How do you feel about staying in the hotel until you leave? Sorry to move you, but Oliver will need your place for his special bed. I won't move your things, but is it okay if I begin to make the villa ready for him? Lucien.

34

GINA

The interior of the basilica was nothing short of stunning. Any revelations that might have been about to happen were shelved for the moment as we took in the vast space.

The vaulted ceiling was covered in mosaics and there was an oriental or perhaps an Islamic feel to the upper sanctuary. There were acres of gold leaf and the mosaics depicted olives and palm trees with exotic birds.

There were paintings showing dramatic incidents like shipwrecks, and civil unrest on the walls of the nave and model boats hung from the ceiling, showing connections with the city's maritime history. In fact, votive offerings from the citizens of Marseille were scattered throughout the basilica – crash helmets, war medals, even life buoys.

Gerald slid into one of the pews with Adele beside him and they crooked their necks upward to take it all in. I walked over to where they sat and joined them, while Meredith hovered in the aisle beside us. *It's going to happen now,* I thought, time and time again, but Adele seemed to have lost her nerve and just hung on to the pearl on the end of her chain that she'd had tucked into her top.

I opened the book again and resumed being a tourist guide for our group.

'Supplicants arrive throughout the year and there is a major pilgrimage to the basilica that takes place on 15 August each year, with torchlight processions and mass,' I said.

'So, it's somewhere to come if you need comfort, or if you have something you want to share,' Meredith suddenly said and her eyes were on Adele.

Adele got up and walked away from us, down the aisle, towards the altar and Meredith followed her. I felt ridiculously nervous and moved along the pew until I was next to Gerald.

'Are you okay?' I asked him, not really expecting a response, which was fine and he didn't respond in words, but he took my hand and held it in his lap. He was watching his wife.

Adele was almost at the altar now, but she stopped when Meredith put a hand on her shoulder. Adele turned to her and I could see she was going to say something. She had it written all over her face.

I held my breath and even Gerald tightened his grip on my hand.

I couldn't hear what Adele was saying, but Meredith took her hand from her shoulder and lifted it to Adele's necklace, held the pearl between her fingers for a moment before her eyes filled with tears and they came spilling down her cheeks. And then she raised her arms up and Adele stepped into her embrace. They stayed like that for some time until slowly Meredith let her go and I could see that Adele was crying too.

Then Gerald looked over at me and said very quietly, 'We thought she was gone, but she is here. Her baby.'

The Old Girls' Chateau Escape

* * *

We took the train back down to the old port and I navigated the harbour to find the restaurant Lucien had suggested for lunch. It was actually on board a boat that was moored right at the end near the harbour wall and offered the best view of the port and out to the sea beyond.

After the revelation in the church I imagined that Meredith and Adele would be in full conversation. Confessions, explanations, recriminations, but they were fairly quiet, happy to walk together with Adele's arm linked through Meredith's. I guessed all of that would come in good time. Perhaps when I wasn't around. I had a million questions, because it was clear that Dorothy and Meredith had differing accounts of their history and what went on between them. I had to pick my moment to tell Meredith that her old friend was here. Would that spoil this moment between mother and daughter? I was pleased that I had, at least, told her I had a connection with Dorothy. That was a start.

I did notice a couple of wary glances Meredith gave Gerald, but he was happily wandering along beside them and anyway, she didn't hear what he had said inside the church.

It was as we walked down towards the restaurant that a message from Lucien came about me moving rooms and how Rose and Hugo were on their way home with Oliver.

'Two pieces of wonderful news in one day,' Meredith said and Adele gave her a shy smile.

I sent him a message back to let him know I didn't mind at all. The thought of going home was welcome. Dorothy and I would have to look into booking flights. It was nice to think we could travel back together.

I wondered about the memoir then. I wouldn't possibly have time to finish the first few chapters as Meredith hadn't actually recorded it all, yet. Perhaps she might change her mind again and ditch the whole thing. Either way, if I was going home it would be out of my hands.

We were offered the perfect table with only a rope to separate us from the sea beyond. A slight breeze had picked up and the rhythmic sounds of the boats rocking in the water could easily have sent me off to sleep. Occasionally bells would chime and the creaking noise of the rigging could be heard. Along with the calls of the gulls, you could close your eyes and know exactly where you were.

Everyone was studying their menus when I spoke. 'I think it's time to address the elephant in the room. And that elephant is me.'

Meredith and Adele both looked up surprised and only Gerald smiled.

'You're not an elephant.' He laughed. 'You're a very nice woman.'

That did go some way to lightening the mood.

'Seriously, though,' I continued, 'I realise something monumental has happened and you must have lots to talk about. I can leave you to it, get a taxi back to the hotel and Adele is very capable of seeing you all home.'

'No,' Meredith said. 'You should stay, Gina, if you want to. I think it's just a lot for us both to take in.'

We ordered some drinks and food and sat back to wait for it to come. I poured everyone a glass of water from the carafe on the table.

'When I arrived into my adoptive mother's arms I was wearing a pale-lemon knitted babygrow with tiny wooden buttons in the shape of strawberries that had been carved and painted red. I also had a pearl strung onto ribbon and a book of fairy tales wrapped in tissue paper. My adoptive mother kept all of these things, even the tissue paper, and I have them all now.'

Her hands went to the pearl hanging around her neck again and she stroked it between her fingers.

Meredith pulled a tissue from her bag and began dabbing at her eyes.

'Of course, I didn't know about these things until my mother was dying. That was when she told me I'd been adopted and where to find my birth mother if I wanted to.'

'I knitted it myself,' Meredith said with a shaky voice. 'The pearl was from a set of earrings that my parents bought me for my eighteenth birthday. I still have the other one, but of course I never wore it on its own and I told my mother I'd lost it. She was not very happy about it, but she said it wasn't the worst thing I had done that year and she wasn't wrong.'

'She meant you having me,' Adele said sadly.

'She did, but when I say she wasn't wrong it was because I did agree the loss of the earring wasn't the worst thing. The worst thing for me was giving you up,' Meredith said and reached across the table to take her daughter's hand.

The waiter arrived with our drinks and a basket of bread and butter. Gerald got stuck in, slathering lots of the butter on a slice of the warm sourdough, but the three of us just sipped quietly at our drinks.

'I don't blame you,' Adele said. 'You were young, it was different times and, really, you gave my mother the opportunity to have a child, which wasn't possible for her. I doubt it was an easy decision for you. Please know, I hold no animosity towards you.'

'Thank you,' Meredith said.

'I'm cross she didn't tell me sooner, though. Think of the years I could have known you.'

'Perhaps she was scared she might lose you.'

'Maybe,' Adele said. 'Do you know she gave me Meredith as a middle name and I aways wondered where it came from. She said it was after the most generous woman she had never had the chance to thank properly for her kindness. She didn't tell me any more than that.'

'You know that one of the reasons I didn't want to move here was because there would be more distance between us and the chance that you might ever knock on my door would diminish. Because I did always hope for that. Even though I had vowed not to interfere in your life, it didn't mean I didn't always hold some small hope you might find me. How *did* you find me?' Meredith said.

'My mum told me that your mother was friends with her mother – my gran – and that was how the adoption came about. Mum said that she couldn't have children and desperately wanted to adopt. Then, when you were pregnant with me, the friends got together and arranged it. So, my mum always had a connection to your family through that friendship. Mum knew when Rose moved to France. It didn't take much digging to find you. Honestly, it was my husband, Jason, who encouraged me. I was the one who was hesitating; it was a lot to take in, but he pushed me once we knew Gerald had dementia. He told me to hurry up and not waste precious time. That there was only one way to find out if you wanted a relationship with me and that was to ask.'

I realised then, that was at the heart of the text message that had arrived on Adele's phone in Aix. It wasn't sinister at all.

'Did you ever see me over the years?' Adele asked Meredith. 'I did wonder if, as our families had that connection, that maybe you saw me.'

'No,' Meredith said, sadly. 'I had to make the decision to stay away. I thought it very likely if I saw you, I'd probably steal you.'

'It must have been so hard for you,' Adele said.

The Old Girls' Chateau Escape

I so wanted to slip away. This was such a personal conversation that I felt I had no right to be listening to, but the food was on its way and they had both asked me to stay. And maybe it was easier for them to talk with me here. There was less focus solely on each other.

I had chosen a glass of local red wine, recommended by the waiter, and it was delicious. It was also slipping down quite nicely. And when my bowl of rich seafood pasta in a spicy tomato sauce came it was the perfect accompaniment.

We all enjoyed our food and wine and made small talk about the city and the harbour, about the success of the festival and how we all hoped Oliver was improving. And then I could put it off no longer.

'There is one other thing,' I said. 'Dorothy flew in to see you. She's at the hotel.'

35

GINA

When we got back, Gerald picked his favourite spot on the patio for his power nap and Meredith and Adele went inside the villa to make tea.

Meredith had been shocked when I told her that Dorothy was here in France, but she had recovered and I was delighted when she said how much she should like to see her.

I told them I would go and get her and disappeared off to the hotel.

Dorothy opened her door almost as soon as I had knocked on it and I guessed she had been waiting for us to return. She was animated and quite dressed up. I also noticed that she was wearing make-up, not something she did often. I remembered us talking about it in the past and her saying that at her age the applying of make-up wasn't the hardest thing. The hardest thing was the excavation of it from her craggy face afterwards, that it was akin to an archaeological dig. I had laughed, but really, Dorothy didn't have a particularly wrinkled face. She looked pretty good for a woman approaching ninety.

'Are you ready to go and meet your friend?' I asked her.

'Yes,' she said. 'I'm more than ready. How did it go in Marseille? Did Adele do what she told me she was going to?'

'Yes, she revealed herself to be Meredith's daughter.'

We left her room and travelled down in the lift.

'Meredith was eighteen when she became pregnant. She didn't tell me until that night of her fifth miscarriage. She was so distraught and thought she was being punished for giving up her baby all those years before. But it was clear to me that she hadn't wanted to. It was her mother who persuaded her to give the baby to a family friend whose daughter couldn't have children.'

'Yes,' I said. 'That's what Adele said.'

'She did it reluctantly, because I do think if her mother had offered any kind of support to her in keeping the child, then she would have. Instead she heaped shame on poor Meredith. The father, Frank, was a married man who had no interest in her or her child.

'I couldn't bear it, Gina – the amount she was suffering, it was intolerable. I suggested we look for the child, see if she could get her back, but Meredith wouldn't entertain the idea. She would have been six or seven then and Meredith didn't want to confuse a happy child, said that she alone must suffer the consequences of her actions. So *I* did something and I went to look for the child myself. I wanted to at least report back that everything was okay and the child was happy. What I found, though, was that the child had died of meningitis when she had been about three.

'I couldn't tell Meredith; it would be too much, but I did tell Gerald and that is what I did that was so wrong. You have to understand that he was in the dark and I honestly thought she might take her own life, she was at such a low ebb. So I told Gerald and he was obviously upset that she had never told him, but he was also glad to understand why she was in so much pain.'

I could hear now in her voice, even after all these years, how much this had upset Dorothy.

'So, imagine my surprise when Adele told me who she was. There had been a mistake; a child had died, but it wasn't her.'

'Don't forget, she thinks you and Gerald were having an affair,' I reminded her.

'I think he might have made a mistake back then with someone, but it wasn't me. But after I told Gerald and we decided between us that Meredith shouldn't know about the child, the next time I saw her I guessed he must have been honest with her because she told me she knew what I had done and shut the door in my face.'

I remembered Meredith telling me this was exactly what happened earlier. Same words, but the wrong context.

'She meant about the affair and you thought she meant about you telling Gerald. God! What a mistake. A friendship dissolved on misunderstanding,' I said.

'A friendship dissolved on lies,' Dorothy corrected me.

'Well, now you can go and put everything right,' I said.

We were at the villa and Dorothy held back as I went to knock on the door.

'Okay?' I asked her and she nodded before taking the last few steps to join me on the doorstep. Meredith opened the door and then without a single word she also opened her arms to her old friend.

I left them then. There was a limit to how many reunions I could witness in one day.

* * *

My villa had a hospital-style bed in the middle of the living room and Lucien was unpacking some boxes of equipment.

'I'm so sorry for the intrusion,' he said as we sat and had a cup of coffee.

'It is no problem at all,' I said. 'It is wonderful news about Oliver coming home. Meredith and Gerald will be glad of having Rose home too.'

'They both seem far happier now. You have done a good thing there.'

I didn't mention about Adele, he could find out in good time from someone who wasn't me. I was ready to pack my bag and vacate, so after we had finished our drinks, I left him to organise the living room while I got my things together.

'We have a room in the hotel ready for you,' he called through. 'When you are packed, I will show you where to go.'

'Thank you,' I called back.

'Lucien, just the man.'

Meredith's voice came from the living room and I poked my head back through.

'Ah, Gina too, perfect. I would like someone to set me up to speak to my daughter on my laptop please. I think it would be good to have a chat before she returns.'

'That is a great idea,' I said.

'And I thought that we could all have a meal in the restaurant tonight. You, Gina and Adele and Gerald and Dorothy, me and you too Lucien if you can manage it.'

'I'm sure I can,' he said, although his face told a story of a man with a lot of other things to do. I smiled at him and he grinned back. 'I have one more box to collect from the front desk and then I will be back to set that up and get Gina settled in to her room for the night.'

After he'd disappeared Meredith looked as if she was going to leave too, but then she turned back to me.

'Thank you, Gina. You have somehow managed to turn my world upside down since you've been here and all for the better.'

'It was really nothing to do with me,' I said.

'I think it is. I think you are someone who is good at bringing people together.'

I thought that this was a little ironic bearing in mind I couldn't keep my marriage together.

'And you and Dorothy have had a chance to talk?'

'Yes, we have made a start and have plenty more to catch up on before you leave. We were on completely different pages and now it seems so stupid what I thought. It was a tricky time and my head hadn't been in the right place. Dorothy thought all this time that Adele had died, which is a terrible thing to have to know.'

'That is awful, but what was the confusion?'

'Adele's mother had a sister whose child died when she was three. The families were living in the same house as they were waiting for her husband's job to take them overseas. They did eventually move to Jeddah, but sadly it was minus a child. Adele was able to tell us all about it.'

'When did you suspect Adele might be your daughter? It wasn't in the basilica was it?'

'No, it was when she was looking after Gerald, after he went for a wander the other day. When she was sitting on the grass, for a second she looked just like her father and it brought me up short. All I could do was stare at her. Then I saw the pearl. I think she usually kept it hidden, but it must have slipped out and I saw it before she tucked it back.'

'Are you okay?' I asked her. 'It's a lot to take in.'

Meredith got up from where she had been perched on the edge of the bed and walked over to me. She clasped my hand in her good one and smiled a warm and genuine smile.

'I'm delighted to know Adele after all this time. I'm sad that

The Old Girls' Chateau Escape

Dorothy and I lost so many years on a misunderstanding, but I'm so happy we have found each other again. I'm devastated to be losing my husband, but happy to have him still with me for now. I'm thrilled to know that my grandson is coming home. And I'm looking forward to seeing my youngest daughter home too.'

'That is a lot,' I said.

'I'm also glad to have met you too, and I think we should have a lovely meal on my son-in-law with some good wine to celebrate the wins in life. I feel like a different woman from the one I was when you first knocked on my door. I have found moving very difficult for a number of reasons and having to rely on help from others is not an easy thing to square. I'm sorry I wasn't very warm to you at the start and well done for sticking with me.'

I felt a little tearful after that speech, but I managed to hold it back until after she had gone.

Once my case was packed I followed Lucien back to the main hotel and into the lift. He seemed ridiculously pleased with himself.

'Have you asked Béatrice out yet?' I said.

'*Oui*,' he said, his grin intensifying.

'Ah, no wonder you are so happy. She obviously said yes.'

'She actually said it was better late than never.'

I laughed as we walked out of the lift and Lucien led me down a carpeted landing with prints of Cézanne's work along the walls. We were on the other side of the hotel from where Dorothy's room was. Then he stopped in front of a room that had double doors.

'Is this the broom cupboard?' I asked him.

He didn't answer, but just opened both doors wide and stepped back so I could enter.

The room was sumptuous. That really was the only word to describe it. Rich mustards, cool blues and warm greys greeted me in the curtains and the scatter cushions neatly lined up on the huge bed. I could see there was a balcony through a set of sliding doors with two reclining chairs and a coffee table with carefully placed magazines and a potted orchid to set the scene. Strung up above was a sunshade of stiff linen-like fabric and before I could stop myself an image of me out there with a glass of wine came to my mind.

There was a bottle of wine on the table, because there *was* a table with four chairs as if I had someone to entertain. A basket of fruit and chocolates were next to it. And when I turned, there was a large and very comfortable-looking sofa behind me.

'This is too grand for me!' I said, as Lucien pushed my suitcase towards the wardrobe.

'Béatrice and I wanted to make sure your last night was special. I think you do a lot for others and then you say things like *I don't mind, this will be fine for me, please don't bother about me.* Please enjoy it,' he said and then before I could protest again, he left.

I walked over to the sofa and flopped back down into its velvety comfort and promptly fell asleep.

* * *

The restaurant wasn't busy. A lot of people had left after the festival and it wasn't the weekend, so we could enjoy the gentle atmosphere.

'I have spoken to Rose and she has confirmed that they're on their way home. Oliver is in high spirits to be coming back and he's looking forward to seeing you, Lucien,' Meredith said.

'That is wonderful,' said Dorothy.

Lucien was taking the cork out of the bottle of Champagne

that Meredith had insisted on having and he poured us all a small glass each.

'I'm hopeful that you will get your watch back,' Lucien said to Meredith. 'The police have confirmed they are searching this woman's things and they also are looking for Cristòu. There is no guarantee of course, but I will cross my fingers that everything will be returned. If not, I promise you will be reimbursed.'

'Thank you, Lucien. To old friends and new beginnings,' Meredith said with her glass raised.

We all echoed her sentiments, and it was quite fitting. Gerald needed a top-up for the toast because he'd finished his before Meredith had even spoken. I caught a glimpse of the man that he was before the dementia in his cheeky smile as he offered up his empty glass.

Adele seemed much more relaxed than she had earlier. The three women together could easily fill in all the blanks for the missing years. They had a lot to catch up on. We dined on the most delicious fish to start and then Helena came out of the kitchen to carve the *Chateaubriand*, which we had with green vegetables and *dauphinoise* potatoes. A chocolate mousse nearly finished us off and then Lucien left us to have a nightcap in the bar before we staggered to the lift, Dorothy holding on to my arm for support.

'What a day,' she said as I deposited her outside her room. I wondered if she might want to talk some more. 'Do you mind if I leave you now? It's been quite a couple of days and I would simply love to get into bed and close my eyes until tomorrow morning.'

'Of course,' I said, thinking that I was very happy to spend some time in my own gorgeous room.

It was a little bit of a shame that I only had one night here. Dorothy and I had decided to leave the following day. Rose was on her way and Adele was here to help Meredith in the meantime.

We were no longer needed. I also felt that once Rose was back, I really would be in the way. They needed to be together as a family. The hotel could prove to be the perfect place to rework a blended family situation. Béatrice had managed to get us on a flight leaving at lunchtime. I made the most of it by opening the wine and taking a glass of it and my book out onto the balcony for an hour, before filling the bath and adding the complimentary bubbles for a long soak. Then I pulled on my pyjamas and slipped in between the crisp sheets to finish the last few pages of my book.

Riley caught his man, fired the most undesirable letch in the office and made it home in time to put his kids to bed. All was well in the world and I could discuss the book quite happily at Erik's next book-club meeting.

I drifted off to dreams of Erik, standing on his boat with a Viking sword in his hand to protect my honour from something that was lurking just under the surface of the water. In the morning when I woke I couldn't remember what I'd dreamed about at all.

36

GINA

I had my suitcase packed and it was standing outside the door to my room. One last look around and I knew I had everything. The beauty of packing up yesterday for the last night in a new room was that I was almost ready to go.

Dorothy and I had eaten a quick breakfast together on my balcony and she had said how content she now was.

'My situation with Meredith has been hanging over my head for years,' she said. 'Every time an emotional situation is resolved it feels so liberating. A bit like finishing a book on your to-be-read pile.'

'With a little more importance,' I said, laughing. 'And I assume you asked her about the New York debacle?'

'Yes, we did find a quiet moment to discuss that. Meredith said that she would never have written about it and fully intended to take it to her grave.'

'That must be a huge relief,' I said.

'Yes, it is and now I'm very much looking forward to going home,' Dorothy said.

I thought about her house in Hampton with my boathouse at

the end of her garden – it did feel a bit more like mine now – and I realised how happy I was to be going home also. We worked well together, the two of us. Two old girls with a new-found enthusiasm for life. Dorothy perhaps more so than me, but I did feel as if I was catching her up.

I took one last look around my room and closed the door before walking to Dorothy's. It was time to start saying some long goodbyes.

We found the others in the spa café having a late breakfast after Gerald's treatment and Meredith's swim. They looked relaxed and happy. Meredith had a sparkle to her that was not there at the beginning of the previous week. Finding Adele had truly been the best thing that could have happened to her. What would transpire once Rose and Hugo were home remained to be seen, but that was for them to work out as a family.

'Will you both join us?' Meredith asked as we approached their table.

'No, but thank you,' Dorothy said. 'We've actually come to say goodbye.'

'Lucien has borrowed Béatrice's car and is giving us a lift to the airport,' I said.

'Are you glad to be going home?' Adele asked me.

'In a way, but I have enjoyed my time here and Aix and Marseille are beautiful cities. It was also lovely to meet you all. What a couple of weeks it has been.'

'You can say that again,' Meredith said. 'I am so glad you came and made sure Dorothy did too.'

'Well, that, I have to say, was Dorothy's own doing.'

'You know me,' Dorothy said, 'once I get a bee in my bonnet. I will say goodbye now.'

Dorothy was reaching out for Meredith's hand when she stood up.

The Old Girls' Chateau Escape

'No, Dorothy, you and I will never say goodbye again. I will say, see you soon.'

The two women embraced and then Adele got up and pulled me into a hug too.

'You made this whole experience a lot easier than I would have managed it alone. Just think, I might never have plucked up the courage to approach Meredith if it hadn't been for you.'

'Adele is going to help me with my memoir,' Meredith said. 'She's agreed to stay on for a while and we can work on it together. We can fill in our missing years.'

'That's wonderful,' I said, wondering how it really would play out once Rose was back.

'And you know I chatted with Rose last night,' Meredith continued and, not for the first time, I wondered if my thoughts showed directly on my face. 'She was surprised, of course, but then she said the most interesting thing. She said she had always felt as if there was something or someone missing from our family. She said I was always a little bit lost. I think it's all going to work out okay.'

'Let's not leave it so long next time,' Dorothy said and it elicited a laugh from them. Even Gerald joined in.

'You've always been a funny one, Dorothy,' Gerald said.

'Thanks, Gerald, I will take that in the manner it was intended, which I assume was with great love and respect, not that you think I'm a bit odd.'

Gerald twinkled at her for a moment. It was indeed with a look of great love and respect. One I had only seen him offer to his wife.

* * *

Lucien looked slightly out of place in Béatrice's hot-pink Fiat 500 with the roof down. He got out to squeeze my suitcase into the boot and Dorothy's on the back seat where I pushed myself in beside it.

'We really do appreciate this, Lucien,' I said.

'To be honest, I have to go home for a bit anyway. My mother has turned up.'

'Oh, has she? How do you feel about that?'

'I don't know. I've said and thought a lot of things about her over the last couple of weeks, but if she really does want to get some help, then I have to give her a chance, don't I?'

'That is really up to you. I wouldn't blame you if you decided not to help her, but I have a feeling that it would be difficult for you to turn her away. Just be careful, though. People with addiction are not always trustworthy and you'd be wise to take it gently and not expect too much, too quickly.'

'As ever, wise words from you, Gina,' Dorothy said as she climbed into the passenger seat.

It was then that I noticed Riley standing underneath a bush in the border. I raised my hand and waved at him while whispering a little goodbye. He seemed to stare at me for a moment and then he was gone.

Lucien switched on the engine and pulled out of the parking space, then we were on our way, with the roof down and the wind in our hair. Lucien lowered his sunglasses onto his face from the top of his head and grinned at his reflection in the rear-view mirror.

'I think this car suits me,' he said and we laughed.

'So are you and Béatrice going to make a go of it? I have to say, you do look very good together.'

'We are going to take things slowly. I don't have much to offer her at the minute. No car, no money.'

The Old Girls' Chateau Escape 243

'None of that is important, though,' Dorothy said. 'She seems a sensible girl. I get the impression that she won't care about any of that.'

'*Oui,* I think you're right. We can still have fun without money, *non*?' he said and then blushed. 'I mean... you know what I mean.'

'I know *exactly* what you mean,' Dorothy said, her voice loaded with innuendo.

I watched the countryside fly past as we picked up speed on the dual carriageway. It didn't seem like only ten days ago that I arrived. It felt as if I had been here for some time. A lot had happened. To see Meredith and Adele connect was not a small thing at all. Also, to know that Dorothy had finally been able to pass on the truth to Meredith was gratifying. Dorothy had carried that around with her for a long time and now she could know the truth about Meredith's baby.

Lucien stamped on the brake when he'd found a parking space at the airport and I was glad we had made it in one piece. There was no denying it, Lucien might well be a gentle man but he was not a gentle driver.

He hugged me after he'd pulled my suitcase from the boot and I felt a little tearful.

'You've been a fantastic person to have in the hotel, Gina. You are quite right, you're a problem solver and I will miss you.'

He then took my shoulders in his hands and kissed me on each cheek, before doing the same to a surprised Dorothy.

'Now I must go and deal with my *mère*. Will you be okay finding your way into the airport, ladies?'

'Of course, and thank you, Lucien. You have been a real friend these last ten days and your uncle is very lucky to have you in charge. You are such a credit to him. And now I will go before I start crying in the car park. Not a memory you need in your mind.'

He laughed as we walked away pulling our cases behind us.

'*À bientôt,* Gina Knight,' he called after me and I raised my hand as a farewell gesture. I didn't turn around because I was embarrassingly tearful and Dorothy must have sensed it, because she slid her hand into mine. I needed to get back home and see my children and grandchildren. I was clearly missing them all.

* * *

Our flight took off ten minutes later than scheduled, as was to be expected. When did they ever take off on time? I had a window seat this time and I had my nose pressed to the glass. We took off over a sparkling sea and I looked back as far as I could, back to the land and thought about those lives I had been fully immersed in. They were all people I would now never forget and yet, they were barely more than strangers. It was the oddest feeling.

'Another adventure completed, my friend,' Dorothy said from the seat next to me. 'I wonder where we will go next.'

'Well, as ever, I will wait for your command,' I said.

I didn't have anything to read as I'd finished the book Erik lent me and Dorothy was now immersed in the pages, so I closed my eyes and folded my arms across my chest and fell into a contented snooze.

It was raining as we landed in London and it was as if I had never left.

37

GINA

I paid the taxi driver and pulled my case up to the door, shaking the rain from my hair as Dorothy leaned forward with her key.

Dorothy's daughter-in-law had been in to load up the fridge with shopping and she'd also left a cake on the counter.

'Such a joy, that woman,' Dorothy said.

We abandoned the cases in the hallway and I made a pot of coffee before we settled ourselves in Dorothy's living room. She had a large patio door which stretched across one wall of the room entirely and through the glass I could see the boathouse at the end of the garden. It was a little house on stilts with Dorothy's late husband's narrowboat moored underneath. They had done a super job renovating the accommodation. It was such a comfortable and cosy little home and I was looking forward to being back inside. For now, I poured our drinks and sliced the cake.

'Dorothy, one thing has been bothering me more than anything else,' I said.

'What's that,' she asked.

'Adele – you carried the knowledge that you thought she had died as a child. Meredith didn't have that knowledge. Only you and Gerald for all the time he could remember. That must have been terribly upsetting.'

'Yes, but that was my fault for sticking my nose in and then not checking the facts thoroughly.'

'Don't blame yourself; you were trying to help your friend through a difficult time.'

'I was interfering, Gina. If there was an Olympic medal in it, mine would be gold.'

'All's well that ends well, though, hey?' I said.

'And you have done a good thing too. Meredith is beginning to enjoy her time in France and is looking forward to exploring the area with Adele.'

'I do wonder how it will all play out when Rose comes back. How will it really be for her to suddenly become a younger sister? She said all the right things to Meredith on their call. I do hope it works out for them.'

'I'm sure they will be able to navigate it. It's over to them now. I have interfered and you have helped. Now they can learn to live with each other in whatever way they see fit.'

'This cake is delicious,' I said after a huge bite.

'We have had the most wonderful food, but a home-made cake is always welcome. You know that Erik phoned me while I was in Barcelona,' she said with a pointed look in my direction, which I ignored. 'He wanted to know how my trip was going and also if I'd heard from you.'

'That's nice. How is he?'

'Very well actually. His son is planning to visit him soon. He's a lovely chap – it will be nice for you to meet him.'

'I doubt he'd want to meet me.'

Dorothy opened her mouth as if to speak, but then she closed it again, a small smile playing on her lips.

***

An hour later I was in the boathouse, unpacking my suitcase and throwing clothes into the washing machine. I stepped out onto the balcony that overlooked the Thames and was pleased to see the rain had stopped and given way to a late autumnal afternoon. The leaves were all gold on the trees that lined the opposite bank and it wouldn't be long before they were gone. There was definitely quite a nip in the air that there hadn't been in France. In truth I didn't miss the Mediterranean warmth as much as I loved an autumn day at home. Pulling my cardigan closer I sat down in one of the chairs and watched the river swirling and flowing beneath me. It wouldn't be long until the sun would be setting, another difference between here and the south of France. They had a good hour more light than us and what with the clouds overhead today, it felt as if sunset was coming early.

I really wanted this to feel like home. I loved being here, but in truth my life felt as transient as the water moving below me. This wasn't mine, whatever Dorothy said, but I did feel determined to enjoy it for as long as I could.

Movement caught my eye and I watched as Erik appeared in his garden. He was wearing a pair of comfortable blue trousers and a grey sweater, his reading glasses pushed up into his soft grey hair. I watched as he opened the door to his shed, then he paused and looked around. He wasn't really looking at me, I didn't think, but I shrunk back anyway so he wouldn't catch me watching him. Then, the next time I glanced over the railings he was gone. I went back inside to phone my daughter.

'Mum!' Alice said when she answered, as surprised as she always seemed to be when taking my call. I smiled. 'Listen, hang up and I'll FaceTime you. The girls want to see your tan.'

'Hi, Granny,' said the grinning face of Lou a few moments

later. 'You don't have a tan at all. What were you doing in the south of France – sitting inside?'

'Hello, darling. Yes I was inside a bit. I was looking after an elderly couple.'

'What, older than you?'

'Yes,' I said, laughing. 'Believe it or not there are people older than me.'

Meg appeared then after wrestling the phone from her older sister.

'Did you have a nice time? We missed you. Can we come and see you soon?'

'I would love you to come and visit. I'll arrange it with Mummy.'

'Did you bring us presents back?'

This was from the discombobulated voice of Lou somewhere in the background.

'You shouldn't ask that,' Meg said.

'Of course I did! I have lovely things for you all and when you come you can have them.'

The girls disappeared then and Alice's face appeared on the screen. She'd had her hair cut into a bob with a blunt fringe.

'I love your hair" I said. 'It really is very stylish.

'I finally did it; I have a mum bob.'

'It suits you and there's nothing mumsy about it.'

'Dad's been onto me about you again. About you being with that man in France?'

I scoffed at the audacity of Douglas, for goodness' sake.

'It's not funny, Mum. Are you sure you don't have a bloke?'

'No, Alice, I do not, but even if I did it's absolutely nothing to do with your dad. He left me, if you remember.'

'I'm getting the impression he might be regretting that.'

I sighed long and deep. I was tired and had the washing to

hang up. I did not want to discuss my marriage, or rather lack of marriage, with Alice, but it was hardly her fault.

'Well, anyway, he said he's going to come round to speak to you as you never seem to want to answer your phone.'

If that was the case, I'd be sorely tempted to stop answering the door as well.

'Okay, well, I guess I'll see him when he pops round. Speaking of which, when do you have time to come with the girls? We could go to Hampton Court; it's only over the road. And then maybe a lovely lunch in my boathouse.'

'Are you happy, Mum? It's been worrying me that you're not settled somewhere. And it's really weird not to think of you in our house in Thame. I keep thinking about you being in the garden and then I remember that you're not there.'

'I'm quite settled here,' I said, ignoring that niggle I had earlier about transiency. 'People move all the time. The older generation downsize to accommodation easier to keep if nothing else. We would probably always have moved anyway. Please don't worry about me. Bring the girls, come for the day and you'll see how lovely it is here.'

38

GINA

Douglas actually knocked on the door the following afternoon. And because I had put it out of my mind and didn't really think he'd just turn up anyway, I opened it assuming it was Erik to say he had the boat ready to go.

Erik had sent me a simple message that morning asking if I fancied a short trip out on Dorothy's narrowboat with him. I assumed he meant me and Dorothy, because all three of us often spent time together, and it was her boat, so I was quick to say yes. But then Dorothy had said her daughter was popping in for coffee and declined. Erik was taking her boat out to give the engine a run as it been some time since it had moved. I toyed with the idea of also declining, but it was too late and it would have looked odd. So I had spent the morning washing my hair and trying on everything in my wardrobe in some pathetic attempt to feel good about myself and the idea of a couple of hours alone with Erik.

'Hello, Gina,' Douglas said and I was so surprised I nearly shut the door in his face.

'Douglas, what are you doing here?'

'Dorothy let me in, told me where to find you.'

The Old Girls' Chateau Escape

This surprised me a little, as she didn't have much good to say about him usually, although they had never actually met, until now. Then I realised that she was probably stirring, because it wasn't in her nature to let him in through her house and down her garden without a motive. She must have hoped Douglas would find me with Erik. I nearly laughed out loud at this thought.

'It's not a good time. I'm just about to go out.'

'It's all very nice here,' he said. 'Dorothy is sitting on a tidy goldmine in that house. Even this poky boathouse is better presented inside than it is out. A nice surprise.'

'High praise indeed, Douglas.'

I picked up my bag and walked past him out of the door, then held it open until he reluctantly followed me out.

'We need to discuss reducing the price of the house, if we're still intent on selling it, that is.'

'Intent on selling it? You were the one intent on selling it, not me.'

'Well, that is something we can discuss then. Maybe we don't sell and have a rethink about our relationship.'

'Gina! All set?'

Erik appeared at the bottom of the steps to the boathouse looking decidedly handsome in an outdoorsy way and Douglas paled beside me.

'I'm ready,' I said, and began walking down the stairs towards him, Douglas hot on my heels. 'Douglas, this is Erik and, Erik, this is Douglas.'

Erik stuck out his hand and Douglas reluctantly took it. They really couldn't have looked more different. Erik had a beard, which was clipped short and tidy. He was slightly weathered from a life of outdoor pursuits, with a permanent golden glow about him and lines around his eyes from squinting into the sun. Douglas was always cleanly shaven and very particular about his clothes. He wouldn't be seen dead in a fleece or any sort of sportswear. He liked his clothes tailored, which unfortunately made him always overdressed and stuffy-looking.

Dorothy appeared then and I could see her smile all the way from this end of the garden like a glowing beacon. By the time she reached us, Erik was onboard Dorothy's boat and had started the engine.

'Are we going to have that discussion then?' Douglas asked me with both of his eyebrows raised.

'No, not now because, as I said, I'm going out.'

And then, in a gesture of defiance that had never really been in me before. I stepped on board.

'You're very welcome to join us, Douglas,' Erik said, and I was reminded again of his Scandinavian roots in the soft burr of his voice. 'No? Just me and Gina then.'

He pulled the rope on board while Douglas just watched on, looking stunned. We moved slowly away from the mooring and just for a moment, I thought Douglas *was* going to jump on board too, but he didn't. His expression darkened, though, and irritation was written all over it. I did feel a little sorry for him for the briefest of moments. He was a man usually in control and it was slipping away from him. It was almost worse than if it had been a high-speed getaway, showering him in a cloud of dust. Instead it was a slow disappearing act and we all had to hold our nerve and eye contact as we inched further and further away.

'We do need to talk, Gina,' he said.

'We will. I'll phone you,' I replied.

Then Dorothy appeared behind Douglas with a wicked grin and her hand out flat as if she was going to push him into the water. I stood up in shock, my own arms outstretched as if I could save him from this distance, but she merely tapped him on the shoulder and the last thing I heard before we were out of earshot was: 'Cup of tea, Douglas?'

Erik was chuckling as he poured us both a coffee from the cafetière a little while later and added a splash of milk to mine.

'I'm sorry, Gina. I don't mean to wind Douglas up, but he made it so easy.'

'I'm just sorry you have to witness my ex-husband behaving as he does.'

'I don't think he considers himself an ex any more. It looks to me like he's trying to win you back.'

'I'd be amazed if he was, and he has a funny way of showing it.'

'Seriously, Gina. You should think about what you really want. I think you could call all the shots now.'

'I hear what you are saying, but the truth is, Douglas decided that he didn't want me. He no longer wanted the woman he married. But I haven't changed. Fundamentally I've always been the same person, but I do feel I've come alive under the care of those who respect me.'

I blushed then and was pleased that Erik wasn't looking directly at me, while he navigated past another boat.

'Does that make sense at all?'

'It makes perfect sense,' he said and then his eyes did land on me and it was a while until he looked away.

* * *

Later, after Erik had moored the narrowboat back at Dorothy's house, we stepped into her garden.

'I hope Douglas has gone,' I said. 'I really don't want him to spoil what has been a wonderful afternoon.'

'It was fun, wasn't it,' Erik said. 'Do you want me to disappear, though, just in case?'

'No, I want to talk you and Dorothy into a takeaway curry and a movie. What do you say?'

'Consider my arm well and truly twisted,' he said with a grin. 'I tell you what, I'm going to pop back home for a while. I've got some washing to do and I need to phone my son, but message me when you've spoken to Dorothy and see if she's up for it.'

And then, before I realised he'd even done it, he bent down and kissed me lightly on the cheek.

'Thanks for a great afternoon, Gina,' he said and then disappeared back through the shared gate into his own garden.

He told me he'd suggested the gate to Dorothy so he could have easy access to cut the hedges both sides, but in truth it was nothing to do with that. He had done it so he could easily get into Dorothy's property if she ever needed some help.

I thought this was a very kind thing to do, but I also realised why he hadn't told Dorothy his true motivation. She was proud and independent; she would not have liked the thought of this at all.

I walked towards the house feeling like a teenager, trying to work out how to get the ridiculously large grin off my face before Dorothy saw it.

Douglas had gone, I was pleased to see, and Dorothy was watching a repeat of *Murder, She Wrote*. I realised, as I looked at her through the window, that she was asleep and I walked round to the kitchen door and tapped gently and then, more loudly.

'Dorothy? I'm back, is it safe to come in?' I called out after I'd given her enough time to rouse herself.

'Of course, Douglas has long gone. Unsurprisingly he didn't stay for that cup of tea with Sophie and me,' she called out, her voice a little croaky. 'Which was a shame really, because my daughter could have wiped the floor with him. She doesn't have any patience with pompous men.'

I walked through and hovered in her doorway.

'Did you both have a nice time?' she asked.

'We did. It was lovely on the river. He took us round to Eel Pie Island and we had a drink with some of his friends who live there. I'd forgotten what a little treasure that island is. It was nice to be back so close to Ham House too.'

'You used to work there many years ago didn't you?'

'Yes, with my mother. I might go properly next time. Be a visitor.'

'I could come with you, if you like.'

'I would like that, every much,' I said. 'What did Douglas have to say for himself, anyway? I hope he wasn't rude to you.'

'No, not at all, in truth, he was quite charming, for an idiot. He said could you please phone him as he really does want to discuss the house.'

I sighed. With two sales now fallen through, we really did need to consider reducing the price. But, after ten days in France I didn't have the energy to speak to my husband about his other options and what they might be. I did, however, have the energy for an evening with Erik.

'You, me, Erik, a curry and a movie tonight. What do you think?' I asked her.

She looked at me for a moment, assessing what, I wasn't sure.

'I'm a bit tired to be honest. I'll leave you youngsters to it, I think.'

'Youngsters,' I said, laughing. 'I'm seventy-one and Erik is sixty-nine!'

'Well, you're both considerably younger than me.'

'Dorothy, I can see what you're doing and I like Erik, a lot, but this is all too much too quickly for me. If you're not up for this evening, then we can do it another time. But, after an afternoon alone with Erik, I don't think an evening alone with him is a good idea. It's sending out a message I am not sure I want to send yet.'

I expected her to tell me to live a little, to take a chance and grab the bull by the horns et cetera, but she didn't.

'Actually, Gina, I do understand. I will join you, then none of us have to eat alone, but I will fight you for final decision on the movie.'

'Deal,' I said. 'I'm going back to mine for a bit, but shall we say six-thirty?'

'Yes, but before you go, I wanted to talk to you about something.'

I sat down in the armchair opposite her, hoping it wasn't going to be something unpleasant. It had hit me recently how much I cared about Dorothy. She was probably my best friend these days. And with that thought came the worry that I might lose her.

'Please tell me it's not another companion job for one of your friends, because they don't need companions, they need emotional support from thick-skinned problem solvers.'

'Oh, Gina, so suspicious.'

'With good reason, Dorothy.'

'You know I was telling you about the group I met on the cruise? Well, they're off again, but this time on a river cruise along the Nile.'

'Well, that sounds nice.'

'It does, doesn't it, which is why I'm going to go with them.'

'I think you will have a fantastic time,' I said, already thinking about how much I'd miss her.

'No, Gina, you misunderstand. I want you to come with me. They are an art appreciation group and I'm not sure they know a damn thing about their subject. You could be our tour guide. But, not only that, I really do feel as if I'd like to go away with a good friend.'

I smiled at her sweet words. I was actually very tempted, but I would have to find out how much it would cost. Also, I did have a family and they needed me occasionally. Could I just take off again?

'I love the idea of that, Dorothy,' I said, 'but there are a few things to think about. Can I let you know?'

'Of course you can,' she said.

As I left her to walk back to the boathouse my head was full. Was it time to make changes? Was it okay to do things that made me happy without worrying about others? I opened the door to my new home and looked around it, taking in how stylish it was, how comfortable and perfect it felt for me. I made a cup of coffee and thought about Douglas and what he might be suggesting. Was he thinking we could go back to how we were before as if nothing had ever happened? How happy Alice would be to have both parents back in the family home ready to welcome her and her family for Sunday dinners and Christmas Day. Could I go back to that to make my family happy?

I could see Erik hanging out his washing on the line at the end of his garden when I stepped out onto the balcony and I smiled to myself at how late in the day it was. He'd leave it hanging out all night and I'd seen the forecast, it was likely to rain.

I closed the door and settled myself on the sofa. I pushed all of my thoughts away. I didn't have to be making decisions tonight. I could think about it tomorrow. Instead I opened my emails and began to draft one to my friend Carmen. I told her all that had been going on in my life recently, how I'd been forced into making some changes, but how much better I felt about myself because of it. I asked her how she was, whether moving home to Malaga had been as good a decision as she hoped it would be. I told her I missed her and would love to visit her at some point.

I closed my email before I sent it. I wanted to dwell on my words for a bit, come back to it tomorrow and reread it. I also wanted to freshen up for an evening with my two newest friends.

I brushed my hair and swept some pale lipstick over my lips. I changed my top for something more comfortable and grabbed the takeaway menu from the drawer in the kitchen. I reached into the bag on the table for the treats I'd bought for Erik and the silver photo frame from the French market I'd bought for Dorothy, then I locked up the door ready to head back to hers. I hesitated for a moment with the key in my hand and I realised how this was the first time in a very long time that I had sole charge of where I lived. I suddenly didn't see it as me being lonely, but rather me living alone with no one to answer to.

It struck me that I was feeling stronger than I had in years. I wasn't just a woman whose husband had left, I was a woman who had been offered an opportunity to change her life. And I was proud of myself for all the strides I had made.

I smiled as I headed down the steps. I was off to have a curry and watch a movie with two friends and life was pretty good.

ACKNOWLEDGEMENTS

How exciting to have written my fourth book!

This also means it is the fourth time I will be thanking people for the huge amount of help they have given me.

Firstly to my editor, Rachel Faulkner-Willcocks who always gets to the heart of the story I'm trying to tell. In fact, to the whole of Boldwood Books! I am so happy to have found a home for my writing with this incredible team of hardworking, enthusiastic and efficient people.

To my agent, Robbie Guillory and to my first readers and supporters. Writing a book can be a lonely occupation, so, to have a group of cheerleaders is a wonderful thing.

Speaking of cheerleaders I'd like to give a huge shout out to the Virtual Writing Group who can lighten up the darkest of days with some of the best chat in town.

To Rebecca Netley for her excellent plot chats and to Marie France for allowing me to pick her wonderful brain!

I'd like to say thank you to The Askett Glass Studio. You are a hugely talented group of artists and I was so lucky to be part of it.

I would also like to thank all the reviewers and bookbloggers who give so much to the writing community!

Finally to anyone who will pick up and read this book in a shop, online, through audio or from their local library. Thank you x

ABOUT THE AUTHOR

Kate Galley is the author of uplifting golden years fiction, including *The Second Chance Holiday Club*. She was previously published by Aria, and is a mobile hairdresser in her spare time.

Sign up to Kate Galley's mailing list for news, competitions and updates on future books.

Follow Kate on social media here:

facebook.com/Kate%20Galley%20Author
x.com/KateGalley1
instagram.com/kategalley1

ALSO BY KATE GALLEY

Old Girls Behaving Badly
The Old Girls' Chateau Escape

BECOME A MEMBER OF

THE SHELF CARE CLUB

The home of Boldwood's book club reads.

Find uplifting reads, sunny escapes, cosy romances, family dramas and more!

Sign up to the newsletter
https://bit.ly/theshelfcareclub

Boldwood

Boldwood Books is an award-winning fiction publishing company seeking out the best stories from around the world.

Find out more at www.boldwoodbooks.com

Join our reader community for brilliant books, competitions and offers!

Follow us
@BoldwoodBooks
@TheBoldBookClub

Sign up to our weekly deals newsletter

https://bit.ly/BoldwoodBNewsletter

Printed in Dunstable, United Kingdom